Here's what critics are saying about
Play Dead:

"Exciting first in a thriller series replete with hit men, high-speed chases, and international crime."
—*Publishers Weekly*

"Starts with a bang and doesn't let up. The action is gripping and the characters are compelling. Four stars!"
—*RT Book Review*

"A fast-paced, easy-to-read thriller that touched my heart. Highly recommended for fans of romantic suspense!"
—*Gumshoe Review*

"Halliday combines investigation with the inevitable romance for a mystery that's enjoyably by the book."
—*Kirkus Review*

"Whew! I don't know when I read such a riveting story that kept me on the edge of my seat. Talk about adrenaline! Kudos to Gemma Halliday for a terrific story!"
—*Lesa's Book Critiques*

BOOKS BY GEMMA HALLIDAY

Anna Smith & Nick Dade Thrillers
Play Dead

Marty Hudson Mysteries
Sherlock Homes and the Case
of the Brash Blonde

High Heels Mysteries
Spying in High Heels
Killer in High Heels
Undercover in High Heels
Christmas in High Heels
(short story)
Alibi in High Heels
Mayhem in High Heels
Honeymoon in High Heels
(short story)
Sweetheart in High Heels
(short story)
Fearless in High Heels
Danger in High Heels
Homicide in High Heels
Deadly in High Heels
Suspect in High Heels

Tahoe Tessie Mysteries
Luck Be A Lady
Hey Big Spender
Baby It's Cold Outside
(holiday short story)

Hollywood Headlines Mysteries
Hollywood Scandals
Hollywood Secrets
Hollywood Confessions
Hollywood Holiday
(short story)
Hollywood Deception
Hollywood Homicide

Jamie Bond Mysteries
Unbreakable Bond
Secret Bond
Bond Bombshell
(short story)
Lethal Bond
Bond Ambition (short story)

Young Adult Books
Deadly Cool
Social Suicide

Other Works
Viva Las Vegas
A High Heels Haunting
Watching You (short story)
Confessions of a Bombshell
Bandit (short story)

PLAY DEAD

GEMMA HALLIDAY

For my people: Nick, Tommy, Zack, and Charlotte

PROLOGUE

***

"Take it off."

Anya looked across the over-furnished room at the man who'd issued the command. General Fedorov. Fifties, salt and pepper hair, eyes as dark as two bottomless pits. He took a deceptively casual position, leaning back in a plush, velvet armchair, one leg crossed over the other. But Anya wasn't fooled. She could see the tension still present in his limbs, as if he were ready to pounce at the slightest provocation. He held a lit cigar in one hand, the smoke tickling her nostrils as she complied, slipping the straps of her dress down her right shoulder, then the left. She shimmied her hips until her clothing fell to the floor, leaving her bare beneath his gaze but for the red, patent leather heels on her feet.

"Like this?" she asked, her voice barely a whisper.

Fedorov nodded, looked her up and down. A flicker of appreciation crossed his sharp features. He took another long drag from the cigar, as if drawing in the sight of her, then slowly blew it up toward the ceiling.

"Come closer."

Her stomach clenched. But she did. Her long legs crossed the distance between them until she was standing directly in front of him, so close she could feel the heat emanating from his body.

"And now?" she asked.

"Kneel down."

Again, Anya did as she was told, her bare knees hitting the cool marble floor. She swallowed a shot of apprehension, noticing the growing bulge beneath his tailored slacks.

You've done this a thousand times before. You can do it again. One last time.

"And now?" she asked. Even though she knew full well what "and now" would be. They'd been watching him for weeks. They knew his habits, his mannerisms, what kind of soap he washed with in the morning, and what color socks he wore at night. What kind of cigars he smoked and what kind of recreation he indulged in. Blondes. Expensive ones. If they were lucky, he let them leave in the morning. Others became just another casualty of war.

Fedorov reached out, trailing a finger down Anya's cheek. His hands were rough, calloused, like him. She shivered but leaned into his touch all the same, doing a kitten-like mew deep in her throat. He gave an answering groan, telling her she'd done her research well. He liked.

His hand left her face, and Anya could swear she felt her skin sigh in relief.

Fedorov moved to set his cigar down, his free hand reaching for his zipper.

"No. Let me," Anya purred, sliding her hands up the expensive wool fabric that covered his thighs. "Please," she begged.

A smirk crossed his features before he picked up his cigar again. As Anya well knew, he liked it when they begged.

She smiled up at him, holding his eyes as she slowly lowered his zipper. She did another feminine coo, letting her eyes flicker to him as she licked her lips.

He chuckled, leaned back in his chair, and closed his eyes in anticipation.

Anya's heart pounded in her chest. Her hands shook. No matter how many times she did this, nerves always hit her. She supposed some small part of her was glad. At least it was a sign she was still human. Still had some notion of right and wrong. She closed her eyes and took a deep breath.

Then she quickly thrust the zipper back upward, jamming Fedorov's scrotum in the sharp teeth.

He howled, hands going to his crotch as he jumped to his feet.

But not quickly enough.

Anya's right hand shot out and grabbed the double-action revolver he always kept strapped to his right ankle. She didn't hesitate, didn't think, didn't feel.

Just aimed and pulled the trigger.

The first shot took out his right knee, sending him to the ground just long enough for Anya to put some distance between them. She backed up, quickly firing off another to his temple. He hit the ground with a sickening thud, and the room was plunged into eerie silence.

Two deep breaths. In and out. Anya's heart pounded in her ears, her hands steady now as they held the revolver straight-armed in front of her. Mission accomplished. It was done.

And done well.

She could almost hear the praise of her handler's voice echoing in her head.

Perfect shot, my dragi, *my darling. Now get out.*

Three seconds. She knew in three seconds his bodyguards would be at the door. A quiet syringe to the neck would have made escape easier, but in the skimpy dress Fedorov had wanted her to wear there'd been nowhere to hide it. She'd had to work with what she had on hand. Noisy as it was.

Two seconds.

Anya grabbed her dress, slipping it back over her head as she dove for the pair of French doors leading onto the balcony. She quickly pushed one open. But instead of jumping toward freedom she moved behind the heavy, velvet curtain at its side, holding her breath.

She heard the doors to the general's bedroom burst open, a cacophony of shouting voices drowning each other out as bodyguards swarmed the room. Anya closed her eyes, trying to make out how many. Three. Maybe four? Heavy footsteps hit the polished floor, running to the body, down the hall, toward the French doors. She was sure her heart was pounding loudly enough to match the stomping rhythm of their boots.

The scent of cheap cologne warned her one of the Russians was approaching her hiding spot. She closed her eyes, letting her knuckles go white as they tightened around the revolver.

He shouted something to his pals, so close that his voice made her jump. He'd noticed the open door. More footsteps, leading out onto the balcony. More shouting. A thin line of sweat trickled down Anya's back as she clutched the gun to her thigh. If they found her, she was done. She was good, but three to one were odds no one could escape from. Especially when the three were trained killers.

Then again, what am I?

She shoved that thought deep into the recesses of her brain, focusing instead on the commands one Russian was shouting to the others. She wasn't fluent, but she'd picked up enough of the language to understand he was telling them she'd escaped over the balcony. Go find her.

Three pairs of feet pounded out of the room, receding down the hallway.

She waited, counting off two beats before daring to move a muscle. Slowly, she drew back the curtain, using reflections in the windowpane to check the room. The general's lifeless body lay slumped in the middle of the floor.

Alone.

She sprang into action, adrenaline pumping through her limbs as she crossed the room, out the door, running left, opposite to the exit, she knew. Deeper into the compound but farther away from the expanse of property outside the general's bedroom window where the bodyguards would now be searching for her. The sound of her heels pounding with practiced speed was muffled by thick carpeting as she counted the doors she passed. Three, four. She'd been studying the blueprint of the house for weeks, but she still held her breath as she passed the fifth door and slowed, opening number six and slipping inside.

An empty office. Just as it was supposed to be.

She quickly shut the door with a soft click behind her, hearing her own ragged breath fill the silence. The room was dark, moonlight filtering through the window the only light. Anya blinked, letting her eyes adjust. The windows faced east, toward the woods, beyond which ran a little used road where a car awaited her. Her handler had set up surveillance on the road to monitor every person who'd gone in or out of Fedorov's compound for weeks. All she had to do was get to the car, and she knew they'd all be watching her on their monitors from their big, safe room that, as far as anyone knew, didn't really exist. Her handler, the generals, the faceless men who controlled her fate.

And she'd finally be safe.

She paused and put her ear to the door, praying she didn't hear the telltale pounding of feet behind her.

Nothing.

She crossed to the window, lifting it open. The bite of night air stung her cheeks, giving her instant goose bumps in the flimsy dress completely ill-suited for Kosovo in the spring. But cold was an indulgence she didn't have time for. Instead, she pried the screen from its frame with her fingernails, dropping it to the floor as she threw one leg, then the other over the sill.

It was a two-story drop. One she'd anticipated, but it looked far higher now that she was straddling the sill, all that empty air below her.

You can do this. You're almost there.

If she thought about it a second longer, she knew her resolve would waiver. So she didn't. Instead, kicking off her shoes, she plunged into the darkness. She hit the ground with a thud, sharp pain instantly shooting up her left leg. Anya bit down hard on her lower lip to keep from crying out, her hands sliding out from under her in the dewy grass. She looked down. Her left ankle was twisted under her. Probably sprained.

But pain was another thing she had no time for.

The taste of blood filled her mouth as her teeth ground down on her lip. She struggled to her feet, favoring her right side. She forced her legs to hold her up then glanced around in the dark, quickly getting her bearings. Ahead of her lay an expanse of grass, a fence to the left leading to the yard where the general carried out his own private training exercises. She shuddered. She'd seen the files on his victims and could only imagine the tortured souls who still haunted those tainted grounds.

Still grasping the revolver in her hand, she turned right. A wooded area lay at the edge of the grass, but it was a good ten yards to the tree cover. Ten yards where she'd be completely exposed. She could only pray that the Russians were still searching the other side of the compound for her.

Ten yards. Ten yards...and then you're free.

Anya dashed forward, running as fast as her injured ankle would allow, half hopping, half dragging her leg along as she kept her eyes on the tree line ahead. Her arms pumped at her sides, her lungs burning, her eyes watering at the sting of cold wind whipping past her. Six yards. Five. She was almost there.

And then she heard it.

The crack reverberated through the still night like lightning as a tuft of grass at her side flew into the air.

They'd found her.

While she'd hoped they wouldn't, she was really only surprised it had taken them this long. The general had been a sadist but a smart one. The men he'd hired were nothing less.

Anya jagged to the right, then left, never decreasing her speed as she made a zigzag pattern across the lawn. Tufts of grass flew at her sides, spattering her legs with mud as bullets embedded themselves into the soft ground.

Three yards left. She was almost there.

Another shot rang out, and fire instantly erupted in her right arm. Anya cried out, falling to the ground. Her left hand instinctively went to the sharp sting slicing through her bicep. She rolled onto her right side in the grass, shot off two wild rounds toward the house. Pain blinded her. She had no idea if she'd hit anything, but the bullet hail stopped for a second. Warm liquid seeped through her fingers, and she bit back a scream. She would not give them the satisfaction.

The gunfire ceased for only a moment, and then the Russians began again. Relentless. The air filled with deafening shots, chunks of grass beside her jumping, spraying cool mud onto her cheeks.

She rolled left, then right, pulling herself up onto her knees as she twisted away from the hail. She looked up. The tree cover was only a few feet way. So close. She could make it.

She *would* make it.

Anya turned, firing two more rounds back toward the house before the revolver made an empty clicking sound. She threw it, making a mad dash for the trees, her bare feet slipping on the wet earth, her teeth chattering against the cold.

Five more feet.

Four.

She heard shouting behind her, the Russians scrambling for their vehicles, their dogs, their spotlights, organizing an all-out search as she reached the cover of the woods. She wasn't home free yet, but the tall pines bought her time.

She tripped over the uneven ground, roots rising up from the earth to slow her pace. Dried pine needles bit into the soles of her bare feet, low branches scratching at her exposed arms and legs. She heard the sound of wings flapping overhead, birds rising angrily from the highest branches at the sudden intrusion into their territory.

But she kept running.

The woods sloped downward, toward the road, but she didn't slow her pace all the way down the hill, tripping the last few feet as she reached the dirty pavement. On the far side, a shiny silver sedan sat up against the bank.

Anya let out a cry of relief. It was almost over.

Freedom.

She stumbled across the road, listening to the sound of Fedorov's loyals in the distance, jeep motors humming as they closed in on her.

She threw the driver's side door of the sedan open, fingers fumbling in the dark beneath the console for the switch to start the car. She found it.

She paused, the pain in her arm spreading into a dull ache as her index finger hovered just above the switch. She knew they were watching her, waiting with anticipation almost as great as hers. Would she make it out before Fedorov's men caught up with her? Or would they be training someone new to take her place? All eyes would be on the screen now, the room hushed, men with grave faces all leaning forward, holding their collective breath as she disappeared inside the car.

Anya slid her bare thighs onto the leather seat, listened to the roar of motors drawing closer, breathed in deeply the frigid night air scented with pine, leather, and her own cloyingly sweet blood dripping down her arm. She stared out the window at the sight of moonlight shimmering off the frostbitten street, creating a deceptively serene scene.

And then she flipped the switch.

An explosion rocked the air, an orange fireball engulfing the shiny, silver car in one giant fist as smoke billowed up toward the top of the pine trees.

CHAPTER ONE

———

"Dammit, would you just do it already?"

Anna shivered, shifting her umbrella to the other hand, her teeth rattling together. Rain fell in fat droplets around her, splashing back on the cuffs of her jeans as she stood on the small square of lawn, shifting from foot to foot. She could feel mud squishing into the grooves of her running shoes and cringed. She'd have to carry them up the stairs unless she wanted her landlord complaining about muddy footprints again. In one hand she held the umbrella, in the other a leash connected to a stubborn-as-hell boxer who was currently being very particular about where he did his business. Anna thought for a moment he might have chosen his sweet spot when he paused to sniff at the azalea bushes flanking her apartment building. But no. He turned up his black nose and continued pacing in the rain. Anna had a sneaking suspicion he was enjoying this.

"Come on, Lenny," she pleaded.

Lenny looked up, trained his black eyes on her, and cocked his head to the side. Then he went back to his pacing.

Anna narrowed her eyes at him. "Jerk."

Originally he'd come to the shelter from a family who'd been moving to Chicago and couldn't take a dog with them. They'd promised he was an excellent watchdog and very companionable. The companion part he'd proven right away. She could hardly walk two steps in her tiny apartment without running into him. The watchdog part had turned out to be the biggest joke she'd ever heard. Lenny's deep baritone bark was impressive, but he was more likely to lick an intruder to death than attack. Still, half the idea of a watchdog was for show, so she hadn't had the heart to unload him on someone else.

She just wished he'd show a little more cooperation.

"Please, Lenny. I'm cold. I'm wet. I'll give you three bacon treats if you just pick a spot and take the dump. What do you say?"

He ignored her completely, sniffing the flowerbeds along the walkway.

Anna wiped a raindrop from her cheek, wrapping one arm around herself to stave off the chill. Normally she didn't mind the rain so much. She loved the smell of water hitting the oil-stained streets, the crisp color of the San Francisco sky that it left behind when the clouds parted. Almost as if the entire city were being washed clean and given a fresh start.

But tonight she wasn't a fan. The rain cut down on her visibility, left her feeling too exposed standing out in the open.

Her gaze swept the street. The dim glow of streetlamps bathed the neighborhood in pale yellow hues, rows of old Victorians lining the block of narrow three-story buildings, over the years painted every color of the rainbow. They banked right up against each other, one after another, trailing down the hill toward the bay. Across the street were a used bookstore, an Asian market, and an all-night Laundromat. Only the Laundromat's lights were on at this time of night, a sole occupant visible inside, reading a book as he waited for his clothes to finish. It wasn't a particularly busy street for San Francisco, one of the things Anna had liked about it when she'd first moved in, but it was close to the park and Muni, and the rent was relatively cheap.

And her landlord hadn't asked any questions when she'd installed a state-of-the-art security system.

Anna tore her gaze away from the street, focusing again on her stubborn partner.

"I swear to God if you don't do it now, you're holding it until morning," she threatened.

Lenny walked over to the azaleas and, miracle of miracles, this time squatted down. Anna said a silent thank you, pulling a plastic baggie out of her pocket. She waited until he'd finished then transferred the leash and umbrella into one hand as she crouched down to pick up Lenny's offering with the other.

But the rain must have made her grip on the leash slip. As she bent over, Lenny gave a tug on the end, and the leather slid out of her hand, the umbrella fell to the ground, and rain immediately pelted her as she lost her balance in the muddy grass.

"Dammit, Lenny," she shouted, throwing one hand out to break her fall. She slid forward, mud streaking down the side of her jeans as she lunged for the dog. He'd taken off like a shot into the dark evening, bounding down the rain-soaked sidewalk.

"Lenny!" she called, her cries immediately swallowed up by the storm.

Abandoning the baggie, she grabbed her umbrella, useless now that she was soaked to the bone, and picked her way back over the square of lawn, hitting the sidewalk just in time to see him shoot across the street into the Laundromat.

"That's it," she muttered to herself. "No bacon treats for you."

Reluctantly she set off after him, crossing the street. As she pushed through the glass doors of the Laundromat, warm, humid air immediately hit her like a blanket. She scrubbed her wet hair out of her face, scanning the room for the dog.

He had the sole occupant of the room backed up into a corner, his book held up like a shield as Lenny tattooed his clothes with muddy paw prints.

"Lenny," she yelled, "get down!"

Which, of course, he ignored, completely enamored with new-person scents.

Anna crossed the room, her wet shoes squishing with every step, and grabbed the end of his leash from the floor. She gave a sharp tug. "Down. Now," she commanded again.

This time he did as told, letting his captive go as he took a step back to sniff a box of detergent on the floor instead.

"Sorry," she said to the man.

He was tall, at least six feet, lean with broad shoulders beneath a cotton shirt, unbuttoned at the top. His jeans were worn at the knees, his shoes dry, indicating he'd been inside for a while. His hair was a warm chestnut color, curling a little at his neck, just slightly longer than current fashion would dictate. His eyes were a deep brown, so dark, she noticed, that they were almost black. He had a square jaw, a day past needing a good shave, and his build was tight, all angles, like an athlete's.

He lowered his book as Lenny stepped away, the corners of his mouth tilting upward.

"No problem. I only peed myself a little," he joked.

Anna felt an answering smile. "I swear he looks more vicious than he is."

"I'll take your word for that." He slowly sidestepped the dog. "I've always been more of a cat person, myself."

"Well, on a night like tonight, I don't blame you." She looked down at her jeans. It would take an act of God to get those grass stains out.

The man reached into a plastic laundry basket and pulled out a towel, tossing it to Anna. "Here. You look like you've been swimming."

"Nearly," she said, gratefully drying her face. "Thanks, but you know I'm just going back out in it."

"Nick." The man stuck his hand out at her. "Nick Dade." Anna looked at it for a minute. Then gingerly took it. "Anna."

His grip was firm, strong, his skin a little rough as if he worked with his hands regularly. Definitely confident. But careful not to hold on too long.

"Just Anna?"

"Smith. Anna Smith."

"Hmmm." He crossed his arms over his chest, leaning back on his heels. "Smith. Very mysterious."

Anna laughed. "No, very plain."

"Well, it's nice to meet you, Anna Smith. You live around here?" he asked, gesturing to the windows.

Anna paused and bit the inside of her cheek.

Don't talk to strangers.

She nodded slowly. "Yes."

"It's a nice place. Quiet at night."

"It is. I like it."

"The architecture's amazing. I love all the old buildings. It's incredible to me that so many have survived not one but two major earthquakes."

Anna nodded, running the towel over her hair, trying to squeeze out the bulk of the rainwater. "That's one of the reasons I moved here," she agreed.

"Where from?"

Anna looked up. "What?"

"Where did you move from?"

Don't talk to strangers. Don't get personal.

Anna looked away, turning her eyes to Lenny, still circling the detergent box.

"Oh, I've lived all over. I'm a bit of a nomad. What about you? Local?"

He shook his head. "No, I'm just visiting a friend in town. Thinking of relocating, though. It's a fun city. You lived here long?"

Anna shrugged. "Long enough, I guess."

"Long enough to know a place for good Chinese?" He took a step toward her.

Without meaning to, she took one backward.

"In San Francisco? You'd have a hard time finding bad Chinese."

He laughed, his eyes crinkling at the corners. "Come on, you must have a favorite?"

"Okay, if I had to pick one, I'd say the Shaolin Palace. Down the street a couple of blocks. They deliver twenty-four hours."

"Oh, definitely my kind of place."

A dryer dinged behind him, signaling the end of the cycle.

"Well, I guess I'll let you get back to your laundry," Anna said.

She dropped the towel on the counter and tugged Lenny toward the door. Having ascertained the detergent box didn't contain anything edible, he complied.

"Wait," Nick said, taking a step forward. "Are you busy tomorrow night? Maybe you could walk me through the Shaolin Palace's menu, huh?"

Anna chewed on her cheek again.

Don't get personal.

"Sorry, I have plans tomorrow. With my boyfriend."

"Oh." His smile faded. "Oh, I'm sorry to hear that."

"Yeah, well, good night," she said quickly, pulling Lenny toward the door.

"I guess I'll see you around, Anna Smith."

She raised a hand in a wave then pushed out into the sheeting rain again. It hit her like ice after the warm, sticky air of the Laundromat. Giving up altogether on the umbrella, Anna crossed the street, ducking her head against the torrent as she ran up the walkway.

He's watching you.

She stole a quick glance over her shoulder. He had his back turned to the windows, pulling clothes from the dryer and dropping them into his plastic basket.

She shook her head. He was just a nice guy trying to get a date. The foul weather was making her paranoid.

"Come on, Lenny. Let's go dry off." She slipped her key into the lock and let herself into the lobby, Lenny barking gleefully beside her. She tugged off her wet shoes before leading him up the two flights of stairs. For all the good it did. Her feet still made a trail of wet footprints on the worn, wooden steps. Not to mention Lenny's muddy contribution. She'd be catching hell in the morning.

Two apartments shared the third floor. Mrs. Olivia, a seventy-three-year-old widow and sudoku addict, lived in the one on the right. Anna was on the left.

She shoved her key into the lock and let Lenny bound into the room ahead of her, skidding to a stop at his food bowl and lapping up the crumbs. Anna shook her head as she keyed her PIN into the security system. That dog had a one-track mind. *We should all have such a simple life.*

She shut the door behind her and locked it, then secured the chain and deadbolt and armed the alarm system again before stripping off her wet clothes and leaving them in a pile by the door. A long, hot shower sounded like heaven.

She padded into the kitchen, throwing a cupful of dog chow into Lenny's bowl then crossed the small studio apartment, pausing briefly at the front window. She pulled the edge of the curtain back and peeked out.

He was still there, folding towels at one of the counters, his head bent over his work, his hands moving in quick, practiced movements. She had a fleeting vision of laughing over a plate of chicken chow mein with him. His eyes crinkling at the corners, mouth twisting up in a warm smile.

But before it could go any further, she quickly shut the curtain. She'd been in San Francisco too long. She was getting too comfortable here. It was time to move on. Maybe somewhere in the Southwest. It had been awhile since she'd been to the desert.

She stepped into the bathroom and turned on the shower, letting the hot water fill the tiny room with steam.

* * *

Liar.

Dade watched her disappear from the window, her thick curtains obscuring her from view. He knew for a fact she didn't have a boyfriend. As far as he could tell, she didn't have any friends. Which didn't surprise him. From everything he'd read, she wasn't exactly the social type.

He grabbed the last of his clean towels from the dryer, folding them end over end as he kept one eye on the window of the third floor. She wouldn't go out again tonight. She'd feed the dog, maybe take a shower, and then sit on her sofa watching TV. At midnight she'd turn out the lights, set her alarm, and go to bed.

He'd watch until then, until he was sure she was down. Then he'd catch a few hours himself before setting up camp outside her work in the morning. An animal shelter near the park. Considering her former life, he found it ironic that she spent her days saving cats and dogs from the needle.

He tucked a pile of towels into his laundry basket. The same pile he'd been washing every other night this week. Though tomorrow he'd have to find something new to occupy his time, thanks to her damn dog.

He shook his head. Dade hadn't intended any contact. He didn't like contact. He liked things clean and simple. He did his surveillance thoroughly, chose his weapons carefully, and did his job quickly, unseen, and without any complications. Contact with the target made things complicated.

Not that he'd really anticipated this one being simple. For one thing, she was a woman. As much as Dade logically knew a woman could kill as easily as a man, he'd been raised to think of women and children as civilians. But once he'd read the file on Anya Danielovich, he'd decided to make an exception.

She'd been one of the go-to agents of the KOS, the former Yugoslavian intelligence agency, a group that had been integral in shaping the faces of power in those years leading up to the Kosovo conflict. Years that were particularly bloody in the former country's history. Factions breaking off from one another, allies becoming enemies. One day you worked for the good guys, and the next they were the bad guys. Politics and race relations thrown together in a stew that resulted in military units without leaders, guerilla factions acting under whomever had the funds to feed them, and power being wielded by those who had no one's best interest at heart but their own. When all the dust had settled, the country had splintered and the KOS was no more.

Officially, that is.

From the file Dade's client had provided, Anya's last known hit was 18 years ago—well after the KOS had ceased to exist in any government capacity. Though, Dade was the first to admit that governments didn't always play within the rules they published.

According to her file, Anya had never served in any government's military, and there was no record of her formal training. In fact, there was no record of her at all up until her first job, where she'd taken out a wealthy Serbian businessman whose funds were being funneled to the wrong people. During the next four years she'd neutralized a total of twenty-four men. Most clean hits, none ever officially investigated. All before her twenty-first birthday.

Dade glanced across the street. The curtains were still shut, but he could see light behind the ones covering her kitchen widows. Grabbing a bedtime snack?

He had to admit, he had a hard time reconciling the woman he'd just met with information in the file. She'd seemed too…normal. Human. If he'd met her under different circumstances, he wouldn't have thought she was anything but your average girl. A little on the skinny side, maybe, but friendly enough not to raise suspicions.

But there'd been no mistaking her. Even with her blonde curls dyed black and several years between her and the baby-faced assassin in his file, there was no doubt in his mind. It was the same pair of huge blue eyes, the same full, pouty, lips. The same high cheekbones, round hips, and long legs she'd worked to her advantage across Eastern Europe. She'd done a good job eradicating any hint of an accent from her voice, but he figured she'd had time to work on it. And if she was half as good as the file said she was, she would have. She wasn't stupid. She'd known what was at stake when she'd left Kosovo.

He wondered if she knew what was at stake now.

Officially, Anya Danielovich had died in a car accident over a decade ago. She'd been a twenty-year-old student out partying too late, drinking too much, and had wrapped her car around a tree along a deserted stretch of the highway. A maintenance worker had found her the next morning, her car burned out, her remains charred to a crisp.

Unofficially, the file said she had died in a car bombing outside the compound of General Fedorov, a man later intelligence reports proved was working all sides of the conflict to his own profit. What she was doing outside his compound was a question no one asked. Though Fedorov hadn't survived the night either.

But in reality…

Dade looked up at the window, watching the light go out in the kitchen and the blue glow from her television glint at the edges of the next bank of curtains.

In reality, Anya was his latest contract. And he'd never been fooled by a pair of legs or pouty lips before. Dade knew that evil came in all sorts of packages.

This time, Anya Danielovich would stay dead.

CHAPTER TWO

———

It was too early for the Beatles. Anna groaned, rolling over to face the red glowing numbers of her alarm clock. 6:15. She threw an arm over her eyes and fumbled in the semidarkness until her fingers connected with the snooze bar, ceasing John Lennon's thoughts on world peace. She rubbed at her eyes, making the slow transition from sleep to reality as she threw her legs over the edge of the bed and into a pair of fuzzy, red slippers.

Lenny perked up immediately from his makeshift bed by the door and barked out a greeting. He loped across the room, stopping just short of knocking her over.

"Hey, buddy," she said, rubbing the stubby, soft fur on his head. "Hungry?"

He barked in response. Then again, Dogzilla barked in response to just about anything.

"All right, breakfast is coming right up," Anna said around a yawn, walking to the kitchen. She filled his bowl again then flipped the switch on her coffee pot, glancing out the window as she waited for it to brew.

The streetlights were still on, dim spots of light dotting the fog as the sunrise struggled to break through. Though the rain had stopped, the streets below still glistened with the evening's downpour. A jogger made his way down the block, his warm breath making visible puffs in front of him as he hurried past her building. The market across the street was opening, the owner pulling back the heavy iron gates to reveal glass windows full of half-priced noodles and canned soup three for a dollar. And the Laundromat's *Open* sign still hung on the door, though Anna couldn't see if anyone was inside.

Forget him.

The coffee pot hissed, signaling the end of the cycle, and Anna grabbed a mug from the overhead cupboard. She poured the dark, aromatic liquid into her cup, sipping from it as steam rose to warm her cheeks.

No doubt about it, it was time to move on.

"What do think of Tucson, Lenny? Or maybe Sedona. Lots of wide open space to run in Arizona."

He answered with a loud slurp, finishing the last of his breakfast, and lumbered to the front door, his nails clacking along the hardwood floor. He sat by the door and made a pathetic whine in the back of his throat.

"Oh no, pal. After what you put me through last night, you can wait until I've had a shower first." Anna set her cup down on the counter and headed toward the bathroom.

She wasn't sure, but she could swear Lenny gave her a dirty look as she closed the door.

* * *

The Golden Gate Animal Shelter was located two blocks south of the park, in the Sunset district. It was a nondescript, square building squatting between a hardware store and a dry cleaner's near the end of the block. Glass windows spanned the front while a hand-painted yellow sign sporting a cartoon dog in lederhosen informed passersby that they were open.

Originally the shelter had been created to handle overflow from the county facilities when they'd instituted their no-kill policy, putting down only the sickest of animals or ones deemed too dangerous to be adopted out. With just fifteen kennels in the back, it was a small shelter by city standards, but it was clean and close to public transportation, so it had suited Anna perfectly when she'd first moved to the city.

A small pang of regret that she'd soon be leaving it behind hit her stomach as she pushed through the front door. An overhead bell jangled in the small lobby to signal her presence.

"It's just me," she called out.

A slim redhead in jeans and a Giants sweatshirt poked her head out from the back room.

"Hey," she answered, wiping her hands on the seat of her pants.

Shelli Cooper had been hired on as office manager at the shelter a couple months after Anna had started there and ran the place like clockwork. At just over five feet, she was a petite little firecracker with enough perk to singlehandedly solve the nation's energy crisis. She had a tendency to talk with her hands and was perpetually bouncing on the balls of her feet. Her red hair was worn long and loose around her face, hippie style, with a pair of green eyes set in skin so pale she reminded Anna of a china doll. A dusting of freckles along Shelli's upturned nose gave her a perpetually youthful look, though Anna put her age somewhere in her early thirties, close to Anna's own.

"You're late," Shelli said.

"Sorry," Anna replied, setting her shoulder bag down on the counter. "Long night."

"Oh yeah?" Shelli leaned in. "You get some?"

"Ha. No, stubborn boxer. Rain. Mud. Not fun." Anna picked up a pile of mail and thumbed through it. Mostly bills and bulk mailers from other local businesses.

"Yeah, it really came down last night, didn't it? My power flickered a couple times during the debates. I was sure it was going to cut out. Did you watch?"

Anna shook her head. "No. I never get into politics."

"You didn't miss much. Republicans crying bleeding heart, Democrats crying corporate corruption. Same old tune. They say Jonathan Braxton's ahead in the polls, though. Not sure how I feel about having a president young enough to be my brother, but there you have it. Oh, hey," she said, switching gears, "we got a newcomer last night after you left." Shelli navigated around the front counter to grab a clipboard from the desk behind it.

"Oh, yeah?" Anna asked.

"Terrier mix. Tiny little thing, freaked half out of his mind. No tags. A homeless guy brought him in just as I was closing up. He was afraid the church wouldn't let him in for the night if he had a dog with him."

"Is the dog in the back?"

"Number fifteen." Shelli handed her a clipboard with the terrier's paperwork before taking a seat behind the counter and jiggling her computer screen to life. "He's all yours, Anna."

"I'm on it."

The shelter's kennels consisted of one large room with concrete floors where fifteen smaller cages were set up. Three-quarters were full, which was less than most shelters in the area that were often overflowing, sometimes even illegally housing animals in the offices and storage rooms. It was hard enough finding cute little puppies homes, but for the older animals that had been abused, neglected, or worse, grown up feral, fending for themselves, it was almost impossible. While Anna did her best to clean them up and make them look attractive for potential new homes, it was often a race against time to get the adoptable ones out and make room for the never-ceasing influx of new animals.

She stopped at the last cage and squatted down next to their newest boarder. He was small, even for a terrier, his fur a shaggy gray color, matted with something dark and sticky along the back. He yipped warily at the cage door, bouncing up and down on all fours.

"Hey there, fella," Anna said, trying to make her voice as low and soothing as she could. "Don't you worry. We'll clean you up."

He yipped again, clearly not convinced.

She slowly opened the cage door, talking in soft tones to the animal as she reached out a hand and let his wet little nose run along her palm. Once his nostrils had gotten their fill, she scooped him up from the floor, running her hand gently along his back as she carried him to the sink. He shivered, and she could feel his ribs jutting beneath his skin. Sadly, he looked like he'd been on the streets for a while.

"It's okay. No one's going to hurt you. Trust me, you'll feel so much better after a nice, hot bath."

She turned on the water, letting it warm up a bit before setting the dog down in the deep, metal basin. He circled a few times, sniffing at the drain as she turned on the handheld showerhead and ran it along his fur. Immediately the water turned brown, rinsing away God knows what. She lathered him in shampoo as he tried to bite the bubbles rising from his coat then rinsed him again until the water ran clear and his fur was at least two shades lighter.

The next step was to scan for ID. Even though he'd come in tag-less, Anna looked for the telltale bulge of the implanted ID chip along his neckline. Nothing. But just for good measure, she scanned the handheld machine over his fur. As suspected, nothing showed up.

"I guess you're Fido Doe, now," Anna informed him.

He looked up at her and licked her chin.

"Oh, you like that name, do you?" she laughed.

She scratched behind his ears as she carried him out into the front room where Shelli would take his picture to broadcast online for a potential new home.

"Ready for his close-up," Anna said.

Shelli's head popped up from her screen. "Oh, isn't he cute! He looks so much better. He's gonna go right away."

"Let's hope."

"Okay, hold him up." Shelli pulled out her phone and aimed it at the terrier. "Hmm…wait. He needs something."

She leaned down and rummaged in her desk.

Fido wiggled in Anna's arms, his little nose twitching, clearly dying to explore the new room.

"I'm not sure how much longer I can hold him."

"Here. Perfect." Shelli stood up, a length of red ribbon in one hand. "Just hold him a second," she said, navigating the ribbon around his neck. The little dog twisted his head to the side, trying to nip at the ends as Anna held him down. Finally Shelli won out, creating a somewhat lopsided bow around his neck. "There, much better."

Anna rolled her eyes and laughed. "Just take the damn picture already. He's going to bolt any second."

Shelli held up the phone. "Okay, big guy, smile." She snapped the shot then checked the screen. "Aw, he's adorable."

Anna peeked over Shelli's shoulder. "Perfect."

"Oh, here," Shelli reached behind the desk, pulling out the morning's copy of the *Chronicle*. "I'm sure he needs fresh paper in his stall."

"Hey, save me the classifieds," Anna asked, juggling the terrier in one arm while she tried to pull the section out from the rest.

"Oh no, not again."

"What?"

"Don't tell me you're moving again?"

Anna turned away, hoping her thoughts weren't visible on her face. "Thinking about it."

"This is the second time you've moved since I've known you." It was true. She was getting antsy faster and faster the longer she stayed in the city.

"My lease is up," she lied.

"Can't you renew? I thought you liked that place."

"I do."

"So?"

"So, it's time for a change."

"Last time it was the plumbing. The time before, the super who refused to fix the AC. God, I hope you find a keeper this time."

Anna cringed. She hated lying to Shelli. Both apartments had been fine. But more than a few months and she started to get that itchy feeling. Like she was too settled, too comfortable. That's when her guard would fall.

"Well, let me know if you want me to go check out some places with you. Oh, hey, my neighbor's sister just rented this condo near the Haight. I think she's looking for a roommate. I could ask?"

Anna bit the inside of her cheek. Then nodded slowly. "Yeah, sure. That would be great."

Liar.

She had no intention of staying in San Francisco. As much as she'd miss the shelter, even Shelli, it was time to move on. Unfortunately, not something she could share. There would be too many questions, promises to keep in touch that would just be another round of lies. She knew from experience that the best way to go was silently and swiftly. One day she was there…the next it would be like she'd never existed.

Like a ghost.

Because, after all, isn't that what she was?

* * *

Dade squinted his left eye closed, his right trained on the image of Anya magnified through his scope.

"Come on, girl. Just put down the damned rat," he muttered under his breath.

He'd been glued to her since she'd arrived. His scope tracking her as she parked her car up the block and walked to the shelter. He'd followed her inside, his entire body focused on the framed image of her dark hair in the lens. But he hadn't been able to get a clear angle. First, she'd had that redhead dancing around her, then she'd disappeared into the back room, and now she was holding some mangy dog that wouldn't sit still.

Dade shifted his weight, keeping his index finger loose on the trigger. He was patient. He knew his moment would come. It would be done today.

The roof of the hotel was the highest point in a three-block radius. It was an area wide enough to make him confident no nosey office worker looking out her window would see him but close enough to his target that he knew he wouldn't miss. He'd been lucky. It was perfect for a long-range shot. Which was exactly how Dade wanted it. He had no intention of getting that close to her again.

He would do it through the window. A bigger mess, no doubt, with the glass. But the noise would confuse people. Make them focus on the point of impact, not the point of origin. They'd be ducking, avoiding debris. Not scanning the street for a guy with a gun.

He'd hauled his rig up to the roof in a guitar case, blending in as one of dozens of the city's street musicians roaming the sidewalks just after dawn. He knew from his mornings parked in front of Anya's building that she woke at 6:15 on the dot every day. She would have been getting her first cup of coffee when he'd set up the scope—the long-range rifle with a sight aligned perfectly to the right front window of the shelter.

At 7:30 the redhead had come in—army bag slung over one shoulder, walking from the bus station up the street—and unlocked the doors, swinging around the yellow sign from *Closed* to *Welcome*. He'd lain on his stomach, sprawled flat against the roof as he'd watched her flip on her computer monitor, paw through a pile of mail, then slip into the back room until Anya arrived half an hour later.

Usually he'd swing in thirty seconds behind her, parking his SUV down the block.

But today he was waiting.

He blinked his left eye shut again, feeling the morning sun begin to melt the layers of fog away. A thin bead of sweat trailed down his temple despite the chill still lingering in the air.

He watched Anya pull out a newspaper and the redhead wave her arms in the air in response. Not a surprise. From what he'd seen, she seemed the high-strung type. Anya was harder to read, though the line of her back seemed straighter, more tense. Whatever they were discussing upset her. Finally the redhead raised both hands in a gesture of surrender. Anya responded with her back to him. Then she leaned forward and passed the dog to the redhead.

Bingo.

Dade felt his muscles relax, his heart speed up, his body focusing, narrowing in on his target. His finger closed around the trigger, his eyes riveted to a spot at the back of Anya's head.

Then she whipped around, her eyes turning his way. For a second, he could swear she was looking right at him. Which was impossible, of course—he'd checked and double-checked to make sure nothing on the roof was visible from the ground.

He blinked hard, shook off the feeling, refocused on his sight. His finger hovered over the trigger.

He counted off one, two...

But he never got to three.

Instead, as his finger lay loose on the trigger, the plate glass window in his scope exploded into a million pieces.

Dade jerked his head up. Bits of broken glass spewed onto the sidewalk. Passersby scattered, screaming, covering their heads as if being attacked from all sides. A man came running out of the hardware store next door, yelling in some foreign language, waving his arms. It was exactly the scene he'd envisioned.

Only a second too early.

Dade grabbed a pair of binoculars from his bag, training them on the broken storefront. Neither the redhead nor Anya was visible, though he spotted the tail of that rat dog peeking out from behind the front counter.

Another shot rang out, and Dade watched the telephone on the counter explode, chunks flying every which way. He dropped the binoculars, left the scope, reached into his bag and grabbed his M9, shoving the handgun into the waistband of his pants as he hurtled himself over the fire escape. His legs pumped down the rusted flights, one thought racing through his mind.

He hadn't pulled the trigger.

So who the hell was shooting at Anya?

CHAPTER THREE

——

They've found me.

Anna dove behind the counter, tackling Shelli to the ground. Her heart thudded in her chest, a fear she'd hoped never to feel again surging through her limbs.

Shelli's eyes were two big saucers, her face ghostly white, mouth hanging open. "Ohmigod. What's going on?"

"Stay down," Anna commanded, covering her head as two more shots ripped through the tiny lobby, embedding themselves in the wall behind her. Shelli nodded and crouched beneath the desk, holding the terrier to her chest in a death grip.

On instinct Anna grabbed for the .32 strapped to her ankle. Only she came up empty. It had been years since she'd worn one. And her Glock was in her purse, halfway across the room. There was no way she could get to it without completely exposing herself.

You've gotten careless.

She frantically ran her hands along the floor, searching for anything she could use as a weapon. Shards of glass cut into her palm as she closed around a paperweight shaped like a Siamese cat. She leaned forward, trying to get a visual around the side of the counter.

The point of impact was clearly the front of the building, but it was too chaotic on the street to get a clear handle on the shooter's position. She did a quick scan of the area, even though she knew it was futile. These were professionals with the best training money could buy. If they wanted to be invisible, there was no way she'd see them. Had she been the one setting up the hit, she'd have done it from the ground, close to the buildings across the street. But it was too hard to tell if anyone was there now.

"Anna, what the hell is going on?" Shelli asked again, her voice shaky. The dog whimpered in her arms.

"Stay where you are," Anna shouted back. "Don't move, just stay down."

She picked a spot on the left side of the room, near the front door, and hurled the paperweight toward the window. It crashed through, bouncing off the sidewalk. A second later gunfire sprayed the window, and Anna lunged to the right, her fingers curling around the strap of her handbag a split second before the shooter redirected her way. She hit the cover of the desk just as a bullet took out the chunk of beige carpet where she'd been.

She leaned her head against the counter, taking one quick breath, then two as she rummaged in her purse for her weapon. An odd sense of calm washed over her when her fingers clamped around the cool metal. She lifted it and held it almost like an extension of her hand. She'd let it lie dormant in her purse for years, never touching it but knowing it was there, loaded, just in case.

Just in case today happened.

Shelli gasped when she saw it, shrinking even farther back under the desk. "Jesus, Anna, you carry a gun?"

Anna didn't answer. She didn't have time to. She knew these weren't the kind of men to play games. They'd be closing in soon. Once the element of surprise was gone, they would rely on time. They must know as well as she did that they weren't in the remote regions of Bosnia anymore; the SFPD would be on scene in a matter of minutes. They had to get to her before then.

Which meant she had to run.

She wrapped both hands around the gun, took a deep breath, then stood up, launching herself vertical like a jack-in-the-box as she fired off half a dozen rounds through the nonexistent front window. She quickly dropped back down to a crouch, listening for the pause as they took cover themselves before returning her fire.

It came swift and hard. Faster than she'd hoped, spraying the back wall of the office, raining pieces of plaster down on her.

Not good.

Fully automatics, AK-74s if she had to guess. How many of them were there? She wasn't sure. All she knew was she had to get out of there. Without an arsenal of her own, she was a sitting duck.

Anna bit the inside of her cheek, panic rising as, one by one, she eliminated escape options.

The gunmen shot three rounds into the computer on Shelli's desk, the monitor exploding with a pop that sent sparks flying into the worn carpet. Shelli screamed. Anna ducked, covering her head with her arms and turning away.

Just in time to see the back door fly open.

A man dressed in all black entered the room, a handgun held tight to his body. He took two steps into the room then ducked behind a column as gunfire erupted again.

Anna's heart froze.

Trapped.

She trained her gun in his direction, mentally counting how many rounds she had left. Eight. She had eight shots left. Enough. She held the gun straight-armed in front of her and shot off three rounds into the column at head level.

She heard him swear, diving backward for cover. He returned fire, and Anna ducked down, narrowly missing a bullet as it bounced off the desk chair. Anna retaliated, shooting off four more shots his way before ducking back down behind cover. Out of the corner of her eye the man darted across the room toward her, hailing more fire from the front of the office.

She turned her gun on him.

But he was faster, grabbing her by the wrist and twisting her arm behind her until she cried out, her hand involuntarily releasing her weapon with a sickening thud to the floor.

"Anna!" Shelli cried out, her voice high with hysteria.

Anna struggled. But the man's grip was tight. It was like struggling against steel, completely unyielding. There was nowhere to go. He shoved her up against the wall, his hard body pinning her there, pressing into her back. His mouth ground up against her ear, the stubble on his chin scraping her cheek. She tried to turn away, but there was no space left to move.

"There are at least two in front, one down in back." His voice was deep, low, and direct, demanding attention. "I'll provide cover. You grab the girl and go out the back."

Anna felt her breath hitch. He would provide cover? *Who was this guy?*

Anna nodded in agreement. What choice did she have? Instantly she felt the pressure on her back let up as he slid away from her. Slowly. As if the lack of trust was mutual. He paused to pick up her gun from the floor, slipping it into the waistband of his own pants.

Anna didn't hesitate. She grabbed Shelli by the arm, hauling her out from under the desk. Her heart pounded, her legs antsy, ready to spring into action.

"Go," the man commanded. "Now!"

He stood, shooting toward the front of the shelter. Anna didn't waste time, shoving Shelli ahead of her and running through the back door, expecting the fiery pain of a gunshot wound to erupt along her back at any second.

Deafening shots ripped through the room, plaster flying off the walls on either side of them as the gunmen returned fire. Their would-be savior continued shooting, sending round after round into the front window until she heard the click of his gun signaling he was out of ammo.

Then he was behind her, urging her forward, past the kennels of dogs barking and cats howling, all whipped into a frenzy over the commotion.

"Go!" he shouted again, punctuated by a swift shove to the small of her back. She stumbled but kept moving forward, all the while listening to Shelli's steady chorus of "Ohmigodohmigodohmigod," as she clutched the terrier to her chest like a security blanket.

They hit the back door, and Anna plowed straight into Shelli's back as she stopped short and let out a strangled cry.

A man in black sweats and a wool cap lay on the pavement just outside the door. A red bullet hole dotted his forehead, eyes staring toward the sky, open and unseeing.

Anna took one look and felt her insides go numb. A hollow yet jarringly familiar feeling. Years faded before her vision, and she was transported back in time. How often had she seen this same scene?

"Move. Now!" The man shoved her forward again.

Adrenaline coursed through her limbs, the panic she'd felt moments earlier converted into trained reflexes. She grabbed Shelli, who was still making gurgling sounds in the back of her throat, and pushed her down the narrow back alley running the length of the building.

Reluctantly, Shelli complied, the two of them covering the length of the block, stumbling over chunks of uneven asphalt, navigating around the teeming dumpsters. Anna felt the man close behind, heard his feet pounding as the gunfire across the street ceased. They knew she wasn't in the building anymore. They'd be on the move, one step behind her.

The sound of sirens echoed in the distance, moving toward them as the alleyway dead-ended against a metal fence at the back of an Indian restaurant. Scents of warm naan bread and curry hit her nostrils as the man shoved both women up against the fence, behind a blue dumpster. He moved in front of them, flattening himself along the grimy metal side as his eyes scanned for an exit.

It was the first time Anna had gotten a chance to really look at him. A broad, sturdy build filled out his black cargo pants and matching T-shirt. His eyes were still as dark as they had been last night, though the stubble along his jaw had grown. The man from the Laundromat. Dade.

She sucked in her cheeks, her stomach knotting, churning over the possibilities.

Who was this guy?

He turned to Shelli, his voice low and commanding. "See the back door of that restaurant?"

She nodded, her teeth chattering as she clutched the shaking dog to her.

"I want you to run to it as fast as you can. Then wait inside for the police to come. Got it?"

Shelli shot a wary look at Anna before nodding again, this time more slowly.

Anna took a step forward.

"No. Not you." Dade turned to her, meeting her gaze. "Just her." Shelli opened her mouth to protest, but she didn't get the chance as he shoved her forward hard enough to make her stumble. She recovered quickly, doing as she was told, racing for the back door.

Anna prayed it wasn't locked, prayed Shelli made it, prayed they wouldn't come looking for the redhead as long as she separated from Anna.

She could hear Shelli's breath echoing off the sides of the alley as she hit the door, tugging at the metal handle. It opened easily, and Anna let out a long sigh as the redhead slipped inside.

As soon as the door closed, gunfire erupted down the block.

Anna felt Dade's body stiffen beside her, his hand clamping around her arm, shoving her back into the fence until the metal diamonds bit into her skin.

"Go. Over the fence," he whispered.

She did, quickly hitching one foot over the other as she scaled the wall, dropping down the other side just a step before Dade launched himself over in one swift motion.

Again, he wrapped his fingers around her upper arm, propelling her north, away from the shelter, down a side street lined with fast food and mom-and-pop bodegas. He slowed to a quick jog, staying close to the cars parked on the street for cover. Every muscle in Anna's body strained for the shout of gunfire behind them.

Halfway down the block, he stopped, pulled out a pair of keys, and remotely unlocked a black SUV. He opened the driver's side door, shoving her in ahead of him, over the console. He slid behind the wheel, and pulled away from the curb, his tires screeching as he made an illegal U-turn, rushing against traffic in the opposite direction. Horns blared and middle fingers rose as they careened down the street.

They made it only four car lengths before shots ripped into the right side of the car. Anna ducked, covering her head. Dade swerved left, cutting across two lanes to make a sharp turn the wrong way onto a one-way street. He jumped over the curb, narrowly avoiding a VW head on. He made another left at the end of the block, then a sharp right, threatening to tip the SUV as it bounded onto Sunset.

Another three blocks and two turns later, Anna finally remembered to breathe. The gunfire had ceased, the unseen assailants silent. Anna scanned the side mirror for any sign they were being followed.

Behind them was a pickup. Beside him, a minivan. To their right, a yellow sports car driven by a guy yelling at his phone. No bullets, no nefarious-looking vehicles. Just the usual rush of San Francisco traffic.

Anna turned her attention to Dade in the seat beside her. His jaw was clenched, his features seemingly set in stone. Eyes straight ahead, hands gripped tightly against the steering wheel, every muscle in his body flexed, poised for action. A far cry from the warm, easy persona he'd displayed last night.

He knew how to handle a gun. Gave orders like he expected to be obeyed. He'd clearly been trained for action. Military? CIA? He didn't have the least hint of an accent; she pegged him as American. But that was all she could know for sure.

"Who are you?" she asked.

He didn't answer immediately, and when he did, his eyes never left the windshield.

"I told you. Nick Dade."

"That doesn't tell me anything."

"No, it doesn't."

His jaw flinched, and he made a screaming right turn. Anna sucked in a breath, fearing the vehicle would rise on two tires.

"You're not some tourist visiting a friend."

"No."

"It wasn't a chance encounter last night in the Laundromat."

"No."

"What were you doing at the shelter?"

Silence. His jaw flinched again, his eyes never leaving the road ahead of him.

"You killed that man behind the shelter, didn't you?"

Again he was slow to respond. When he did, it was just the slightest nod of his head.

While she'd already known the answer, the fact that he didn't even try to deny murdering a man left a familiar chill in her bones.

"Why are you doing this?" she asked, her voice barely a whisper.

He turned to look at her for the first time, his eyes so dark they were black pools, hooded and unreadable.

A slow shake of his head was his only answer.

Anna swallowed, white knuckling the armrest as he took another turn.

"Where are we going?" she asked.

"Your apartment."

Her head whipped around. "*My* apartment? Why?"

"You've been made. They're going to expect you to leave town. But if they've done their homework, they know you won't leave without your dog."

Lenny!

Anna's heart leapt into her throat, and tears immediately sprang behind her eyes. She'd forgotten all about him. He was just a dumb animal. The thought of anything happening to him…

She sniffed loudly, pushing back the tears, grasping again for the numb feeling that had been her savior, her safety, for so long.

She took a long breath. Then another.

"They'll be waiting for you at your place," Dade continued. "That's where we'll catch up to them. I want to know who these guys are."

As much as her instincts told her to run, run like hell, she knew he was right. She wanted a face-to-face with them, too, though for entirely different reasons. She already knew who they were. She wanted to know how they'd found her. How they'd penetrated the illusion of safety she'd worked so hard to build around herself. She'd been careful. But somehow, somewhere, she'd slipped up. She needed to know where.

Because if she got out of this alive, she vowed she'd never slip up again.

"You're out of bullets," she said, amazed at the false calm in her voice.

"Glove box."

She pulled the compartment open, lifting a box of ammunition onto her lap. She reached across the console, grabbing for the empty gun still shoved, along with hers, in his waistband.

Immediately his hand covered her skin, fingers closing around her hand like a vice grip.

She winced. "I'm loading your weapon for you."

He looked down at her hand, then up at her eyes. His still dead black.

He paused a moment, then nodded and let go of her hand.

Gingerly she took his weapon, loading the ammunition into the magazine, then set it down on the console between them. She would have given anything to be able to reload her own gun, but at the moment that wasn't an option.

One bullet.

She glanced across the interior of the SUV at him again. If it came down to it, that would be all she needed.

She leaned against the headrest, her mind turning over a million different thoughts, questions, and scenarios. Dade had been watching her—that much was apparent. It was unnerving, jarring, knowing that someone had been peeking into her life uninvited. How much did he know about her? How long had he been watching? Was her apartment bugged? The shelter?

And, maybe most importantly, why?

She took a deep breath, forcing questions she couldn't answer now out of her head as they approached her street. Questions could wait. What she needed now was focus. Keen focus on the threat at hand.

They've found you.

No matter how many deep breaths she took, that thought had her biting back desperation and panic. Nausea grew in her belly, and tears she wanted desperately to shed threatening the back of her eyes. Deep down, she'd always known this day would come. But somehow she'd tricked herself into hoping that knowledge was wrong. That she really could live a normal life, that Anna Smith was her future and that her past didn't matter, didn't exist. A distant memory she never needed to call up again. Now that little kernel of hope had been completely crushed. The normalcy she'd pretended to live had shattered in an instant. It was clear now that her life in San Francisco had all been an illusion, a failed round in a game she couldn't hope to win. Today had proven beyond a doubt that as hard as she tried, there was no denying who she really was.

She'd never be able to outrun Anya.

CHAPTER FOUR

———

Dade turned the corner, and Anna leaned forward in anticipation as her apartment building came into view. In the early morning sunlight the tall, yellow building trimmed in white wooden latticework looked bright and fresh, the last of the rain clinging to the paneling and Victorian moldings along the roofline. It had once supported a large, wraparound porch, long ago demolished to make way for a more modern lobby when it had been converted to apartments. Now the face sat back mere feet from the street, nondescript squares of lawn separating it from the sidewalk. Cars lined both sides of the street, making it impossible for Anna to check the interiors of each for signs of life as she would have liked.

For signs of her attackers lying in wait.

Her hands twitched in her lap, feeling oddly empty without a weapon.

Dade double-parked the SUV beside a green Chevy dotted in rust spots and motioned Anna out of the car. She opened the door and stepped out, head down, using the Chevy as cover. Dade crouched low, moving with catlike stealth as he came around the car, keeping his back close to the SUV. He held his gun in both hands, tight to his body, though she could see his index finger rested loosely on the trigger. His eyes scanned the street. He quickly assessed the terrain before giving the slightest nod of his head in her direction, motioning for her to follow.

She did. One eye on the front door of her building, one on Dade's back, silently calculating just how fast she'd have to be to outrun him.

He moved quickly, fluidly, across the grass, up the front steps, pausing only briefly at the wood and glass door before motioning her forward.

"Key?" he asked.

Anna shook her head. "It was in my purse."

Dade didn't hesitate, ramming the butt of his gun down hard on the door handle, splintering the old wood surrounding it. He shoved a shoulder into the door, and it easily pushed open, allowing him inside.

She followed. But she took just one step before he blocked her path with a sturdy arm, flattening her against the front wall as he scanned the interior. She held her breath, felt her fingertips tingling with that familiar surge of what was to come.

Satisfied, he turned to her, nodded toward the stairway. He moved forward, gun trained above his head as he ascended. She was a quick step behind him, wishing like anything she had a weapon. It was like walking into the lion's cage armed only with a juicy flank steak. She could draw them to her, but once they got there she had no recourse but to trust Dade's aim.

Trust. The word instantly made her nervous.

They reached the second-floor landing, opening up to three apartments, all three doors shut. The smell of frying bacon wafted under the door of the first, the third vibrating with the loud bass rhythms of her downstairs neighbor's stereo. Dade gave them only a quick glance before continuing on, climbing the next flight. As they neared the top, he put a hand out, urging Anna to wait as he took the last three stairs, stepping onto the tiny landing.

It was empty. Silent. Anna was sure her ragged breath echoed like screams in the still air. But Dade didn't seem to notice, his full attention riveted to Anna's front door. He took slow steps forward, his sneakers squeaking against the hardwood. One hand reached out, pushing on the door.

It easily swung inward.

His eyes immediately cut to Anna in a silent question. She shook her head. There was no way she'd leave her place unlocked.

They'd beaten her there.

Dade took a step forward, over the threshold, and then froze, his eyes cutting to the apartment on the left. He stiffened. Anna followed his gaze.

A thin line of red liquid oozed out from under her neighbor's front door.

Anna's stomach seized. Her right hand twitched again for the comforting grip of a nonexistent gun.

Mrs. Olivia.

With a backward glance at Anna's door, Dade moved to the left, gun straight out in front of him, his body rigid. Anna left her crouching position in the stairwell and followed a step behind, keeping one eye on her own door, expecting armed gunmen to jump out at any minute.

"Stay close," Dade whispered, untucking his shirt and using the hem to cover his prints as he slowly turned the doorknob to Mrs. Olivia's apartment.

Anna did, standing just at his back.

The first thing she saw was a foot. It was encased in a pink house slipper, worn on the sole, twisted backwards at an unhealthy angle. Mrs. Olivia was wearing a matching pink housecoat, buttoned clear up to the top, the shade pale, like her halo of white curls, still perfectly coiffed in place as she lay sprawled on the floor just inside the door. Her eyes were open wide behind her bifocals. A deep red stain spread across her chest, leaking onto the floor, creating a trail of sticky red as it congealed along the door frame.

Numb. Just go numb.

Dade did a silent sweep of the apartment, moving quickly through the tiny room. A television sat in the corner, muted as *The Price Is Right* flickered across the screen. A glass of milk, half finished, sat next to a faded armchair, and the bed along the far wall was unmade.

The kitchen was a carbon copy of Anna's, though the bathroom was situated to the left, opposite Anna's apartment. Anna watched Dade enter it, only to emerge a moment later lowering his weapon. The apartment was clear.

He leaned down beside the body and placed two fingers at the side of Mrs. Olivia's neck, even though it was obvious no blood pulsed there now. He looked up and shook his head silently from side to side.

Anna nodded, took shallow breaths, and tried not to remember the last time she'd spoken to Mrs. Olivia. She'd been complaining about the noise, saying that Lenny's barking was so loud she couldn't hear *Jeopardy!* Anna had promised she'd do her best to keep him quiet. She'd ended up feeding him close to an entire box of bacon treats just to keep him complacent enough to stave off an angry call to the landlord. She'd cursed Mrs. Olivia all night long as Lenny's digestive system had protested, emitting enough noxious gases to warrant a hazmat. The woman had been nosey and annoying.

But she hadn't deserved this.

Dade let out a breath through flared nostrils before standing.

"You knew her?"

"Not well," she answered truthfully.

"There's nothing we can do for her now," he said. Then he moved past Mrs. Olivia's prone form, raising his gun in front of him again as he stepped back out onto the landing.

Anna followed, forcing herself not to look at the body of her neighbor.

I'm sorry.

Instead, she focused on the rigid line of Dade's back, moving toward her apartment, pushing the door open, and disappearing inside. Again the thought occurred to her to flee. Run now. Run as fast and as far from here as she could. But she knew she stood little chance of escape against these men. None if she fled unarmed. So instead, she crossed the threshold a beat after Dade, staying as close to his back as possible.

They'd broken easily through her locks, the brass fittings dangling uselessly in their splintered wooden settings. Her security chain had been snapped in half, the alarm box ripped open, exposing a jumbled mass of wires, completely disabled. All the measures she'd installed to protect herself were laid bare as the childish illusions they were.

And they'd been just as thorough with the rest of her belongings. Every dish in Anna's kitchen lay in pieces on the floor, knives, silverware, utensils littered throughout. Every piece of clothing from her closet was strewn haphazardly across the apartment. Her bed had been plucked clean of sheets, the mattress upended. Stuffing from her sofa covered every surface, cushions slit systematically one after the other. A pile of bullets sat near the linen closet where she kept her stash of emergency ammo. The chaos was designed to distract her, but she knew already what they'd taken. The laptop from her desk, bills from the table by the door, and a toothbrush from her bathroom. Recent activity, records, DNA. That's what she'd take.

Dade did another sweep, even though they both knew that if someone had been in the apartment, they'd have been targets by now. The gunmen had come and gone. They were too late.

"Lenny?" Anna called softly, not entirely trusting the steadiness of her own voice.

Silence.

Tears pricked the back of her eyelids, but she refused to shed them, hanging on instead to that blessed numbness.

"Lenny?" she asked again, scanning the room, praying to see some pile of clothes shift, some whimper from beneath her bed, any sign of life.

Dade circled the room, pausing in the kitchen. He shoved his gun into his pants and reached down to pick up the discarded bag of dog chow. He held it up and shook it, the few remaining pieces of kibble bouncing around inside.

A wet, black nose emerged from the closet next to the bed. Anna sucked in a breath, diving toward it.

"Lenny!"

She threw open the doors, wrapping her arms around his neck as he regaled her with wet, slobbery kisses. This time she couldn't help it. Warm, wet tears slid down her cheeks as she hugged his furry neck to her face. Jesus, he was just some dumb animal. She didn't know why it meant so much to her to see him alive. But it did. As if he were the one thing in the world she still had. The one thing that hadn't been ripped from her this morning.

Dade's rough voice cut into her relief. "We have to go."

Reluctantly she released her grip, using the back of her hand to wipe at her cheeks.

"There's a body next door. The police won't be far behind us."

Anna sniffed and nodded. "Let me get some things first."

Lenny followed her as she dug through the mess. She spied a duffel bag in the corner and grabbed a change of clothes at random, quickly shoving them in. Then she crossed to the dresser on the far wall.

The drawers had been pulled out, two of them smashed into unrecognizable splinters. She stuck her hand into the top opening, slipping her fingers into the crack between the body of the dresser and the top rim. It was a tight fit, one that she knew large masculine hands wouldn't be able to manage. She ran her fingers along the edge until she felt a raised edge. She dug with her fingernails, prying a plastic ID card away from the wood. She quickly shoved it into the back pocket of her jeans.

He gave her a questioning look but said nothing. She assumed he had his own stash of false ID cards at the ready. Anyone as good as he appeared to be would.

She moved into the bathroom. Again, cupboards lay open, purged of their contents. Cosmetics, cleaning products, and reams of bathroom tissue lay mingled on the tile floor. Anna stooped down, pawing through the mess until she found the box of overnight maxi pads. Half had already spilled onto the floor, but she reached inside and removed the one stuck to the bottom of the carton, carefully unwrapping it from its powder pink shell. She unfolded the pad, revealing a slit along the right side. She slipped two fingers into the cottony interior and came out with a micro SD card the size of her fingernail. It went into her pocket with the ID.

Dade raised an eyebrow in question again, but she ignored it, instead brushing past him back into the studio, stopping at her linen closet to scoop a handful of bullets from the floor. Then she plucked a leash from a nail on the wall and crossed to the kitchen to grab the bag of dog chow, rolling the top over with a crunching sound, and shoved them both into her duffel.

"Ready?" Dade asked, crossing the room to face her.

She nodded. Then held out her right hand, palm up. "My gun."

He looked down at her hand, then up at her, something akin to amusement flitting momentarily across his features. "I don't think so."

"I'm not leaving here unarmed."

"You're not unarmed. You have me."

Anna squared her shoulders. "I don't need you. I don't need an escort."

"I disagree."

"Give. Me. My. Weapon."

Dade looked down at her and crossed his arms over his chest, his eyes an impenetrable wall of black. He shook his head very slowly, side to side.

"You don't get it. I'm not asking you. I'm telling you," she said.

All the fear, panic, guilt, and regret she'd felt that morning converted into pure, undiluted anger as she stared him down.

"You really think you're in a position to do that?" he countered, taking a step toward her. She took one back, the small of her back coming up against the cool tile of her kitchen counter.

"Look, I don't know who you are, but I know how to handle these guys myself," she said.

His voice was low and even, refusing to respond to her growing agitation. "I'm not sure you do."

Anna laughed, a hollow sound completely devoid of humor. "You have no idea who you're talking to, do you?"

In one quick movement, her hand shot behind her, latching onto a paring knife, flicking it out in front of her.

Dade looked down at the shiny tip, pointed at his chest. His jaw tightened. Anna saw his Adam's apple bob up and down, his chest rising and falling a little faster.

"Actually, I do," he countered.

She opened her mouth to protest, but he rode right over her, silencing her with one simple word.

"Anya."

She felt her insides turn to ice, her heart lurch. "Who the hell are you?"

"I told you. Nick Da—"

"Shut up!" She shoved the knife menacingly toward him. He closed his mouth. But he still held his ground.

"I'm leaving," she said. "With my gun. Now." She held out her hand again, wielding the knife in the other.

Lenny barked in the background, sensing the tension in the air. Anna prayed he stayed put. Already, she knew the disadvantage she was at. Dade had her by close to a hundred pounds, all trained muscle from what she could tell. Trained by whom and how well, she could only guess. But she knew her upper hand was hanging on by a thread.

"Put down the knife," Dade commanded.

Anna opened her mouth to reply, but again he didn't wait for her response.

"Or I'll have to take it from you. And I don't want to hurt you."

Adrenaline surged through her at the threat and, without thinking, she lunged forward, her hand flicking with practiced speed, slashing an angry red line just below his collarbone. He flinched, hands shooting out to capture her wrist, twisting her arm behind her again, and shoving her body forward until she was bent over the counter. She retaliated with a mule kick backward, catching him in the groin. He groaned in response, his hold on her loosening just enough for her to twist sideways and bring her elbow up into his solar plexus.

He swore on a whoosh of air, doubling over.

She twisted to the side again, breaking free of his grip. She spun around.

To face the barrel of his M9. She froze.

Of course he'd pull his gun. Of course he wasn't fazed by a superficial cut, and of course she couldn't have expected to get away while he still held both their weapons.

You're out of practice, Anya.

Though she did notice that his breath came hard, his nostrils flared, telling her the effort had cost him something. She took some small satisfaction in that.

"Until we know who these guys are," Dade ground out, "you're coming with me."

"I know who they are," she retaliated defiantly.

"I don't think you do."

"It's the KOS," she shot back, amazed at how easily the words flowed from her mouth, the secret she'd kept for so long practically spilling out of her. Words she'd been trained never to speak to anyone. Words that she'd tried desperately to forget everyday for the last decade and a half. "Members of the former Yugoslavian—"

"I know who the KOS are," he cut her off.

"And they know who *I* am," she said, the truth of it stinging like a slap. "They've tracked me down. They've hired these men to kill me."

Dade shook his head, his eyes steady on hers. "No. They haven't. Not these men."

Something in his voice changed. Almost imperceptibly. Yet there, enough to pause her arguments, and instead prompt Anna to ask,

"How do you know?"

He took a step toward her, his gun still steady in his hand, still trained on her midsection. His eyes holding hers— black, flat, void of all emotion.

"Because I'm the man the KOS hired to kill you."

CHAPTER FIVE

———

Dade watched Anya's eyes go round, a million questions flickering behind them. Then, without warning, her free hand shot out, slapping at his cheek. It was an act of pure instinct, he could tell. She was trained better than that. He had a gun on her for Christ's sake. But she wasn't thinking logically. In fact, he had a feeling she wasn't thinking much at all. She was in shock.

Which surprised him. The trained professional in his files didn't seem like someone who indulged in emotion, shock or otherwise.

"Stop it," he commanded, grabbing both of her wrists in one of his hands. They were tiny, and her body shook under his grip.

"You sonofabitch," she spat at him. "Do you know who these people are? Do you know what you've done? They'll find you. They'll find you, too!"

She was rambling. Bordering on hysterical. And he didn't have time for it. In the distance he heard sirens. A common enough sound in the City, but considering the dead body next door, they were anything but comforting.

"We have to go." He tightened his grip on her wrists.

She let out a bark of laughter. "You're kidding, right? I'm supposed to go quietly with you to my execution, is that it?"

"We're running out of time. The police will be here any minute. Do you want to explain the dead woman next door to them?"

Something flickered behind her eyes. An emotion that, in someone else, he might have mistaken for regret. It lingered only a split second before they clouded over with pure defiance again. "I have nothing to hide."

"That's bullshit, and we both know it." Dade grabbed her duffel bag, shouldering it himself, then moved his grip to her upper arm, steering her toward the broken front door.

"I'm not going anywhere with you," she protested, jerking her arm backward, trying to wiggle from his grip.

But he held on tight, sure his hand would leave a mark later.

"You don't have much choice."

"Shoot me."

"Excuse me?"

She took a wide stance, feet flat, shoulders back, chin lifted. "If you're here to kill me, do it. Shoot me."

He paused a moment, searching her face. It was a dare. But he wasn't entirely sure she wasn't prepared for him to take her up on it. He could read emotions, surging behind her eyes now, clear as day. Anger, frustration, and desperation were all undercurrents running beneath a thick layer of defiance. But no fear. Whatever she thought he was about to do, she was beyond fear.

He had to respect that.

"I don't have time for this," he answered, propelling her forward toward the splintered front door.

"You don't have time to shoot me? It's easy," she said, leaning in close, invading his personal space in a very deliberate way. "You just pull the trigger." She held her index finger and thumb up to his face. "And...pow!" she finished, shooting her mock finger-gun at him.

"Don't tempt me," he ground out then gave her a hard shove toward the front door.

She stumbled as he pushed her forward, the dog bounding along at her side. Her limbs were stiff, fighting him every step of the way, and he could feel energy roaring just below the surface. She was not going to "go quietly" that was for sure.

Still maintaining a firm grip on her upper arm, he propelled her down the stairway, pausing at the building's entrance to scan the yard before moving quickly to his SUV.

Anya was a good six inches shorter than he was and slim. It wasn't hard to manipulate her physically, and he had to remind himself not to get too comfortable in his ability to overpower her. She'd taken down men larger, stronger, and more dangerous than he was, as her file indicated. And he could feel her waiting for an opening to repeat that experience now.

He had to be sure he didn't give her one.

"Where are we going?" she asked, her eyes on her dog as they crossed the small square of lawn.

Dade squinted against the glare of crisp sunlight off the buildings across the street, acutely aware of the sirens growing louder now as he pulled keys from his pocket.

"Did you hear me?" she persisted. "I demand to know where you're taking me."

"Jesus, would you just shut up and get in the car?"

He pulled open the back door, motioning the dog in. Quite frankly, the animal was the last thing he needed right now. But it was clear that the dog was the quickest path to Anya's compliance. While he was an encumbrance that was almost comical at this point, he was Anya's one weak point. And Dade needed all the chips on his side he could get. At least until he figured out what the hell had gone wrong with his hit.

He shoved Anya into the passenger side, shutting the door behind her. The sirens were almost on top of them as he slid into the driver's seat and pulled away from the curb. It took all he had not to speed away from the scene, to keep his pace even—a few miles above the speed limit to avoid appearing guilty but considerably slower than he'd have liked to put distance between himself and the mess this job had become.

His contact had said nothing about multiple shooters. Dade had been assured he was the only man working the job, a job designed to "tie up loose ends," or so he'd been told. Either he'd been lied to, or someone else had Anya in their sights as clearly as his employer did. Which wouldn't be outside the realm of reality, considering the deeds outlined in her file, but it was a hell of a coincidence that they should both decide to neutralize her at the same time.

And Dade was not a man who believed in coincidences.

He'd already taken half payment for the job—the other half was payable when he'd neutralized the target. Anya's location had been disclosed by his contact and a timeline set for completion of the job. Dade had planned it quick and easy. No contact, no mess, and one bullet the only evidence left behind, traceable to a gun that would have been at the bottom of the San Francisco Bay by now.

Only nothing had gone according to plan today.

Dade glanced across the console at Anya. Her jaw was still clenched in defiance, arms crossed over her chest in an unconsciously protective gesture.

It would be the easiest thing in the world to drop her right now. Finish the job, toss the body into the bay.

But something was holding him back.

Sitting this close to her, watching her arms wrap around herself, her hands clench and unclench with tension, he had to admit it was hard to think of her as the anonymous target she'd been this time yesterday. A complication he hadn't counted on. Just like the dead neighbor, the ransacked apartment, the animal shelter full of bullet holes, and a witness to it all in that redhead.

Dade drew a breath in through his nostrils, letting it out slowly between his lips.

But one problem at a time. He'd take care of the redhead later. Right now…

He cut his eyes to Anya, again. While her posture was stoic, her eyes were busy scanning the interior of the car, the street in front of them, and the map on the GPS unit attached to his dashboard. Ready to jump at the first opportunity he gave her.

Right now there were too many unknowns. Like who was after her, why, and what, exactly, they might do if Dade shot her first.

Until he knew what he was dealing with, he couldn't risk making those kinds of enemies. This was purely business to him; the last thing he needed was to paint a target on his own back by pissing off some lunatic bent on eliminating Anya himself.

No, what he needed were answers. And, like it or not, Anya was going to give them up.

* * *

No matter how she tried to block them out, questions flew through Anna's brain faster than she could formulate answers. Who was Dade? Where was he taking her? How long would he wait before finishing the job he'd been hired to do? And, most importantly, if he was the KOS's man, who were they running from now?

She didn't know. Only one thing was certain.

Escape.

She stole a glance at her captor as he turned left onto Van Ness, searching his face for some clue as to his plans. His eyes were dark and focused on the road, mouth a straight line, and jaw clenched shut. A calm, unreadable wall.

He was numb. He'd been trained well, too.

"How did you find me?" she asked. Not that it mattered now. But if she could get him talking, she might be able to glean some information.

"I was given your location," came his clipped answer.

"By who?"

"Whom."

"What?"

"The correct word is *whom*."

She blinked at him. "I don't need a goddamn grammar lesson. I need some answers."

"Join the club," he mumbled, eyes still straight ahead on the road.

Anna took a deep breath, willing herself to rein in her emotions. Pissing off the guy with the gun was not going to get her anywhere but dead—and fast. She closed her eyes and counted to five.

"Who hired you?" she asked, making a concerted effort to keep her tone calm and even.

"I told you. The KOS."

"The KOS doesn't exist anymore. Give me a name."

He clenched his jaw tightly and kept his eyes straight ahead. No answer.

Which honestly told her more than she'd hoped. She'd bet anything that he didn't know who had hired him. If he had, he would have at least tried to protect his employer's identity with some lie. As it was, the slight twitch of his eyelid now told her that he wished he knew, too.

"How much did they pay you?" she asked.

Dade turned on her. "Excuse me?"

"I want to know how much my life is worth. What did they pay you to kill me? Twenty grand?"

"This is insane. I'm not having this conversation."

"Fifty? A hundred?"

He stared straight ahead.

"Two hundred?"

He didn't move. "Two-fifty?"

Anna watched his right eyelid twitch again.

"Two-fifty," she settled on. "Not bad. But if I were you, I would have held out for five."

His eyes shot to her. "Why? Is that *your* going rate to complete a job?"

"I don't have a rate," she answered quickly. "I don't kill for profit. And if you want to know, it's been seventeen years, three months, and four days since I last pulled the trigger of a gun."

"That's pretty exact."

Anna swallowed. She hadn't meant to say so much, but the moment had gotten the better of her. Her emotions were running high. Too high. She chose her next words carefully, willing her thoughts to slow down before speaking.

"You could say it left an impression."

"I take it this gun was pointed at someone?"

She bit the inside of her cheek. *Tread carefully here.*

"Yes." She nodded, trying to eradicate all trace of emotion from her voice.

"Someone who is now dead," he asked, though there was little question to it.

She closed her eyes, willing her mind to block out the image of her last kill—his eyes wide with surprise, face contorted with pain, color quickly draining from his cheeks as the life seeped out of him, staining his general's uniform a garish red.

"Yes," she answered slowly.

Dade was quiet a moment, and when he did speak his tone was lower, deeper. "You know, there are some people who make the world a better place dead than they did alive."

She opened her eyes to search for the empathy that might have been behind his words, but his gaze was straight ahead on the road. His mouth was a tight line—nothing soft or yielding in his demeanor at all.

"And who gets to decide that?" she asked him. "Who gets to play the anonymous judge and jury when it comes to their fate?"

"People who know better."

"People like you?" she asked.

He didn't answer, but his jaw tensed, a nerve just below his chin pulsing.

"You think you know me, don't you?" she continued. "You think you know me well enough to decide if I live or die."

"I've read your file," came his clipped response.

"I'm more than the contents of some damned file," she countered. Even though they were words she only halfway believed herself.

If her life as Anna had been such an easily shattered illusion, what did that leave her with now? Who was she really?

She shoved that disconcerting thought down as Dade turned left, pulling onto The Embarcadero. Anna craned her neck out the window and saw sparkling blue water peaking through warehouses lined up one after another to her right.

"Where are we going?" Visions of being tied up and thrown into the bay, lungs filling with frigid water, assaulted her. She shivered despite the sunlight filtering in the windows.

"Pier 39."

She knew the popular tourist attraction. She'd been there a handful of times since moving to San Francisco. The pier consisted of a wide, wooden walkway jutting into the Bay, lined with souvenir shops, seafood restaurants, and novelty attractions. It was a sightseeing must-see.

And not exactly the deserted dump site she'd imagined.

"You're going to kill me at a tourist spot?"

He shot her a look she wished she could read before turning his eyes back to the traffic in front of him.

"No. We need to talk, and I need somewhere safe to do it."

"Kind of crowded."

He nodded. "That's the idea."

He turned left at the light, pulling into a four-story concrete parking garage. A machine spit out a parking stub at him then raised its wooden arm to allow him access to the garage. The lower level was full, not surprisingly. He followed a ramp upward, finally finding an empty spot on the third level between a minivan and a Prius. He cut the engine and grabbed a pair of sunglasses from the dash and a jacket from the back seat. "Let's go." He got out of the car, motioning her to do the same.

She did.

And for a split second she was standing on one side of the car with Dade on the other. And a hunk of bulletproof metal between them.

Run. Go. Duck behind the parked cars. Weave through traffic. You can lose him.

But she stayed rooted to the spot. Lenny stared at her through the tinted back window, his tongue protruding, head cocked to the side, and big black eyes wet and ignorantly grateful to be out of the cramped apartment for the day.

She couldn't leave him behind. And Dade knew it.

"Come on," he said, suddenly at her side, a leather jacket covering the bulge of his gun from view.

She took a deep breath, her moment of opportunity gone.

There will be another one. Wait. Be patient.

"What about Lenny?" She gestured to the boxer. His face was pressed against the window, making slobber prints on the glass.

"He's fine."

"He might get hot."

"I cracked a window."

"What if he's hungry?"

Dade gestured to the bag of dog chow that Lenny had already liberated from her duffel.

"He gets lonely. He barks when he gets lonely."

"Nice try. The dog stays," he said, grabbing her by the arm again and propelling her away from the car.

With little choice to do otherwise, Anna fell in step beside him. A pedestrian bridge spanned The Embarcadero from the garage to the Pacific side. Several piers lined the road there. Some were home to storage warehouses and others to cargo ships unloading crates from Asia. Still more with overflow parking for tourists. A few were set up as attractions filled with kitschy shops, street performers, and bay cruises to Alcatraz, Angel Island, and the ocean beyond where most months of the year the migrating whales could be seen by marine enthusiasts.

Dade led the way across the bridge to Pier 39. It was a weekday, but during the summer that hardly mattered. The wide wooden walkway was already crowded with visitors wearing cargo shorts, backpacks, and sunburns. Anna and Dade blended into the throng of people moving down the pier, passing the Hard Rock Café, the aquarium, and the Infinite Mirror Maze. Normally the crowd would have made Anna feel comfortable— the mass of people mitigating the loneliness of keeping a secret she harbored most days. But today, every person that passed by was a potential threat. Every pair of eyes on her a spy, every elbow that jostled hers as they threaded their way through the crowd an attack, making her jump both physically and mentally.

While Dade's eyes were covered by dark glasses, Anna could tell by his body language that he was on alert as much as she was. His grip on her arm was tight, his shoulders tensed, all his peripheral senses scanning the area for unknown assailants.

"I don't like this," Anna said. "I feel too exposed. There are too many things we can't control."

"We're not staying on the pier."

"Where are we going?" she asked, feeling like a broken record. She didn't like being kept in the dark any more than she liked feeling overexposed.

"We're getting on a boat."

Her feet froze. "Are you crazy? We get on a boat and we're trapped. Sitting ducks."

Dade tightened his grasp on her arm, pushing her forward, even as her feet stumbled to catch up. "Calm down," he ground out, his eyes still focused straight ahead. "Think clearly."

She swallowed.

Right. Calm. No emotion. Emotions are weak. And weak agents make mistakes.

She cleared her throat. "I'm calm. I'm just not sure that a pleasure cruise is a good idea right now."

"Once we get on a boat, we're also enclosed. No one gets on or off until we return to the dock. As long as they don't follow us on, we've bought ourselves two hours."

She bit her lip. He made a certain sense. "*If* they don't follow us on."

"So keep your eyes peeled," he said, making his way through the crowd.

As if she hadn't been doing just that for the past seventeen years.

But she did as he instructed, her gaze scanning the face of each person they encountered as they threaded their way down the pier. A German family with two teenagers sat on a wooden bench eating chowder from bread bowls. A guy in a Hawaiian shirt was buying a miniskirted brunette a pair of coral earrings from a vendor cart. A couple kids in puka shell necklaces and baggy shorts stood in line to ride the carousel.

None of the benign-looking day-trippers screamed "assassin." But Anna wished she had her weapon back all the same.

She stuck close to Dade as he led the way toward a small, covered shack on the right side of the pier near the end. A ticket window took up most of the front, a sign next to it listing tickets available for various bay cruises. Dade purchased two tickets on the Blue & Gold Fleet's next cruise around Alcatraz. Cash. The boat was to leave in half an hour, jacking up Anna's paranoia. Thirty minutes was plenty of time for anyone to catch up to them.

"I need to change," Anna said, once Dade had shoved the tickets in his back pocket.

"Into what?"

"I need a fresh shirt."

She gestured to her clothes. It was true. The T-shirt she'd thrown on that morning was cut in several places, the shattered glass from the shelter having made its mark. A smear of her neighbor's blood graced her sleeve, and her right side was streaked with dregs from the Indian place's dumpster. Curry, if she had to guess from the smell.

Dade followed her gaze. "Fine."

He looked up, and Anna watched him scan the shops along the walkway. Several sold souvenir clothing, ranging from pricey designer items to made-in-China T-shirts. He settled on the latter, nodding toward a place two doors down with a sign proclaiming everything inside was ten dollars or less.

"Can you find something in there?" he asked.

She nodded. At this point, any place she could change in private would do.

Two seconds when he's not watching you. That's all you need.

Dade strode purposefully across the walkway, his hand still firm on Anna's arm. The front of the shop was open, racks spilling out onto the pier to entice visitors farther inside. Two college kids in Stanford sweatshirts pawed through the closest one. Dade paused, and Anna saw him doing a slow sweep of their bodies before navigating around them. A visual weapons check. He didn't trust anyone.

That thought made her feel both protected and deeper in danger all at once.

"Let's make this fast," Dade instructed, hovering next to her as Anna quickly gravitated to a rack labeled women. She grabbed a shirt at random. It was white, proclaiming that she had left her heart in San Francisco in scrolling purple script. It would do for now.

She handed it to Dade. "This one's fine."

Dade's eyes flickered to the shirt, then back up to her. "Kind of big isn't it?"

"I'm not entering a wet T-shirt contest."

For a half a second he looked as if he wanted to smile, but it never quite made it to his lips. Instead, he took the shirt from her, getting in line behind the college kids. When he got to the front of the line, he paid the clerk cash, exchanging only the barest minimum of words before taking their purchase and steering Anna back out of the store.

Once outside, he handed the bag to her. "Here. Knock yourself out."

Anna pulled the shirt out of the bag and took a step toward the restrooms to the far right of the carousel.

But Dade's grip stopped her.

"Where are you going?" he asked, pulling her into his chest.

"I need to change," she answered, gesturing to the shirt.

He shook his head. "You can put it on here."

"Really? You think it would be less conspicuous if I stripped down here in the middle of the pier?" Anna thrust her chest out toward him.

"Just put it on over the old one. It's big enough."

"That kind of defeats the purpose of a clean shirt. I'm still wearing the evidence."

Dade's grip tightened on her arm. "You're not going anywhere alone."

"You wanna come with me into the women's restroom? Because I'm sure no one will notice you there."

Dade clenched his jaw, and she could see his nostrils flare at her sarcasm.

But she stood her ground.

"Look, I need to change. It will only take a couple of minutes."

He paused. "Fine," he finally spat out. "You have two minutes. You're not out of that restroom in exactly two minutes, I'm coming in guns drawn. Understood?"

She nodded, letting him propel her forward until they reached the ladies' room door. Women with fanny packs and toddlers in tow navigated around them as Dade paused at the entrance. His grip tightened momentarily, as if having second thoughts about letting her out of his sight. But clearly the less evidence from the shelter she carried on her person, the better for them both. A point he must have realized as he slowly let go.

"Two minutes," he repeated.

Again she nodded in compliance before slipping through the door.

The second she was alone, Anna scanned the room for an escape route. The door she'd come in was the only one visible here. It was crowded. Woman were two deep at the mirrors, sidling awkwardly around each other to reach the sinks and automatic hand dryers.

She pushed through them, surveying the row of stalls at the back wall. Ten in all, lined up along the right side of a rectangular room. No back door.

A small row of windows lined the back wall at the end of the row. But they were at least six feet off the ground. Even if she could have reached them, she wasn't sure she could have pried through the layers of paint and grime to open one, let alone fit through.

90 seconds.

The only way out was the way she'd come in—through Dade.

She bit back disappointment and pulled open a stall, eyes roving instead for anything that could be used as a weapon. Paper seat protectors, small squares of toilet tissue in a metal dispenser that was bolted to the wall above a tiny metal garbage container for feminine hygiene disposal. Nothing she could take with her. Nothing she could hide in a pocket.

60 seconds.

She felt desperation begin to bubble up in her throat as she ripped her tainted clothing off, shoving the clean T-shirt over her head. She exited the stall, depositing her cast-offs in the nearest trash can beneath a pile of dirty diapers and used tissues. She was clean but no closer to escape.

30 seconds.

Anna's eyes shot around the busy room. Sinks were affixed to the wall on one side, hand dryers on the other. A plastic foldout diaper changing station and a metal feminine products dispenser sat on the far wall. Anna crossed to the metal machine. For ten cents she could purchase a sanitary pad or a tampon. For fifty, a single dose packet of Advil or SPF 15 sunscreen. And for a dollar, a condom or a plastic pouch of Chanel No. 5 Imposter.

Anna quickly dug into the pocket of her jeans, coming up with two fives and a one dollar bill. She pulled the one out, sliding it into the machine.

The machine spit it back out.

She smoothed the dollar on the thigh of her jeans, noticing the damp layer of sweat her palm left there as she carefully fed it into the machine again.

Again it spit the dollar out.

15 seconds.

Desperation was an almost palpable thing, her stomach clenching, her limbs tingling, everything she had focused on keeping her hands from shaking as she took a deep breath and, with excruciating slowness, fed the bill into the machine again.

Thank God, this time, the bill stayed put.

A sigh of relief escaped her as she quickly turned the metal knob beneath the perfume photo. She heard a click inside the machine then a second later a small plastic pouch fell out of the metal chute and into her outstretched hand. Anna shoved it into her back pocket and spun around toward the entrance.

She was two steps away when Dade's frame filled the doorway, his hand hovering at the waistband of his pants where she knew his gun still sat concealed from view.

Anna pasted a smile on her face.

"All changed," she told him, swallowing down fear as she let her captor lead her away again.

CHAPTER SIX

———

The Blue & Gold Fleet was one of San Francisco's largest tour companies on the water, with sixteen vessels including catamarans, speed boats, and Bay tour cruises. Three of those signature yellow and navy blue boats were tethered to the right side of the pier, down a level from the shops and restaurants. A rickety wooden staircase led to the water level where large, tar-coated ramps were pulled into place to allow easy access to the boats.

Anna stepped carefully over the wet surface, letting a weathered man in a pair of yellow overalls take her hand as she boarded the boat. Dade was a step behind, keeping close enough that she could feel the heat from his body at her back. It was unnerving at best, and she had to make a conscious effort not to run from him. Not that there was anywhere to run. The boat was larger than some of the fishing boats tethered to the pier, featuring both an outdoor area for sightseeing and an indoor section where guests could take refuge from the wind as they crossed the Bay to the main attraction. But packed with bodies, there was little room to navigate.

Dade steered Anna to a spot at the stern then positioned himself with his back to the rail. His eyes were shaded behind his glasses, but Anna could tell he was watching intently as each passenger stepped over the threshold. Scrutinizing each face, assessing the danger level.

A steady stream of people boarded, mostly families with young children and older couples. Anna dismissed them quickly. The people after her could be anyone, but considering they had little time to plan, she couldn't see her pursuers coming up with an entire fake family to play tourist with.

A young guy with a backpack boarded, and Anna felt herself stiffen. But as soon as he pulled out a digital camera and started snapping photos of the sun-bathing sea lions on the rocks nearby, she dismissed him as a harmless amateur photographer, one of dozens who flocked to the spot each day.

Fifteen long, tense minutes later, the crew finally pulled up the anchor, and a cheery-sounding captain came over the loudspeaker.

"Welcome aboard the world famous Blue & Gold Fleet's Escape from Alcatraz tour. I hope you're all in for a great escape today!"

If he only knew.

Anna struggled to steady herself as the boat pulled slowly away from the dock, the engines churning up froth on the water's surface. As the vessel sliced through the cool water, past barnacle-encrusted stilts of the pier, Dade moved from the stern, nodding Anna toward the front of the boat. Several people crowded the area, pointing out sights along the coastline, eager to be the first of their party to spot a lounging sea lion or playful otter. But as the engines picked up speed, water began to spray over the helm, covering the deck in a salty mist. Both the damp and noise of the boat slapping through the rough waters sent most of the passengers filtering inside, leaving Dade and Anna in sparse company.

Anna leaned into the chipped railing. The metal was cold beneath her palms, but she clung to it anyway, an anchor as she let her weight shift naturally from foot to foot with the rocking waves. The roar of the water drowned the conversations of the few diehards left outside to a low hum. She closed her eyes, lifting her face to the wind. Saltwater flavored her lips as her hair slapped at her cheeks, the sharp wind stinging her skin. It felt good. Like a cool, refreshing shower. Physical sensation slapping away the cloud of emotions hanging over her thoughts.

"Time to talk." Dade's voice was low in her ear.

She dragged in a breath of damp air, reluctantly opening her eyes again as she turned to him.

"About what?" she countered.

"Everything."

A loaded answer. And not one she was willing to oblige, considering the circumstances.

"What do you want me to say?" she asked, wishing he would take those glasses off. Wishing she could see his eyes and had some hope of reading the thoughts behind his clipped words.

"Someone wants you dead, Anya."

"Anna," she corrected automatically. "My name is Anna."

He raised an eyebrow at her.

"Anya is dead," she said. And she meant it. No matter what feelings had risen to the surface today, long thought buried, she would not let that life leak back into her world.

"That may be," Dade responded, "but someone apparently wants Anna dead, too." His voice was raised above the roar of the ocean, but the tone was low, even, and much more calm than Anna felt.

She didn't answer him. Instead she looked past him to a point out on the water, trying not to internalize that statement.

At twenty years old, death had been an abstract. The finality of it obvious in her line of work yet not fully real to someone who had yet to experience much life. Something to be feared in theory, with no concept of how much she'd be missing out on. Only now, having had a taste of what life could be, it was not only real but terrifying.

"Who is after you?" Dade persisted.

She turned her eyes back to meet his. "I don't know. God, if I knew, you think I'd be sitting here on a boat with you? I'd be out there returning the favor."

He narrowed his eyes at her, trying to decide if she was telling him the truth. She didn't know what conclusion he came to, but he switched gears, asking, "Tell me about your life."

She sighed. "Why?"

"Because you're not very popular at the moment, and I'd like to know why."

"Why do you care?" she asked.

"Because I don't like complications."

"So you only kill uncomplicated targets. Is that it?"

Dade shot her a warning look. "Let me explain something to you. I ask the questions; you provide answers. That's how this is going to work. Got it?"

She bit down the snide remark on the tip of her tongue, reminding herself how easy it would be for him to give her the slightest nudge over the railing right now and be done with her. She needed buy time. The longer she could stave off the threat he presented, the better her chance at finding a way around it.

She pursed her lips together and nodded as demurely as she could manage. "Got it."

"Good. Tell me about your last job."

"What last job?"

"The last job you completed. Was it here in the states?" he clarified.

"No," she said emphatically. "I told you I don't do that anymore. I left that life behind."

"Apparently not far enough behind."

She paused. "Point taken."

"You faked your death in Kosovo," he said.

She nodded slowly, the memory of that day flooding back to her faster than she would have liked.

"Who knows that you're still alive?"

She shrugged. "Up until today, I didn't think anyone did." Which was the truth. For seventeen years she'd looked over her shoulder every day, but no one had ever appeared there. It had almost been long enough to become comfortable with the idea that she really had pulled one over on the KOS.

Almost.

"You haven't had any contact with anyone from your former life since then? Friends? Family?"

She shook her head. "I grew up in the KOS. I didn't have friends or family."

"Could it be someone current, then?" he asked. "Someone who has a grudge against you as Anna?"

She let out a bark of laughter, though again there was no humor behind it. "You're kidding, right? I'm a glorified dog washer. I'm not exactly pushing people's buttons."

He nodded. "So whoever is after you is after Anya."

"So it would seem."

"Did you have enemies?"

She shook her head. "I was an assassin. It's not exactly a friendly profession." She paused. "As you well know."

He ignored the comment, instead asking, "Anyone in particular seem *un*friendly?"

She closed her eyes, leaning her head back, calling up memories she'd just as soon forget. "I don't know. I don't remember their names. As soon as I closed the files, I blocked them out." She opened her eyes again and trained them on his. "Besides, they're all dead."

It was a hollow statement of fact, and it disturbed her just how easily she said it.

"What about the people you worked with. Who trained you?"

"I told you. The KOS."

"A name."

"Goren Petrovich was my handler," she said, finding the words tasted odd in her own mouth after so many years. "But he's dead."

"What about the others? The ones who supplied your targets?"

She shrugged. "I don't know. It's not like I could keep in touch after I left. Besides, most of those people didn't officially even exist then; it's hard to know if they do now."

Even as she said it, she couldn't help wondering. She'd asked the same thing hundreds of times herself. Once the Yugoslavian government had collapsed, everything she had ever known had fallen apart. She'd been lucky to get out when she had. Some of her counterparts hadn't been so fortunate, ending up taking the fall for the people who issued their orders—the real hands on the triggers. Not that she'd known any of them personally at the time. They'd all been as nameless as she was. Anonymous, interchangeable agents that the government had churned out like clones, putting them into service as long as they stayed useful, making sure no trace was left behind once that usefulness ran its course.

As if he could read her thoughts, Dade asked, "Who else did you work with?"

She pursed her lips together, forcing her thoughts backward in time. "There was another agent I worked with a couple times. Peter. I never knew his last name. And a doctor I saw once. Mishakeal."

"Anyone else?"

She realized what he was doing. He was fishing for a name that sounded familiar, a link between her and his contact.

"Who hired you?" she asked, turning the tables on him.

He gave her a hard look. But said nothing.

"So, I'm supposed to trust you with my life story when you give me nothing in return?"

He shrugged, his shoulders lifting ever so slightly. "I have the gun."

For now.

"Look, I did a lot of bad things to bad people with bad tempers," she admitted. "I have no idea where any of them are now or who might have been the most angry. It was years ago, for God's sake."

"Fine." He drew in a deep breath. "Then tell me this: who could have found you here?" he asked.

"I don't know." She paused. "How did your employer find me?"

Predictably, he ignored the question about himself again. "Tell me about your friends."

"I don't have any."

"Boyfriends?"

"No."

"Your neighbors."

She swallowed down the sudden raw memory of Mrs. Olivia's body, twisted under itself on the cold floor of her apartment.

"I wasn't close with anyone. I only knew them to say hello."

"How long have you lived there?"

"Almost four months."

"Who have you—"

"Look, there's no one, okay?" she cut in. His game of twenty questions wasn't doing her any good. He was giving her nothing, and she was spilling everything in return. Not something she'd intended to do, but somehow once she opened her memory a crack, the truth was hard to contain again. "I don't spend time with anyone, I don't talk to anyone, and I don't engage with anyone. I'm not that stupid."

But even as she said it, she knew that wasn't entirely true. As careful as she'd been, she must have messed up somewhere. Or else they wouldn't be where they were now.

"What about your coworker?" Dade asked. "The redhead."

"Shelli? What about her?"

"How well do you know her?"

Anna shook her head. "Shelli's harmless."

She felt his eyes narrow behind his shades again. "You didn't answer my question."

"I know her well enough to know that she's harmless, okay?"

"How long have you two been friends?"

"We're coworkers, not friends. I told you I don't have friends," she corrected. "And she was hired on a couple months after I was."

Dade stiffened, his posture shifting to attention.

"*After* you were?"

"Yes." She nodded slowly. "But that doesn't mean—"

"Where did she work before that?" he asked, cutting her off.

"I…I don't know. Why is it important?" But even as she asked the question her mind jumped on the same track as Dade's. Someone had been watching her. They had put together the pieces linking her painfully nonexistent life now to the one she'd left in flames. Had Shelli been planted to gather those pieces? She'd never seemed anything but casually interested in Anna's life. She'd never pried beyond friendly inquiries into Anna's past, her social life. At least, they'd seemed friendly enough at the time…

"Where does Shelli live?" Dade asked, breaking her out of her own sudden suspicions.

"A place in the lower Haight."

"You've been to her house?"

"Not inside but, yeah, I dropped her off at her apartment one day when the busses were down."

"I thought you said you weren't friends?"

"We're not. I just gave her a ride. That's all."

"Does she know where you live?"

Anna opened her mouth to respond in the negative, paused mid-thought, and then shut it. "Maybe."

He raised a questioning eyebrow her way.

"I never gave out my address," she explained. "But I guess it's possible she could have looked up my employment info. My checks had to be mailed somewhere."

"Checks?"

"Paper. I don't do digital trails."

He nodded, seemingly agreeing. "Did you ever meet any of her friends? Relatives? Anyone who knew her ever drop by the shelter?"

She slowly shook her head, feeling the sickening suspicion build. She didn't want to believe it. She didn't want to believe that the first person she'd even been casually friendly with in her adult life might turn out to want her dead.

Shelli had seemed genuinely scared when she'd been crouching under the desk at the shelter. But if she'd been playing Anna since they'd met, was it really a stretch that she'd been playing at scared this morning, too?

Her questions must have shone in her eyes as Dade nodded, resolution clear in the straight line of his shoulders.

"We start with Shelli."

*　*　*

They rode the rest of the trip in silence, the boat slowing as they rounded Alcatraz, causing tourists once again to flock to the railing with their cameras as the captain detailed some of the island's most infamous inhabitants. Al Capone, The Birdman of Alcatraz, and George "Machine Gun" Kelly, the prohibition gangster. Anna only halfway listened, lost in her own thoughts. By the time they hit dry land again, she was antsy—tired of standing still, and ready to move.

Once again, Anna watched Dade's stoic posture, scanning the people at the dock as the boat pulled back into its slip. He slowly assessed each body leaning against the wooden railing above them, checking for weapons, for anything out of place, anyone too interested in the inhabitants of the boat as it docked beside the pier.

As far as Anna could tell, only the same sea of pleasure seekers stared back at them. Benign, harmless, one face blending into the next. Whoever was after her, they hadn't followed Anna to the pier.

"Let's go," Dade commanded, his hand again on Anna's arm as the crowd of people surged toward the back of the boat. He guided her through them and up the gangplank and the short flight of stairs leading back up to the pier.

She let him lead her as far as the brightly colored carousel again, located at the widest point of the pier and still tinkling an overly cheery tune, before the urge to move overwhelmed her.

It's now or never, Anya.

She deliberately halted her pace, jolting Dade backward.

"Ohmigod, it's them," she said, letting very real fear taint her voice.

Dade's hand shot down to his waistband, hovering over the hidden butt of his gun. "Where?" he asked, his voice sharp and clipped, easily slipping into combat mode.

"There." Anna pointed toward a corner shop hidden in the midday shadows. "Just behind the candy store. I saw a gun muzzle."

Dade took his sunglasses off, squinting into the darkened corner.

Which was exactly what Anna had hoped he would do.

In a second she had her hidden perfume packet out of her pocket, ripped open with her teeth, and pointed directly at Dade's face.

She squeezed, watching a sharp spray of fake Chanel No. 5 hit his eyes.

"Sonofabitch!" His hands immediately went to his face, his grip on her arm gone.

And Anna ran.

CHAPTER SEVEN

———

Anna took off at a full sprint, weaving through tourists. She knocked into shopping bags, jostled past strollers, and tripped over feet—both her own and those of the people she shoved out of the way. She could feel Dade behind her, and panic spurred her forward.

The perfume must have stung, but she knew it wouldn't faze him for long. It was a single moment of surprise. One she knew she had to take every advantage of quickly, putting as much distance between them as she could. He was taller, stronger. He'd be on her in a second.

As if to confirm her thoughts, footsteps fell behind her, loudly, hammering down on the wooden planks like ominous thunder. Gaining on her, gobbling up her advantage much faster than she'd hoped.

Pushing her to run faster.

She passed a row of take-out stands, the scents of chowder, raw fish, and fried calamari filling her nostrils as her breath came faster and faster. Her limbs pumped, her eyes darting ahead, calculating her next move—weave to the right to avoid the woman in the backpack, swerve left so you don't knock over that toddler, move around the double stroller and don't trip on the wheels. She knocked into a woman, jostling her purse to the ground. She hit a guy in khakis with a camera in hand. They were slowing her down.

She could only hope they were slowing Dade as well. The pier was a long structure with only one way in and one way out. While there were plenty of nooks and crannies between the shops to hide in, hiding was all she could do there. She'd be stuck, waiting for him to find her. It was possible she could outrun him to the end of the pier, but then what? She knew he'd easily catch up to her before she could get to Lenny. And, as he well knew, there was no way she was leaving him behind.

No, she couldn't outrun Dade.

But she could outsmart him.

She quickly jagged left, darting through the maze of wooden shops lined up two stories high along the water. She ran around the back side of the stores, between the wooden buildings and the frigid Bay lapping at the wooden pylons. There were fewer people here, fewer obstacles between her and her destination.

She pushed on past three more shops then took a wooden staircase leading to the second level of stores and attractions on the east side of the pier. She heard Dade rounding the back of the stores behind her, and knew he'd spotted her on the stairs. It wouldn't take long before he was on top of her. She had thirty seconds. A minute, tops. She needed to hide, to lose him somewhere. And ahead of her was the perfect place—the entrance to the Infinite Mirror Maze.

Anna had been in once before, when the attraction had first opened, curious to see if it was really as difficult to navigate as the review in the *SF Gate* had hailed it. To her delight, it had been. Room after room of floor-to-ceiling mirrors reflecting dozens of images of herself from every direction, obscuring the exit in a challenge that she'd thoroughly enjoyed at the time. On that visit, Anna had been issued a pair of vinyl gloves in order to touch the mirrors in front of her to find her way out. Only today Anna had no time to wait in line, no time to pay, and no time to worry about putting on gloves.

She shoved through the line of patrons at the front entrance, jumping over the turnstile before the attendant, a pimply college student, could do more than yell, "Hey!"

Once inside, a kaleidoscope of glass stared back at her, instantly distorting her sense of reality. She saw herself several times over, mingled with snippets of images of other people in the maze. Though which direction they were coming from she couldn't tell. Voices bounced off the glass—children screeching with laughter, men and women calling out to their companions swallowed up by phantom images. She tried to walk through an opening to her right, only to run up against a solid wall.

She bit her lip, took a deep breath, and willed her body to calm down now. The fight-or-flight hormones had served her well running down the pier, but now she needed a level head and a steady hand to find her way out before Dade found her. She reached in front of her, feeling her way along the first wall, turning left around a corner. Two more false starts, and she found herself turning left again, hoping she wasn't going in circles.

She wasn't sure how long she felt her way through the cool, sleek walls, but soon a new voice broke through the odd echoes surrounding her.

"Anya. I know you're here," came the calm, confident tone.

Anna froze, eyes instantly scanning the dozens of distorted images around her for Dade's. Nothing. Just a pair of blond kids to her right, an Asian couple to her left. Or at least their images reflected from directions unknown.

Panic filled her as she felt her way left, then right, not sure if she was walking deeper into the maze, trapping herself, or moving closer to the entrance and freedom.

"Anya. I can hear you breathing." A chill ran up her spine.

He's trying to rattle you. Scare you into answering and making a mistake.

She took a slow, steadying breath, willing her mind to ignore Dade's taunts. If he wanted to find her, he'd have to do it on his own. She was not giving anything away. Instead, she closed her eyes, reached her hands out in front of her, and slowly felt her way forward.

She'd done the maze before, so logically she knew all she had to do was let her body feel its way out. Let her fingers tell her where the walls were and let her feet follow the same path she had before. If she could tune out the panic, she knew her body would remember the direction to go. She very slowly and deliberately breathed in then out, in then out. Clearing her mind of thoughts long enough to let her body take over.

It felt like an eternity later before she finally rounded a corner and saw the sweetest sight she'd ever laid eyes on—the green, glowing exit sign.

She quickly pushed through the door, blinking against the sudden sunshine. She didn't waste time, knowing he could be right behind her. She bolted down the wooden stairs, two at a time, and raced toward the front of the pier.

Her feet pounded on the wooden boards, soles slapping on the ground, her ears perked, waiting to hear the sound of Dade chasing her.

The end of the pier was in sight. A woman in a flowy dress was playing a guitar. A guy with a sitar sat beside her, a music case open with dollar bills inside. Anna ran past them, hitting the pedestrian bridge, fairly flying over the traffic on The Embarcadero below. Once on the other side, her footsteps echoed in the parking garage, giving away her location to anyone nearby. But it couldn't be helped—speed was more important than stealth now.

She took the stairs to the third floor, not waiting for the elevator. Dade's SUV was parked at the end of the row at the back, just as she'd left it. She paused just long enough to take off her left shoe, shove her hand inside, and use it as a glove to smash the driver's side widow.

It took three tries before the glass shattered under the force of her thick-soled boot. Lenny barked wildly in the back seat, bouncing up and down on the leather, though whether it was because of the noise or because he was happy to see her, she wasn't sure.

Anna reached through the shattered window, unlocking the door manually. Ignoring the glass shards, she slid into the driver's seat and looked under the steering column. The outline of a square panel sat just beneath the wheel. She stuck her fingernails into the crack at the side, pulling, only to break a nail painfully close to the skin.

Instinctively she slipped the injured tip of her finger in her mouth, sucking as she quickly looked around the cab for anything slim and rigid she could use to pry the panel open. She dug into the pocket of her jeans until her fingers closed around the fake ID she'd swiped from her place. She inserted the edge into the crack between the panel and the steering column. On the second try, it finally popped off.

She said a silent *thank you* that the car wasn't the latest model. That would make things easier. She grabbed at the wires exposed beneath the steering wheel, locating the two red ones she was looking for. She stripped down the ends of both with her teeth then twisted the exposed metal together, connecting the ignition switch's primary power supply to the car's electrical circuits.

Feeling time slip away form her, she shot a glance out the window. No sign of Dade.

Yet.

Anna sifted through the remaining wires, locating a brown ignition wire, stripping it with her teeth as she had the others until she had a half inch of bare metal exposed. Taking care not to let her red wires touch anything metal along the column, she gently touched the exposed brown wire to the twisted section of the red. A cough sounded from the engine. She tried again, this time letting the brown wire sit for just a second more. A longer cough.

She hit the wires a third time, letting out a sigh of relief as the engine caught. Her right foot hit the gas pedal, revving the machine to life.

She quickly put the car in reverse, letting the exposed wires dangle at her knees as she backed out of the parking space, swerving right toward the garage's exit.

Not a moment too soon.

As she pulled left into traffic on The Embarcadero, cutting off a minivan, she spied Dade on the pedestrian bridge above. The van's driver hit his horn in response to her line jumping, and Dade's gaze immediately shot her way.

The last thing she saw in her rearview mirror as she drove away was the satisfying look of surprise on Dade's face as he watched his own car race down the street away from him.

* * *

Shelli lived on a quiet street in a section of the City called the lower Haight, located along the famous Haight Street, just this side of Divisidero. East of the bohemian Haight-Ashbury, the neighborhood was home to trendy nightclubs, restaurants, coffee shops, and galleries, making it a popular neighborhood for studio apartments and single people craving a true urban experience.

Or looking to pose as one such person.

Shelli's building had once been a motel, since converted into cheap housing. Four units on the ground floor faced a courtyard of square concrete tiles flanked by flowering agapanthus. Two more stories above made a total of twelve units.

Anna circled the block, scanning the windows of all twelve for any sign of Dade, her attackers, or anyone else who might add their name to the list of people who wanted her out of the picture. Nothing jumped out at her as off. Ditto the surrounding buildings. She circled around the back and parked a block and a half down on a side street. Afraid to leave Lenny in the car with a busted window, she pulled the leash from her duffel and clamped it on his collar, taking him with her as she walked back toward Shelli's place.

As much as she wanted to believe Dade was wrong, Anna'd had the short drive over to realize that her "wanting" was clouding her judgment. Shelli was the one person who might have been close enough to Anna to learn the truth about her identity. She'd been painstakingly careful about building Anna Smith. But no one was infallible. Wherever she'd made the mistake, whatever had tipped them off to her real identity, it would have taken someone close to her to be sure that Anna was a fake. Why they wanted her and who "they" were, she had no idea. It amazed her that after all these years, anyone would care. Anya had known lots of secrets about lots of people then, but she'd thought the need for secrecy had died long ago.

She wondered at the timing. Had someone been looking for her all this time, or was there something special about *now*? What she'd told Dade about her current life was true—she'd done nothing important enough to upset anyone. So why now? Why decide she was such a threat today? She didn't know.

But she was damned well going to find out.

She followed the uneven sidewalk to Shelli's apartment complex and paused at 2A, the ground floor unit on the far right. It was a simple wooden door with a brass number affixed beneath a peephole. A window sat to the left, white, plastic blinds shut tightly. None of the interior was visible from the outside. No sound from beyond the door giving a clue to its occupant.

Anna rang the bell, ready for just about anyone to open the door. Shelli, a masked gunman, a gang of thugs. At this point not much would surprise her.

She found herself clenching and unclenching her fists as she counted off the seconds, alternating between feeling brave and ready to fight and being terrified at the unknown and the fact that she stood unarmed against it.

Ten Mississippi, eleven Mississippi, twelve....

She rang again, listening to the chimes echo inside. But again no movement greeted her, no sound at all indicating Shelli was there.

Anna turned around, her eyes scanning the small courtyard. A cool breeze from the Bay ruffled tall grasses and native wildflowers between the buildings. A car drove by on the street beyond, and the sound of a trolley two blocks over echoed in the distance. A dog barked from somewhere nearby.

Anna stiffened.

A small, scared, yelping bark. She couldn't be sure, but it sounded a hell of a lot like the dog Shelli had left the shelter with that morning.

Anna cocked her head to the side, putting an ear to Shelli's door. But as the dog continued to bark, she realized the sounds were not coming from Shelli's apartment but from 1A—the unit across the courtyard.

Anna quickly crossed the paved distance and knocked on the opposite door.

A minute later it opened to reveal an Asian woman in her sixties. She wore a red velour sweat suit, and her hair hung loosely to her waist, a grey color mingling with sleek strands of jet black.

"Yes?" she asked, blinking up at Anna, her eyes squinting ever so slightly as if trying to call up a name to go with the face before her.

"I'm sorry to bother you," Anna started, "but I'm a friend of Shelli's. I work with her at the shelter. Anna." She stuck her hand out, doing her best to present a friendly, causal demeanor.

Despite the panic and fear that had been tumbling inside her all morning, she must have pulled it off as the woman's features softened, her hand reaching out to shake Anna's.

"Karen. Nice to meet you."

"You, too. I was wondering if you've seen Shelli today? She doesn't seem to be answering her bell."

The woman nodded. "Yes. She was here just a little while ago. She asked if I could watch a dog for her."

"I thought I heard Fido in there." Anna forced a smile. "Why did she need a pet sitter? Was she going somewhere?"

The woman nodded. "She said she'd be out of town for a few days. Needed to clear her head or something like that. She was only home a few minutes before she left with a backpack over her shoulder."

Anna forced the smile to stay on her face, forced herself not to display any of the sickening betrayal seeping into her belly. Shelli had fled.

Maybe she was just scared? Maybe she's staying with a friend. Going home to family.

Or maybe she was fleeing before the police realized she was involved in the shooting. Before Anna had a chance to put two and two together.

And come after her.

"I don't suppose Shelli told you where she was going?" Anna asked the woman.

She shook her head, hair falling softly over her shoulders. "Sorry, she didn't say. But she said she couldn't take a dog on the plane with her."

"The airport," Anna said, more to herself than the neighbor.

"That's what I'd guess," she answered.

"How long ago was this?"

The woman pursed her lips and shrugged. "Not long. Maybe an hour?"

"Thank you," Anna said. "Listen, if she comes back, can you tell her that I'm looking for her? Anna?"

She nodded. "Sure. Does she have your number?"

Anna nodded. Unfortunately, in more ways than one, it seemed.

She heard the woman's door close behind her, but Anna was already jogging back to her stolen SUV, Lenny bounding happily alongside her.

If Shelli had been there recently, it was possible Anna could catch up to her at the airport before she boarded a flight.

The San Francisco airport was actually located south of the City, down Highway 101 toward Silicon Valley. Anna wasted no time, pointing the car in the direction of the freeway.

Lenny started pacing the back seat, and Anna had a bad feeling that the bag of dog chow he'd been flirting with all morning was finally catching up to him. Unfortunately, a bathroom stop was something she couldn't take right now. She crossed her fingers that the dog could hold it as she merged onto the freeway.

Twenty minutes later she pulled into short-term parking at SFO. As much as she hated leaving Lenny exposed, there was no way she could take him into the terminal. Instead, she looped his leash around the front seat, leaving him enough slack to move around the back but not enough to leap out the busted front window as she could tell he desperately wanted to do. She rubbed him on the head.

"Sorry, boy. I'll be back soon, I promise," she said, hoping it was actually true.

She quickly jogged across the walkway into the main terminal. SFO was an international hub, housing hundreds of flights per day, to and from every corner of the globe. Anna took a deep breath as she confronted a towering wall of monitors displaying departure information.

If she were fleeing the city, Anna would want to hop on the first flight out. She automatically homed in on the airline with the most flights departing that day. American.

There were seven leaving that afternoon, two within the next hour: Boston and Toronto. The next most populous airline had three: Bakersfield, Beijing, and Chicago.

She immediately weeded out the international flights. More security. If Shelli was looking to get out of town fast, she'd want to avoid that.

That left Boston, Chicago, and Bakersfield.

She bit her lip. If it were her, Bakersfield would be too close for comfort. And too small. She'd want to disappear—not something easy to do in a small town.

Which left Chicago and Boston.

Anna let the two cities roll around in her head as she scanned the list of airport services posted on the next bank of monitors. If she was going to get through security and get to either of those flights, she was going to have to purchase a ticket. And for that, she needed funds.

Located in the international terminal was a vending machine filled with prepaid phones. Anna made a beeline for it, and quickly purchased one with the remaining cash she'd had in her pocket when she'd come into work that morning.

Which seemed like a lifetime ago now. In some sense it was. A life that was gone for good now.

She quickly slipped the micro SD card she'd taken from her apartment into the phone, and accessed the program she'd stored there. It was a simple program, crude by real hacker standards, but it allowed her temporary access to credit card numbers and security information. Just long enough to pluck a random set of numbers for a one-time purchase that was unlikely to be large enough to warrant any investigation by a credit card company used to absorbing losses.

At least not quickly enough to catch her before she disappeared again.

She made a gut decision and quickly purchased a ticket on the next flight to Chicago before ditching the pre-paid in the nearest trash receptacle and quickly heading toward the self-service check-in kiosk with her confirmation number.

* * *

"Good afternoon…" Dade looked down at the name badge on the fortyish woman behind the ticket counter

"...Glenda." He shot her a smile with lots of teeth. Friendly, bordering on flirty. But only just bordering.

As he'd hoped, Glenda smiled back, slight wrinkles forming at the corners of her eyes. "Good afternoon, sir. Can I help you?"

"Oh, I sure hope so, Glenda."

She was slim and toned enough that the gym was obviously on her daily schedule. Her blonde hair was cut in a short shag and shot through with platinum highlights. Her makeup was tasteful, her diamond earrings fake, but most importantly her left finger was naked, making her a much better choice for his attentions than the young guy behind the ticket counter next door.

As soon as Dade had seen Anya driving away in *his* car, he'd known she was long gone. Considering she hadn't even officially existed before, his chances of tracking her down now were slim, bordering on downright impossible. He'd briefly contemplated calling his employer, but considering the mess this job had become, he scrapped that idea. At least until he had a better handle on just *what* this job had become. Instead, he'd decided to take the easy route to finding Anya...find the people following her.

Namely, Shelli.

He'd started by calling San Francisco Animal Care & Control to lodge a complaint against a woman named Shelli at their Golden Gate facility. After several minutes of ranting on the nonexistent customer service, he'd been able to pry from the flustered woman on the other end that Shelli's last name was Cooper, and that an official complaint would be filed against her on his behalf.

Armed with a last name—at least the one she'd been going under for the last few months—he'd quickly switched gears, calling the police precinct for the Sunset area, asking to speak with his daughter, Shelli Cooper, whose place of work he'd just learned had been victimized that morning. After being transferred to a series of different desks, he finally ascertained that no witness named Shelli Cooper had been involved in the shooting at all.

It was all the confirmation Dade needed that he was on the right track. Shelli hadn't stuck around to talk to the police any more than he had. That didn't speak to her innocence in the matter.

Dade then logged onto the NCIC, the National Crime Information Center, database on his phone, typing in Shelli's name, location, and approximate age. While NCIC was usually reserved for police use, one of the skills Dade had learned in the military was that every computer program—from U.S. law enforcement sites to Afghani schematics databases—had a back door. And Dade had become skilled at finding them. Depending on the program, some doors where hidden more cleverly than others, but he'd found that, by and large, Fortune 500 companies could afford state-of-the-art digital security, while government entities could not.

Making NCIC a piece of cake.

Unfortunately, no records came back with Shelli's name. Which could either mean she was a professional who had the good sense not to be caught or that she'd only been "Shelli Cooper" for a short time. He scanned through several other databases including hospitals, DMV, credit. He finally hit pay dirt with a bank account linked to her name, opened just before Anya said she'd started at the shelter. Most of the charges were expected enough—rent, electrical, groceries. However one recurring charge caught his eye. An auto pay from her checking to the Clipper website. Clipper was a prepaid transportation card, good on any of the City's Muni busses, trolleys, trains, or the Bay Area Rapid Transit, known locally as BART. After slipping into the Clipper's system back door, he ascertained that the bar code of her particular card had been last scanned half an hour ago at the SFO BART station.

Shelli was on her way out of town.

And now, so was Dade.

"I would be happy to help you purchase tickets, sir," Glenda told him, pulling up a screen on her computer behind the desk. "Where are you traveling today?"

"Boston," he said, taking a guess.

"Boston it is," Glenda said, turning to the computer screen. She typed a few keys, pulling up the flight info. "We have a couple seats left on a flight departing in half an hour."

"Perfect."

"How many passengers?" she asked.

"Just one," he said, flashing her a smile again.

"Wonderful." He watched her pull up the screen. "Do you prefer aisle or window?"

"Actually," he said, leaning in. "My fiancée is already booked on the flight. I didn't think I was going to be able to join her, but my plans changed at the last minute, and I'm hoping to surprise her. I was wondering if you could sit me next to her?"

The woman's eyes held a flicker of hesitation, but another bright, warm flash of teeth from Dade pushed her over the edge. "That's very sweet of you," she said. She pulled up a new screen on her monitor. "Do you know where your fiancée is seated?"

He shook his head. "No. But her name's Cooper. Shelli Cooper."

"Shelli Cooper," the woman repeated, looking through her roster. Dade watched as her eyes scanned down the list. Then a small frown settled between her eyebrows. "I'm sorry. I don't see a Miss Cooper listed on our flight. Is it possible you have the wrong day?"

Day? No. City? Absolutely.

He let a small frown settle between his brows. "Okay, I feel like an idiot here, but between you and me, Glenda, I might not have been listening too carefully when she told me which city she was heading to." Dade leaned in, putting his elbows on the counter. "The Giants were playing, they were down by two, and my fiancée picked then to give me her travel itinerary." He did a sheepish shrug.

Glenda chuckled. "Oh, I know how that goes."

"Yeah, well, as you can imagine, that conversation ended in an argument about how I never listen. Which, this time, was totally true. But now I really want to make it up to her. Is there any way you could check the other flights you have leaving today to see which one she's on?"

Glenda hesitated. She looked to her left where a coworker was helping customers at the next counter. "We're really not supposed to give out that information."

"Please, Glenda." Dade clasped his hands in front of him in a begging motion. "You'd be saving my hide. Big-time."

She sucked in her cheeks and shot a second look at her coworker. Then she pursed her lips and pulled up a new screen on her computer.

"We're really not supposed to do this," she repeated, her voice low.

"I won't tell if you don't." Dade shot her a quick wink.

A small smile tugged the corner of her lips upward. It might be that she wasn't supposed to do this, but he could tell she was enjoying breaking the rules a little.

"Okay. Flight two-thirty-five," she finally said, looking up from the screen. "It leaves from gate sixty-three in forty minutes for Chicago. That's where your fiancée is booked."

Dade grinned. "You are a lifesaver, Glenda. Seriously, without you, there might not have been a wedding at all."

After paying for his ticket, and praising Glenda's skills several more times, Dade made his way through security without incident, calmly giving up his ID and ticket as he stepped through the scanners like every other passenger. Once on the other side, the main thoroughfare of the airport spanned before him. Souvenir shops, magazine stands, coffee shops, and bars lined the walkway on one side, while rows of plastic chairs took up residence on the other, creating wide-open waiting areas. Dade slowly walked toward gate sixty-three, scanning the faces of each person he passed for the redhead from the shelter. While her hair would make her stand out like a sore thumb, there was no guarantee she hadn't taken the time to dye it, cut it, or simply smash it into a hat.

He found his gate and made a slow sweep of the plastic chairs, quickly filling with waiting passengers to Chicago. Once he was satisfied that none were the girl from the shelter, he took up vigil in the bar across the walkway to wait for her.

He ordered a draft beer and fiddled with the glass on the table in front of him as he kept his eyes glued to the waiting area.

An older couple entered, a pair of carry-on suitcases on wheels pulled behind them. A woman with a small dog in a lap bag was next, though she had fifty pounds and twenty years on his girl. Two Asian men in business suits speaking Mandarin took up residence by the windows. No one that could pass for Shelli.

Dade lifted his glass to his lips. As much as he could use the drink right now, he forced himself to sip at it. The last thing he could afford was dulled reflexes.

As he watched passengers filter down the walkway, Dade vaguely wondered how many miles Anna had put between them at this point. The perfume had been a dirty trick. One he had to admire. She was good at using whatever means were at her disposal. He'd give her that.

He wasn't sure how much time passed, but his glass was almost empty by the time a voice came over the loudspeaker announcing that flight two-thirty-five to Chicago would now begin preboarding. And he'd seen no sign of Shelli.

Dade stood and crossed the walkway, leaning against a column near the first row of plastic chairs. The second the flight had been announced, most of the seats had suddenly vacated, passengers lining up like cattle at the gate to board. Dade slowly let his eyes scan the waiting line, just in case Shelli had somehow slipped past him.

By the time he'd passed over the last person in line twice, Dade was positive Shelli was not among them.

But just to cover all bases, he approached the flight attendant at a desk to the right of the boarding gate.

"Excuse me, Diana," he said, reading the woman's nametag, and making deliberately familiar use of her name.

The woman with a brunette bob looked up and flashed him a smile. "Yes?"

"I'm sorry to bother you, but I've got a bit of situation here."

Her smile faltered for a second, obviously not enamored with the idea of dealing with a customer "situation" today. "I'm sorry to hear that, sir. What can I do for you?"

"My fiancée and I kind of lost each other in the terminal, and now she's not answering her cell. We're both supposed to be on this flight. I was just wondering if you could tell me if she's checked in yet or not?"

She paused, about, he could tell, to recite some company policy to him.

But before she could, he jumped in with, "Please, Diana? If she's held up somewhere in the terminal, I don't want to get on the plane and end up in Chicago without her, you know?"

Diana paused.

Dade shot her a smile. "You'd really be saving me here."

"Well, I guess I can at least tell you if she's checked in," she finally relented. "Can you tell me which seat she was in?"

He passed his ticket across the desk to her. "Right next to mine."

She nodded, checked the flight info, and then clicked a few more buttons. She nodded. "Yep, she checked in forty minutes ago, but she hasn't boarded yet."

Which meant she was still in the airport somewhere.

"Would you like me to page her?" Diana asked.

"No, that's okay," he said, quickly taking his ticket back from her. "I'll just wait for her here. She's a little nervous about flying, so she's probably just holed up in the ladies' room or something. I'm sure she'll be along."

He shot Diana another grin then went back to his spot at the column where he had a clear view of the now packed waiting area.

An announcement came over the speakers saying that general boarding was now in progress. People began walking through the gate, one small boarding group at a time. A few stragglers joined the waiting line, dragging their carry-ons behind them at breakneck speeds. The gate next to theirs, sixty-four, started filling up, passengers waiting for the flight to Tampa mingling unhelpfully with his Chicago crowd.

He scanned each face, wishing people would just sit still and quit jockeying for a better spot in line. People were crossing in front of him, moving to the other side of the gate, jostling their luggage, and making it hard to keep track of who he'd seen already and who was new.

So much so, that he almost didn't see the slim woman in jeans and a heavy, shapeless hooded sweatshirt walk out of the ladies' room. The navy blue sweatshirt disguised her body type, adding a boxy shape and at least ten pounds to her frame. She wore a backpack over one shoulder, looking to all the world like any other college student flying home for a summer visit. Her hair was a jet black, cropped short in a choppy cut that he could only guess had been done moments before in the ladies' restroom. Because as she turned her face toward him, he recognized her instantly, despite the absence of the long red hair she'd worn that afternoon.

Shelli.

CHAPTER EIGHT

Dade took a step forward, making an effort not to move too quickly and scare her off. He watched as she got in line behind the other passengers waiting to board the plane, shifting her backpack to the other shoulder, keeping her head down.

She hadn't spotted him.

She had the hood of her sweatshirt bunched around her neck to obscure her profile. Her shoulders were slumped forward, her body language saying she was doing everything she knew to seem small and inconspicuous.

He slowly made his way forward, walking the long way around the crowd now spilling into the walkway to avoid her eyeline. He had to grab her before she boarded. A confrontation in the airport would be bad enough. He wasn't taking this on a crowded, enclosed plane. He moved along the line of waiting travelers, sliding between the Asian businessmen, past the older couple. He was two people behind Shelli, almost close enough to reach out and grab the backpack off her shoulder, when he passed by the woman with the lap dog. The animal must have smelled Anya's dog on him, because it immediately went into a frenzy in its little cage, barking like it was the end of the world.

Several passengers spun around to see the noise.

Including Shelli.

Her eyes immediately locked onto Dade's, surprise registering before she could hide it. Unfortunately, her initial reaction was followed quickly by trained instincts.

She jumped out of line, shoving the rolling suitcase of the man behind her in Dade's path before taking off at a dead run in the opposite direction of the gate.

Dade swore under his breath, navigating around the woman with the damned noisy dog, and took off after her.

The airport was crowded at this time of day, with vacationers as well as long-distance commuters—people rolling luggage behind them, texting as they walked, creating a sea of human obstacles blocking his pursuit. A family of four with a blond toddler got between them, and Dade nearly tripped over the kid, trying to avoid a head-on collision. He lost Shelli for a moment, frantically scanning the walkway in front of him, eyes darting from the back of one head to the next. A brunette in a turtleneck, an older lady in a hat, a teenager wearing braids. Finally he caught sight of the navy sweatshirt, the hood now pulled up over her head. She was a few feet ahead of him, ducking behind a magazine rack displaying the latest issues of *People* and *Us Weekly*.

Dade surged forward, eyes glued to the spot at the front of a shop. He got within a couple feet before Shelli jumped out from behind the magazines, shoving the stand as hard as she could, sending it careening forward toward Dade.

Instinctively he put his hands up, catching the metal shelving before it brained him on the head. By the time he'd thrown it to the ground, Shelli was gone again, dashing toward the baggage claim area.

Where his height and longer legs might usually have been an asset, here Shelli's smaller size had her slipping between travelers with an ease he couldn't emulate. He knocked into shoulders and bounced off irate passengers, each one slowing him down. Dade could hear them protesting, but he barely registered it, his entire being focused on Shelli, sprinting at a full run now through the terminal.

As she raced past the security checkpoint—going the opposite direction from the scanners—a portly security guard in an ill-fitting uniform shouted at her to slow down. Which, of course, she completely ignored. The guard grabbed a walkie-talkie from his belt shouting a series of numbers into it. Dade consciously slowed his pace, still keeping one eye on the hooded figure ahead as he slipped past the checkpoint.

Shelli hit the escalator to the lower-level baggage area, knocking a guy in a baseball cap off the last three steps. Dade followed, gaining ground as she rounded the first baggage carousel.

And she knew it, too. She glanced over her shoulder, running into an overweight woman with a cart full of bags. The bags toppled over, and Dade quickly leapt over them, narrowly avoiding the woman himself as he ran after Shelli.

The passengers were thick here, standing two and three deep as an alarm blared over the next carousel as a signal that bags were about to be loaded in. The belt started moving and people crowded forward, barring Shelli's progress.

Unfortunately, they also barred Dade's. He pushed between two guys in suits, keeping one eye on the back of Shelli's head as he pressed forward. He was close, and she was out of places to run. He positioned himself between her and the wall of glass doors to the outside where taxis and hotel shuttles sat waiting at the curb. If she was going to leave, she had to go through him.

Her eyes darted left and right, realizing she was trapped. She paused a moment, and he could see her contemplating options. Then she pulled herself up onto the carousel, stepping out onto the conveyer belt.

Several passengers yelled in protest as she ran in a large circle with the belt's momentum. A security guard appeared from nowhere, tracking her progress, and yelling, "Hey! Get down!"

She did, leaping from the belt as it came around at the point nearest the glass doors. She landed with a tumble but quickly popped up to her feet and took off for the doors.

Dade swore, pushing toward her, knowing he was too far away to make it before she bolted into the sunshine.

"Stop! You can't do that!" the guard shouted at Shelli again, chasing after her. He called ahead to another guard positioned by the doors. The second guard planted his feet square, facing Shelli, and reached for something on his belt. Probably a Taser, though Dade never got to find out for sure since, instead of stopping as suggested, Shelli ducked her head down and rammed forward, shoving her backpack right at the guard. He caught it in the chest, stumbling backward. Shelli plowed forward, past him and out the glass doors toward the busy pickup curb.

Dade shoved through the crowd of onlookers, who were now more riveted to Shelli than on their circling bags. He hit the glass doors just in time to see Shelli's navy sweatshirt dive into a yellow cab.

He sprinted toward it, and might have had a fighting chance of at least getting the license plate number of the car, if a dark-haired woman in a white T-shirt hadn't come barreling out of the baggage claim area at exactly that moment, knocking squarely into him.

"Jesus, watch where you're going," he shouted, disappointment sinking in as he watched the cab pull away from the curb. It melted into traffic with the fifty other cabs circling the airport.

The woman took an immediate step back as Dade transferred his attention to her. And, getting a good look at her face, he realized why.

It was Anya.

Her eyes registered the same shocked recognition, going round and wide. She turned to run back inside, but he was faster, his hand shooting out to catch her before she had the chance.

"Imagine my luck," he said.

"Let go of me," Anya shouted in response.

A pair of passengers getting into a Hilton shuttle turned to stare. One glanced to the glass doors, the security guard who'd caught Shelli's backpack standing directly on the other side.

Dade pulled Anya in close, wishing he had his weapon on him. "I swear to God," he whispered, "if you call that security guard over here, I'll snap your neck before he even makes a move."

She paused a moment, as if trying to decide how serious he was. Honestly? It was at least an option.

"Let go of me," she said, this time her voice low enough that the group heading for the hotel dismissed them.

"Not a chance," he murmured back.

"Shelli's getting away."

Dade looked down the circular roadway. "Honey, she's long gone."

"I'm not your honey," she snapped back, trying to wriggle from his grasp.

"No," he agreed. "You're the pain in my ass. What are you doing here?" he asked, steering her down the sidewalk, away from the security guards and other passengers.

"Clearly the same thing you were. Looking for Shelli."

This surprised him. He'd expected Anya to run as far and as fast as she could. To get the hell out of town in a hurry. Out of the country, even. But instead, she'd run right toward the very person who was after her.

It was a ballsy move. But, if he stopped to think about it, probably exactly the same one he would have made in her position. You could only run so long before someone caught up to you. Confrontation might be a lot messier, but it was also a lot more final.

"Well she's not here now," he said, stating the obvious.

Anya took one last look down the concourse, eyes scanning the sea of yellow cabs before the slump of her shoulders conceded defeat. "Let's go," she said, spinning around.

"Go?" he asked.

"To Shelli's place. She left in a hurry. Maybe she left something behind. Some clue to where she'd go now."

He paused. As much as he wanted answers about who was after his target and why, he wasn't willing to lose Anya again. He'd underestimated her at the pier, and that wasn't a mistake he was going to make twice.

Anya must have sensed his hesitation as she added, "Someone hired Shelli to watch me and hired those men to kill me this morning. And I damned well want to know who."

He looked down at her eyes, flashing a deep blue with determination. Finally he nodded. "Okay. We'll grab a cab to Shelli's place."

"No need. Your car's in short-term parking."

"Fine." But instead of moving toward the structure, he paused on the sidewalk, pulling Anya in close to him. "But first thing's first." He put both hands at her waist, skimming the sides of her body upward toward her breasts.

"What the hell are you doing?" she ground out, jerking away from him.

But he pulled her back in tightly. "Checking for any more perfume."

She paused, her eyes meeting his. Then she slowly put her arms out to the side, submitting as she let him pat her down.

He did, making a thorough job of it, skimming his hands along her sides, down over her hips, feeling at her pockets both back and front. He had to admit, it wasn't an altogether unpleasant job.

"Satisfied?" she asked when he finally stepped back.

He nodded. "Where's my car?"

"Level three, in the back."

He grabbed her by the arm, steering her across the pedestrian walkway to the domestic terminal's short-term garage. Forgoing the elevator, he pushed her ahead of himself, up the three flights of stairs, letting her lead him to a slot near the rear. It wasn't until he was standing outside the driver's door, keys in hand, that he noticed his missing window.

Perfect.

He shot a look toward Anya, but she was carefully studying a piece of lint on her shirt.

He wrenched open the door, sending a small spray of shattered glass falling onto the ground from the vacant frame, and slid into his seat.

As if the broken window—and dangling collection of wires he noticed coming from his steering column—weren't enough to brighten his mood, an ominous scent immediately hit his nostrils, causing a gag reflex in the back of his throat. He spun around. In the center of the back seat was a small, dark log soiling his leather seats. Lenny squatted as far from the offering as he could get, wearing the same evasive look as his owner.

"What the hell is that?" Dade asked.

Anya turned in her seat. "Looks like shit to me."

He ground his teeth together, shoved his keys in the ignition, and turned the engine over.

And he could have sworn he heard Anya whisper a "Good dog" to the animal as he backed out of the space.

CHAPTER NINE

———

Anna sat still in the front seat as Dade drove out of the garage. Only instead of angling the car down toward the street level, he followed the garage's ramp upward, toward the top of the structure. He drove the car into a slot near the elevator on the fifth floor then hopped out. Anna watched as he lifted the lid off of a garbage can, reached inside, and pulled something wrapped in newspaper out.

She was about to ask what was in it, when he shed the paper, revealing both her Glock and his M9.

Right. He would never have gotten through the airport with those.

Anna's hands itched to reload her weapon. The bullets she'd grabbed back at her place were still sitting at the bottom of her duffel bag, just behind her seat.

But Dade quickly stuck both guns in the waistband of his pants, eradicating any fantasies she might have had of being armed. He quickly used the empty newspaper wrapping to extract Lenny's offering from the back seat, then left the garage and drove as far as the nearest gas station. He pulled up to the pump and began cleaning the back seat with paper towels and a windshield wiper squeegee. Anna took the opportunity to grab Lenny's leash and pull him from the car.

"What are you doing?" Dade barked, his eyes shooting up to her.

"He needs a walk."

She could tell he was about to protest, but she gestured to his seats and asked, "You want a repeat performance?"

He paused then nodded. "Two minutes. And stay close."

She gave him a mock salute then led Lenny to a small square of grass near the bathrooms. She watched him sniff, circle, sniff some more. Finally he picked a spot and squatted, doing his business. By the time she came back to the car, Dade had the seat cleaned, though a slight scent still hung in the air as they pulled away from the station.

"Where does Shelli live?" Dade asked.

She rattled off the address, watching Dade punch it into the GPS system on his dash.

"Thank you," Anna said as he navigated north. He turned a questioning look her way. "For helping me find answers."

"I'm not doing this for you," he said quickly.

She shrugged. She knew that. Whatever Dade's motivation in tracking down the people after her might be, she knew it had nothing to do with her well-being and everything to do with his own. She was keenly aware of the fact that there were not one but two parties out there who wanted her dead.

"You don't know who hired you, do you?" she asked, watching him closely.

Dade kept his eyes squarely on the road ahead of him.

"And you don't think it was a coincidence that both your employer and Shelli's tracked me down at the same time?" she added.

Dade shot her a look. "Do you?"

"No."

His eyes went back to the road. "Coincidence is just a word people use when they don't have all the answers. I prefer answers."

"Me too."

He shot another look her way, this one reading like he wasn't entirely comfortable thinking they had anything in common.

"Listen, how about we share some answers," she said slowly, watching his reaction.

He narrowed his eyes, though they stayed on the road ahead of him. "Such as?"

"You answer a question of mine, and I answer one of yours."

He paused, seemingly weighing the pros and cons of her proposal for a moment before slowly answering. "Okay. You first."

Anna cleared her throat. "If you don't have a name for your employer," she asked, "how do you know he's KOS?"

"Your file," Dade answered quickly. "It was clear that it had to have come from inside the agency. No one else would have that kind of information on you."

She nodded. That much sounded true. Dade knew more about her than anyone else she'd encountered since leaving Kosovo.

"How did he contact you?"

Dade shook his head. "Sorry, that's two questions. My turn."

Anna bit her lip. "Fine. What do you want to know?"

"Why a dog shelter?"

The personal question surprised her, and she blinked in response. "What do you mean?"

"I imagine you acquired a varied skill set in your line of work. One that could earn you a hell of a lot more money than you make washing dogs. So why a nonprofit shelter?"

She licked her lips, letting the question sink in before formulating an answer. "I like dogs."

He raised an eyebrow her way. "That's it?"

She shrugged. "Dogs don't care who you are or where you've come from. Their affection is unconditional, and as long as you feed them, walk them, and give them a pat on the head now and then, their loyalty is undying. They're a lot less complicated than humans, and a hell of a lot more honest."

Dade glanced across the console at her, his eyes assessing her as if trying to read something deeper into her words.

She shifted uncomfortably in her seat. "Besides," she quickly covered, "the shelter didn't ask a lot of questions on their employment application."

He nodded, seemingly satisfied. "Fair enough."

"And I don't have as many skills as you might think," she added. "That was a long time ago."

Dade gestured to the wires dangling from his jimmied steering column. "You seem to have remembered a few."

She bit her lip again. "Sorry about that," she said, at least halfway meaning it.

He cut his eyes back to the road. "Just don't touch my car again." He paused. "Or I *will* shoot you."

She nodded in agreement, not entirely sure he wasn't serious.

They lapsed into silence for the rest of the drive, and twenty minutes later they pulled up to Shelli's apartment complex.

The building looked the same as she'd left it a couple hours earlier. Three school-aged kids were skateboarding along the sidewalk out front now, but there was no visible sign that Shelli had returned to the apartment. Not that Anna would expect her to. She'd clearly been made by Dade. If Anna were in her shoes, she'd be hiding out in the busiest corner of the City she could find, the farthest away from any part of her former life, until things died down enough to slip out of the country unnoticed.

Dade parked two buildings down, and Anna quickly tethered Lenny to the front seat again before following Dade to 2A. He knocked, one hand hovering over his weapon as they waited. As Anna expected, no one answered.

Dade looked over his shoulder at the kids out front. "Stand behind me. I don't want to draw attention."

Anna did, obscuring the kids', or any other passerby's, view as Dade pulled his gun from his waist and took the butt of it to the cheap doorknob. It broke off immediately, the wood surround splintering. He pushed his hand through the opening, manually manipulating the lock until the door swung open. One hand on his gun, he moved into the room, gesturing for Anna to do the same.

She did, eyes scanning what was visible of the apartment from behind Dade's back.

The front room was standard issue rental: low ceilings, brown carpet, a little natural light struggling in through the vertical blinds. A small living room had been set up to the right, a narrow galley style kitchen to the left. Both were painted in off-white, the kitchen floor was covered in a cheap laminate, and the counter in yellow tiles from the '80s. The kitchen was tidy, with a coffeemaker, toaster, and wooden wine rack sitting out on the counters. The living room held a small sofa and love seat combo pointed at a TV sitting on a modern black chest across the room. A reproduction oil painting hung above the sofa, and a potted ficus took up residence in the corner. Black lacquer shelves covered the far wall, a smattering of framed photos decorating them.

Dade moved to the TV consol, shoving his weapon into the waistband of his cargo pants as he pulled open the top drawer, rummaging inside.

Anna moved into the kitchen. It was neat and clean. Too clean. There wasn't a single crumb on the floor, no stray coffee rims on the counter, the stovetop burners immaculate. No pot had ever boiled over here, and Anna had an eerie feeling no one had ever eaten here before either. She opened a couple drawers. Silverware lay in a caddy. Glasses were stacked in the cupboard above the sink. A stack of white plates filled the cabinet next to the refrigerator. Everything a normal kitchen should have, but something felt off. As if she expected price tags to still be attached.

Anna opened the refrigerator. A carton of milk and a takeout box were all it contained. Not that those really meant anything. There were days when her refrigerator looked the same.

"Check out these photos," Dade called, breaking into her thoughts.

She backed out of the underused kitchen to find Dade standing in front of the wall shelves, a photo of Shelli at the Grand Canyon in one hand.

She joined him, looking at the rest of the collection. Frames in various sizes, half a dozen or so, were tastefully arranged. All were of Shelli with what looked like friends and family—enjoying a summer picnic, lounging at the beach, out at a nightclub somewhere. On the surface, proof that Shelli lived a normal life.

On the surface.

Anna homed in on what she didn't see. Variation.

Shelli's hair was the same in each photo, her age approximately the same as it was now. They had all been taken within the last year, if Anna had to guess. In the nightclub photo, her coloring was slightly paler than her friend—the hues more yellow than rosy. It was a subtle difference, but it flashed like a neon beacon to Anna. The friend was photographed in different lighting. Shelli had never been in the nightclub. She'd been photoshopped into the scene.

"They're fake," Anna said.

Dade nodded. He gestured to the one in his hand. "The shadow's off on this one. It's close," he said, pointing to the dusty ground at Shelli's feet, "but it's a few inches to the right of her friends'."

Anna looked down. He was right. To the casual observer, not enough to notice. Subtle. Done by a professional.

"None of it's real," Anna said, trying to shake off an unnerving feeling at being confronted with hard evidence of Shelli's duplicity.

You should have known. For months she fooled you. You should have seen through her. You're better than that.

At least she used to be.

"I'm going to check out the bedroom," Dade said, moving through the narrow doorway to their right.

Anna followed, taking in the similarly uninhabited feel there. A queen-size bed filled the space, a cheap floral-printed comforter covering its surface. A pair of ruffled pillows sat at the head. A chest of drawers in oak leaned up against one wall, and a pair of sliding closet doors took up the other. A small nightstand next to the bed held an alarm clock and a ballpoint pen.

Dade went to the nightstand, pulling open the drawers.

Anna looked on. She should have felt intrusive, invading someone's personal space like this. But she didn't. Maybe because the room didn't feel like anyone's personal space.

Dade abandoned the nightstand, seemingly not finding anything of interest there, and moved on to the bed. He threw the comforter off and ripped up the sheets.

Anna was tempted to comb the pillowcase for hair samples, but she knew that if Shelli had gone this far, there was no point collecting her DNA. She wouldn't exist in any databases. She was a ghost, just like Anna.

Anna looked up at her companion. And possibly like Dade.

It hadn't escaped her noticed that he was looking for exactly the same things she was. He'd been trained the same way. His accent was clearly American, so he couldn't be KOS. But he'd been trained to kill, to know how to disappear.

Again, she wondered just who he was.

Dade slid the mattress off the box spring. In the center of the bed the surface sagged. Dade grabbed the pen from the bedside and stabbed a hole in the thin material, ripping it toward him. As he pulled it aside to reveal the interior of the box spring, a small arsenal of guns stared Anna in the face.

She felt her stomach drop.

You trusted her. You should have known.

Anna felt sick as the truth was hammered home. Every meaningless conversation Shelli had engaged her in about the weather had been carefully calculated to gain Anna's trust. Every casual question about Anna's apartment, her family, and how she'd spent the weekend now took on sinister meaning.

Dade pulled a handgun from the box spring. He flipped it over in his hand and clicked the magazine free, dropping five bullets into his palm. He was clearly comfortable with the weapon. He picked up another one, disarming it the same way.

Anna looked from Dade to the small arsenal. Three guns left. If she could distract him for just a minute, she might be able to get her hands on a weapon...

"She didn't have time to dispose of these properly," Dade observed. "She left in a hurry."

"Maybe she planned to come back?" Anna asked. She inched closer to the hollowed bed. There was a Sig pistol sitting near the edge. It was small, slim, and would fit easily in the pocket of her jeans. All she needed was a second to slip it on her person.

Dade shook his head. "I don't think so. Would you have come back?"

No. She would have run as far as she could. Probably what she should be doing now.

"Check the bathroom," Dade directed.

Anna wavered a minute, eyeing the pistol.

But, as if he could read her mind, Dade snatched it into his hands and relieved it of ammunition just as he had the others.

It had been a long shot anyway. If Dade was as good as he appeared, no way would he have let her sneak the gun into her pocket.

Don't worry. There will be another opportunity. There always is.

She did as directed, leaving Dade to examine Shelli's remaining weapons as she slipped into the adjacent bathroom. Dade left the door ajar, she noticed, keeping one eye on her as she opened the bathroom drawers and medicine cabinet. As with the kitchen, everything was in order to look like a typical single woman's apartment. Tylenol, Midol, and a pack of Band-Aids sat in the medicine cabinet. None of them ever opened.

She pulled open the bathroom drawers. Comb. Brush. Both void of any hair or sign of use.

Anna sighed and shut the drawer. It was futile. If Shelli had ever had personal effects here, she had taken the time to dispose of them thoroughly.

"What do you think of these?" Dade asked, coming into the room behind her. In his hand was a stack of postcards. Three were decorated with pictures of the wharf. One showed Coit Tower and another Chinatown. Dade handed her the one of Chinatown.

Anna flipped the card over in her hand. Sprawling script in ballpoint pen filled the back.

Had a fab time. You must come next time to check out the people. See you soon!
Kim

Nothing odd. Nothing sinister.

Yet, Anna didn't trust it for a moment.

"Where did you find these?"

"Her closet," Dade answered. "She ever speak of a 'Kim'?"

She shook her head. Now that she thought of it, she wasn't sure Shelli had ever mentioned names of any of her friends or family. It wasn't as if Anna had asked. She'd only halfway listened the entire time, to be honest, too worried about giving something away herself to pay attention to what Shelli had been giving away.

"They must have been important if she kept them," Anna said. She flipped the card back over. "This one was postmarked just last week."

Dade flipped through the others. "They're all postmarked within the last two months. Meeting sites?" he asked. "You think maybe she was meeting 'Kim' in Chinatown?"

Anna shrugged, handing the card back to him. "It's possible. If so, the last meeting was recent."

He shoved the stack into his back pocket. "Well, she's not coming back here," he said. "Whatever she was doing here, she's done. She left the extras, took what she needed."

"Cash. Her phone."

He nodded. Then he pulled his own cell from his pocket. "So let's call her."

"Why?"

"Ask if she's okay. You're concerned after what happened at the shelter, and you want to check up on her. We need to find out where she is."

"You really think she's going to tell me?"

Dade shook his head. He flicked his index finger across his touch screen. "No. But we can trace the call."

She looked over his shoulder. "Don't tell me there's an app for that?"

"There is on my phone," he said, pulling up a clearly homemade program. "What's the number?"

Anna rattled off Shelli's cell from memory. She and Shelli had often called each other if one or the other was running late—a common issue with city public transportation what it was.

Dade dialed it in then hit the speakerphone button. "Keep her on as long as you can."

She nodded, listening to the phone ring once…then twice. Four times in she began to worry Shelli wasn't going to pick up. Finally, the unfamiliar number must have piqued Shelli's curiosity, as her voice came through the receiver.

"Hello?"

Now knowing what Shelli really was, the sound of the familiar voice brought a jump of emotion to Anna's throat. She ignored it, swallowing hard and focusing on the task at hand.

"Shelli? It's Anna."

There was a pause on the other end. "Anna. I didn't recognize your number."

"I lost my phone at the shelter. I'm on a friend's," she quickly covered. "Are you okay? I've been so worried about you."

"I'm fine. Shaken, but I'm physically fine," Shelli answered, playing the role.

"Oh, I'm so glad."

"How are you?" Shelli asked. "Where are you?"

"I'm…" Anna looked to Dade. He made a motion with his hands to keep her talking. "I'm fine. I'm staying with a friend."

"What friend?"

Anna looked to Dade for direction. His face was stony, staring at the phone. Anna could see a grid on the screen, the area slowly narrowing.

"She's in the City," he mouthed.

"Um, just an old friend," she said into the phone. "From college," she lied.

"Where are you?" Shelli pressed again.

Where are you, *Shelli? For that matter,* who *are you?*

"Daly City," Anna lied again, giving her a location just south of San Francisco. "I'm staying at her house for a while."

"Good plan," Shelli said slowly. Anna could feel the questions in the statement. "Listen, I'm glad you're okay, but I have to go," Shelli said.

Dade shook his head violently. "Keep her on," he whispered.

"Wait! Uh, Shelli…the dog. The new recruit. Is he with you? Is he okay?'

There was a pause on the other end. "He's fine," Shelli said slowly. She was beginning to suspect something, Anna could tell. She was asking too many questions. Chatting too long for no reason.

"Is the dog with you? Where are you?" Anna asked.

"We're both safe."

"Are you in the City?" Anna asked.

Shelli paused. Then said, "Good-bye, Anna."

And hung up.

"Shit!" Dade turned away from the phone.

"Did you get it?"

He shook his head. "Somewhere north of Market Street. That's as close as I could get. I needed three more seconds."

"She didn't believe me. She knows I know."

He gave her a hard look. "You pressed too hard. You scared her."

"What was I supposed to say?"

"I don't know! Jesus, what do you usually talk about?"

"It doesn't matter now," Anna said. "She knows."

Dade shoved his phone in his back pocket. "There's nothing left to see here. Let's go."

Anna followed him out the door, waiting while he pulled it closed behind him. Anyone who saw the knob lying on the ground would know the apartment had been broken into, but by the time they could report it, Dade and Anna would be long gone.

Though, gone *where*, Anna had no idea.

They arrived back at the SUV to find Lenny whining in the back seat, pacing and pressing his nose to the windows.

"He needs to go to the bathroom," Anna said.

Dade glanced in the rearview mirror. "Again?"

"He's been grazing on that dog chow all day. Besides, he needs some exercise."

Dade cracked his neck from side to side. "Fine."

Anna reached for the door handle to let the dog out, but Dade's hand clamped down over hers.

"But, I'll take him. You stay here."

She paused. "It won't take long."

"Good. I don't have long."

"I can walk him."

Dade gave her a hard look. "As long as I have the dog, I know you won't bolt."

Unfortunately, true. And he'd read her intentions correctly. While Lenny clearly did need to find a square patch of grass soon, she'd hoped to create an opportunity to slip away. She was going to have to be craftier than that.

"Fine," she agreed, slipping into the passenger seat as Dade opened the back door and unwound Lenny's leash from the front seat. As soon as he was freed, Lenny leapt from the car and bounded across the street to sniff a small patch of grass outside Shelli's building, pulling Dade behind.

Anna took the opportunity to flip on the radio, scanning the AM news stations for any mention of the shelter. One station had a correspondent on the scene but knew precious little about the situation, speculating that maybe gang activity was involved. Which suited Anna fine. The less the authorities knew about the whole thing, the better.

Ten minutes later, Dade loaded Lenny back into the car and slid behind the wheel again. He turned the engine over and pulled into traffic, heading north.

"Where are we going now?" Anna asked.

"We need somewhere to regroup. Eat, sleep, plan our next move."

"A motel?" she asked.

He nodded.

While what he said made sense—it was growing dark now, and they couldn't very well drive forever—the idea of sitting in one place for any length of time made her instantly antsy. The more stagnant she was, the easier it was for someone to catch up to her.

That had been her motto, to a greater or lesser degree, over the last few years. She'd never stayed in one place more than six months, often staying far less than that if something began to feel unsafe. Like two years ago in New York when she'd overheard a snippet of Bosnian spoken in a bar one night. Chances were it was coincidence, but it was enough to convince Anna to flee the East Coast. She'd spent two weeks checking into various motels, spending her meager savings making plane reservations she never kept and buying train tickets to destinations around the country, all the while plotting a steady path toward California. She'd landed in Los Angeles first, easily blending into the masses there. She'd taken an apartment in Burbank, then a loft in Santa Monica. Rented a room in the San

Gabriel Valley, moved south to a complex in Orange County, and then spent three months in a mobile home park just north of San Diego before deciding she'd left too many footprints in Southern California. She'd been in San Francisco since then, bouncing from one end of the city to the next, covering her tracks at each spot, starting over again at the next.

Though, clearly she'd left too many footprints here, too.

"This place will do," Dade said. He pulled off the main road into a small parking lot and cut the engine.

Anna looked up. They were just outside the Mission area of San Francisco, older buildings running up against new developments, creating an eclectic mix of antiques and modern architecture. High dollar real estate competed with seldom-maintained eyesores. Beside a pair of high-rise condos sat the Bayshore Inn. It struck Anna as a typical motor inn—a two-story, L-shaped building with rooms running the length on the top and bottom. A swimming pool sat out front, dead leaves floating over its surface and a couple of rusted lounge chairs sitting pitifully at its side.

Anna waited in the car while Dade again clipped the leash on Lenny, taking the dog with him as insurance as he entered the motel's office and secured them a room. She watched him through the front window, bringing out the same charming smile for the clerk on duty as he'd worn in the Laundromat the previous night, playing the happy tourist. He handed the man a stack of bills—dealing only in cash again, she noticed—then took a room key from him.

The entire exchange took less than ten minutes, and Dade was back, grabbing a black duffel bag from the back of the SUV.

"Let's go," he directed, motioning Anna out of the car.

She complied, grabbing her own duffel before following Dade to a unit on the bottom, in the corner of the L.

The room was small, but it worked. A pair of double beds with white metal headboards were flanked by nightstands, and a TV sat on a dresser on the opposite wall. A small bathroom was through a door. Anna walked through to the bathroom first, filling a plastic ice bucket with water for Lenny, who immediately plopped himself down in front of the TV and lapped gratefully.

"Sit down on the bed," Dade instructed.

Anna paused. She didn't like being told what to do under the best of circumstances. And this was clearly not the best. But, since she had little choice, she slowly sank down onto the pastel bedspread of the double closest to the door, keeping her eyes on him the entire time.

Dade reached into his bag, emerging with a pair of metal handcuffs. He then crossed to her, securing one of the bracelets around her left wrist and the other to the metal headboard.

"Just in case," he said.

Anna wriggled her wrist, testing the bonds. Her hands were small, but not small enough to slip free.

She watched Dade open drawers, checking the contents of the room almost as if by habit. While there was no way anyone could have anticipated their stay here, he was clearly a guy who didn't trust anywhere to be secure.

He pulled a menu from a Chinese place out of the nightstand and turned to her.

"Hungry?"

She wasn't. But she knew that whatever stretched in front of them, she should take her chance to refuel now. She nodded then listened as Dade ordered Kung Pao chicken for two to be delivered to their room.

"Make mine tofu," Anna cut in.

He paused. "Tofu?" he asked her.

"I'm a vegetarian."

He cocked an eyebrow at her.

She shrugged. "I don't like the idea of eating animals."

"You're joking, right? An animal rights assassin?"

"Ex-assassin," she corrected him.

He shook his head, but repeated her order into the phone. When he hung up, he said, "I'm going in the shower." He grabbed his gun and cell then disappeared into the bathroom.

* * *

Dade shut the door behind him. He turned on the water then grabbed his cell and dialed. Three rings in it was answered.

"Dade," the man on the other end said, recognizing the number.

"What the hell is going on?" Dade asked, trying to keep his voice low.

There was a pause. Then, "What do you mean?"

"I mean, who else did you hire to take out my target?"

Another pause. "Just you."

"Bullshit. Someone else is stalking her."

"What do you mean?"

"I mean, I went to take my shot this morning, and someone beat me to it."

"She's dead?" the other man asked.

Dade shook his head in the empty bathroom. It was starting to fill with steam, distorting the reflection staring back at him in the mirror above the chipped sink. "No. She's not. But apparently there are several people who are working on that."

"Who?"

"That's what I want to know."

Dade could hear the man on the other end inhale, breathing deeply. "That's not important right now, and I urge you to remember what is."

"And that would be?"

"The job is supposed to be done by the end of the week."

Dade ran a hand through his hair. "I know."

"Anything else is outside your realm of concern."

"Like hell it is," Dade said.

But the man ignored him. "Your only concern is doing the job you were hired to do. Our employer will not be happy if it isn't done. And when he's not happy, there will be consequences."

"Don't threaten me," Dade growled out between clenched teeth.

"That's not a threat. It's fact."

"Let me talk to our employer," Dade said.

He could hear the man on the other end shifting. "You know that's not possible. I'm your contact. Anything you have to say to him you can say through me."

"Fine. Tell him I'm not making a move until I know what the hell kind of game he's playing at," he ground out then stabbed at the *Off* button.

* * *

The second she heard water running, Anna sprang into action.

She jumped off the bed. Stretching her left arm as far as she could while remaining tethered to the headboard, she used her right hand to look through the nightstand drawers for anything she could use as a weapon. A pen, a Bible, a stack of postcards featuring a painting of the motel that was much more wishful thinking than reality.

She pocketed the pen then grabbed Dade's bag, quickly going through its contents. Mostly clothes, almost all in black. She dug into the side pockets. The first two yielded nothing, but the third contained a pack of nicotine gum and a Muni ticket stub. She tried a fourth. Empty. One small pocket on the inside left was zipped shut. She glanced at the bathroom door, still hearing the water run. She unzipped and stuck her fingers inside. Cool metal greeted her, and she pulled out a silver pendant on a chain. No, not a pendant, she realized as she held it up. Dog tags. Two silver metal ovals on the end of a ball chain. So he *was* military trained.

Anna quickly memorized the info on the tag.

DADE
NICK W. O POS
601811982
USMC M

She shoved the tags back into the zippered pocket, setting the duffel back on the bed just as she'd found it.

"Food here yet?"

Anna jumped, hoping guilt wasn't as etched on her face as it was her psyche.

"No."

"Good." Dade came out of the bathroom and sat down on the double bed opposite hers. His hair was wet, curling around his neck, and his shirt was left untucked. But even in this casual pose, he seemed ready to strike, to jump to attention at any second. She wondered if he ever relaxed.

Dade flipped on the TV, scanning different news stations. It didn't take long before he landed on one broadcasting the shelter shooting story. According to the reporter, it was still being investigated as possible gang activity, a random shooting as part of some initiation rite. There was no mention of either Anna or Shelli.

Anna wasn't sure if she found that comforting or not. On the one hand, the fewer people looking for her the better at this point. On the other…it was an odd feeling that you could disappear so easily and no one would miss you.

Anna started as a sharp knock sounded at the door.

Dade was up and across the room in one swift movement, his gun drawn.

"Who is it?" he called through the closed door. Anna watched him put an eye to the peephole.

"Hungry Panda," came the muffled reply. "I have your Kung Pao."

Dade pulled away from the door and turned to Anna. He put a finger to his lips to indicate her silence then opened the door a crack.

"How much?" Dade asked.

"Twenty-two fifty," Anna heard a young man with a heavy accent reply. She was tempted to cry out, alert him to her presence. But then what? He was an unarmed delivery boy. Most likely, Dade would just shoot him too. So she sat in silence, watching as the man handed Dade a paper bag in exchange for cash. Dade then quickly shut the door and pulled the chain lock shut behind him.

They ate in silence, watching the news and then a debate between two politicians vying for their party's nomination in the upcoming election. Anna only halfway paid attention, closing her eyes, lying back on the pillows, and feeling the exhaustion of the day seep into her bones. She consciously forced each muscle to flex and unflex, letting tension drain.

Two hours later Dade turned out the light, plunging the room into sudden darkness. She heard him shift on the bed. Could imagine him stowing his weapon nearby as he laid his head down on the pillows.

Anna waited in the darkness, listening to him breath. Listening to the muted sounds of a television in the adjoining room, people laughing outside on the sidewalk, cars pulling into slots in the parking lot. As her eyes adjusted to the dark, Anna glanced at the other bed. Dade lay on his back, his hands clasped over his chest, looking almost as though he'd been staged by some mortician. She waited, forcing her eyes to stay open as she listened to his breath. Finally it slowed and deepened, coming in long, rhythmic waves. He'd fallen asleep.

Now's your chance.

Anna moved slowly at first, eyes on Dade's still form. He was fully clothed, sleeping on top of the pastel spread. She prayed he was a deep sleeper as she reached her free right hand down her leg, slipping it inside her front pocket. Dade didn't move. Didn't stir, his body completely still, and his breath coming slowly and steadily. She pulled the pen from her pocket, bringing it up to her mouth. She bit off the top, letting it drop onto the blanket beside her. Next came the tip, which she dropped into her lap, then she dumped the lose ink cartridge next to it. She put the cartridge into her mouth, using her teeth to bite at the plastic end. It took several minutes, but she finally had it molded into a sharp point. She slowly transferred it to her right hand again, inserting the pointed end into the keyhole of her handcuffs. They jangled against the bed frame, and she froze, eyes darting to Dade.

His breath shifted, stuttering for a moment.

Anna closed her eyes.

Please stay asleep.

She waited for what felt like an eternity, but Dade didn't open his eyes. Didn't move. Instead his breath once again slowed and fell into a deep, steady rhythm.

She said a silent thank you then put a pillow between her wrist and the headboard, hoping to mute any further noise as she worked at the lock. The plastic was more pliable than she'd hoped, bending when she would have liked it to stay rigid, yet too rigid to fit all the way into the hole. She didn't know how long she quietly worked the lock, but sweat was trickling down the side of her face by the time she finally heard the telltale click and felt the metal ease on her wrist. She slowly pulled the cuff open, sliding the remaining bracelet down the metal headboard to rest silently on a pillow. She rubbed at her wrist, shaking circulation back into her hand.

"What are you doing?"

Anna spun around in the dark to find Dade staring at her, eyes open and alert, gun in hand aimed at her heart.

Adrenaline coursed through her as she opened her mouth to respond.

Just as the window beside her bed shattered.

CHAPTER TEN

———

Anna dove for the floor, covering her head with her arms as glass rained down on her. A series of sharp gunshots followed, ripping into the bed where she'd just been tethered, feathers and tufts of polyester batting flying into the air.

"Jesus." She felt Dade hit the floor beside her, his body rigid, weapon held close to his chest. He put two rounds through the shattered glass then ducked back down behind the bed.

Lenny barked from across the room, as startled awake as his human counterparts had been.

"Stay!" Anna yelled, hoping for once the dumb animal listened to her. "Do not move. Stay!"

The TV shattered as a bullet hit it, sparks flying across the room. Anna moved closer to Dade. Not that he was any better than whoever was shooting at her now, but once again she was the only one in the gunfight without a gun.

She'd be damned if that happened again.

"The bathroom," Dade yelled. His words were clipped, shouted as rapid fire as the rounds hailing the room. "I'll provide cover."

She nodded.

He silently counted off *one*, *two*, and then popped up from the floor and shot through the broken window again. The return fire stopped for a second, and Anna took the opportunity crawl on her hands and knees toward the tiny bathroom.

As soon as she hit the door, she whistled, prompting Lenny into action. He bounded through the room just as the gunfire started through the front window again.

Dade shot back, creeping backward on his butt as he fired toward the front of the room. It seemed as if she was watching him in slow motion, but in reality it was only a couple of seconds before he hit the bathroom door.

As soon as he was inside, Anna slammed the door shut. It was wooden, thin. A BB gun could blast through it. They needed to get out. Now.

"The window." Dade shot the words out.

But Anna was already on it. She stepped into the bathtub, pulling the small window above the mildewed tiles open. She pried the screen off with her fingernails, breaking two painfully in the process.

The opening was only a couple of feet square. She was confident she could fit through...Dade was another story.

"Will you fit?" she asked him.

"Go, just go," he instructed, lifting her off the ground so she had little choice but to do as he instructed.

She propelled herself through the opening. Arms first, followed by her torso. She wiggled her feet behind her through the window. She hit the ground hard, scraping her palms in the process but quickly scrambled to her feet.

"Hand me Lenny," she shouted.

She thought she heard Dade mumble something derogatory in response, but the dog's head popped up in the window a second later. Anna lifted him over the sill, grunting under his weight as she pulled him to safety on her side.

Run. Bolt. Leave him. You're free.

"Grab my hands and pull," Dade yelled, shoving his torso through the opening.

Anna paused. Dade had been hired to kill her. He was holding her hostage.

But the truth was, people with guns—and just how many she had no idea—were firing at her. And Dade still had her weapon. At the moment, he was the lesser of two evils and her best bet at getting out of here alive.

She swore under her breath at her lack of options but braced her foot on the side of the building, tugging Dade through the opening with both hands. In her peripheral hearing, she realized the gunfire had ceased. Not a good sign. They knew the couple wasn't in the hotel room any longer. In a second, they'd be running around the back of the motel looking for them.

Dade landed on the ground with a grunt, quickly springing to his feet and grabbing Anna by the arm.

"Go," he instructed with about as much finesse as he had at the shelter.

"No, I think I'll wait around to get shot at," she mumbled.

But if Dade heard her, he elected to ignore the sarcasm.

They took off running down the length of the hotel, passing the side alleyway, and continuing on toward the back of the next building. There was a door, a service entrance. Dade ran toward it, pausing to jiggle the handle. Locked.

Dammit, that had wasted precious seconds.

As if to confirm her thoughts, a bullet raced past Anna's ear, lodging into the building beside her. Chunks of plaster flew into the air, followed by more gunfire. Dade shoved Anna ahead of him, ducking around the side of the building. This time he did run the length of the narrow alleyway between buildings. They hauled past two overflowing dumpsters. Anna tripped on an empty take-out box, but Dade still had her by the arm, half dragging her up and onward. Lenny barked, running alongside them, his breath coming in hard snorts as he tried to keep up.

Ahead of them, the alley gave way to the main street again. They'd made it two buildings down from their motel. An all-night liquor store sat across the street, two dark office buildings beside it, and a coffee shop with a metal gate drawn in front of it to their right.

Sirens sounded, signaling that one of the hotels' other occupants had called the police at the sound of gunfire.

From their vantage point, Anna could clearly see the motel's parking lot bathed in streetlamps. Two shadowy figures ran past the pool area, assault rifles in hand, climbing into a black van. They were both dressed in black pants, black tops, and black baseball caps, blending into the night. As soon as they were inside the vehicle, the engine roared to life, tires spinning as they peeled out of the parking lot.

Anna scanned the back of the car for any distinguishing marks. The license plate had been smeared with mud. Clearly deliberate, considering the immaculate condition of the rest of the vehicle. The only marks she could make out were a 7 and a

B. The windows were tinted, so it was impossible to see inside even if it hadn't been dark.

"Let's go," Dade said, grabbing her by the arm as he turned back toward the motel. "We need to get the car and get out of here."

She squared her shoulders. "No."

He turned to her. "What do you mean, 'no'?"

Anna took a breath. "I mean, I'm getting sick and tired of being told what to do." Which was the truth. And she had a far better chance of changing that here on the street than she did back in his car again.

"You don't have much of a choice," he said, gesturing with the gun in his hand.

She paused. Took another deep breath. "I could have killed you in your sleep."

He narrowed his eyes. "Excuse me?"

"You may have the big bad gun, but I've killed without one before, and I could do it again. Before the gunmen arrived you were sleeping. I could have killed you then. So don't think you have all the power here."

It was a brave speech. Far braver than she felt, if she were honest.

He took one menacing step toward her, gun first. "I wasn't asleep," he countered.

She swallowed, not sure if he was telling the truth or trying to intimidate her.

"I don't like being held a prisoner, and I don't like putting my fate in the hands of some guy who won't tell me anything about himself except that he's been hired to kill me."

"I don't care what you like," he said, his voice coming out in short puffs that heated the air in front of his mouth.

"Fine. Then I'm out of here," she said. She spun on her heel, quickly walking in the opposite direction. She steeled herself for the sound of his gun, the heat of the bullet ripping into her. They were on a main street, in full view of dozens of windows. The police were already on their way to the scene. Odds were on her side that he wouldn't kill her here.

She hoped.

She heard him mutter an oath under his breath then felt his presence behind her, jogging to catch her. He did, grabbing her by the arm and spinning her roughly to face him.

"We don't have time for this. The police are on their way."

"Let go of me." She wriggled in his grasp, but, as always, it was iron tight.

She retaliated by kicking him in the shins. He winced but didn't let go. She tried again, lifting a knee to his groin, using all the force she had.

This time he moaned, doubled over, and let go of her arm.

She bolted, running down the block. She got as far as the next building over before he was on top of her again, grabbing her by the shoulder and slamming her body up against the wall.

"Help!" she screamed at the top of her lungs.

But at this time of night there was no one else out on the street to hear her but the man currently grinding her into the gritty brick wall.

"Get off," she yelled, kicking backward. She connected with his shin, but he didn't let up the pressure on her from behind. His fingers dug into her upper arms, and his breath was hot on the back of her neck.

"Try that again, and I will shoot you," he ground out.

She spun around, moving her face so close to his that her nose was almost touching.

"I don't think you will," she challenged, forcing herself to meet his eyes. They were dark, angry, and dangerous. "I think you need answers, and you need me to get them."

"Don't flatter yourself," he shot back. "I'm tying up loose ends, and I can do that with or without you."

She leaned forward until she could feel his breath on her lips. She saw something behind his eyes shift, cloud over, almost soften as her breath mingled with this.

"Then do it without," she whispered.

She lifted her foot and brought it down with force, scraping down the inside of his leg and hitting the instep of his foot. He winced, lifted it, eased off the pressure on her.

She shoved at his right shoulder, pushing past him, and he fell backward against the wall, gritting his teeth together as he crumpled to the ground.

Way too easily.

Anna looked down at her hand. It was covered in a wet, sticky substance. Her gaze shot to Dade's shoulder. A red stain was darkening the sleeve of his T-shirt.

"You've been hit," she said to him, almost as much as to herself.

CHAPTER ELEVEN

———

She looked into his face and saw beads of sweat gathering on his forehead and not, she now realized, from the exertion of chasing her down.

"They shot you," Anna said.

He nodded. "I'm fine."

"You need a doctor."

"What I need is for you to get in the damned car and get the hell out of here," he said, his breath coming hard as he struggled to an upright position again.

"You need medical attention. You need a hospital."

He let out a short bark of laughter. "Questions about a gunshot are the last thing I need."

She pursed her lips together. He was right. This kind of wound would definitely beg a call to the authorities from emergency personnel.

"I'm fine," he repeated unconvincingly. "I can take care of it myself."

"No, you can't." Which was clear as he swayed on his feet, leaning into the brick wall again. She could tell he was in pain. Losing blood. Not to mention that even if he were in the state of mind to operate on himself, he'd have to close the wound one handed.

"We need to get the car," Anna said. She realized she was echoing the very words she'd protested against a moment ago, but with the sirens growing closer, their window of opportunity to disappear was shrinking.

Dade nodded, letting her lead the way the two blocks back to the motel in silence. They navigated the parking lot, Lenny bounding along at their side, and quickly slipped into the SUV. As much as she would have liked to grab their bags from their damaged room, the sound of approaching sirens was loud enough to tell her there was no time for that. A fact that was confirmed as Dade turned the engine over, pulling out of the lot just as flashing red and blue lights appeared around the corner. Dade drove slowly past them, pulling over to the right to let them by as any law-abiding citizen would. As soon as they screamed past, he slowly drove the rest of the block, waiting until they took the corner to push down on the gas, speeding through several lights.

Four blocks and several turns later Anna dared to let out the breath she'd been holding. She looked over at Dade. His skin was a garish white under the glow of the streetlamps, sweat beading on his forehead and cheeks.

"We need to pull over," she said, her voice low and calm, trying her best at sounding commanding.

She was surprised when he didn't argue, instead nodding in compliance and pulling the SUV over to the side of the road on a quiet residential street.

"Take your shirt off so I can look at the wound," Anna instructed.

Dade paused. Clearly he was not used to being given orders. But, considering the circumstances, he complied, wincing as he lifted his right arm out of the T-shirt, exposing his hit shoulder.

Anna inspected the wound. She couldn't tell how deep it was, but it was large, covering at least three square inches of flesh, digging a neat pathway out across his skin.

"You need stitches," she said.

Dade nodded. "I can do that."

"It's on your shoulder. There's no way you can stitch yourself one handed. I'll do it for you."

"Right. Like I'm gonna trust you."

"You don't have much choice, now, do you?" she asked.

He grinned, the movement costing him some effort, she could tell. "Touché." He looked from her to the blood oozing down his arm.

"I'm serious," she said quietly. "You need help."

"Fine," he relented. Though she could tell it was because he saw the logic in her argument, and not that he did, in fact, trust her. As witnessed by the fact his left hand still had the M9 clutched in a vice grip.

"We need to get to a drugstore. I need some supplies," Anna said.

Dade nodded then moved to turn the car on again.

"And I think I should drive," Anna said slowly.

"No."

"You're half unconscious," Anna pointed out.

Dade shot her a look. "I'll let the conscious half drive, then."

Anna bit her lip. "Look you can point the gun on me the entire way, okay? Shoot me if I make a wrong turn. But shut up and get in the passenger seat before you bleed to death, please?"

Dade blinked, taking longer than Anna would have liked to open his eyes again. His mouth quirked upward. "Okay. You win," he said, his voice low. Too low. He really was losing blood.

"Move over," she said, pulling him out of the seat.

He did, shifting into the passenger seat, as she got out of the car and rounded to the driver's side.

Anna turned the key in the ignition, pointing the car toward Van Ness, driving through the darkness until she saw the lights of a 24-hour drugstore. She pulled around the back, into a small lot, and cut the engine. She glanced over at Dade.

His brow was covered in sweat, his breath coming slow and deep. The gun hung limply in his hand. He looked more pathetic than threatening at this point.

Go. Run. He'd never catch you like this.

"I'll be right back," she said.

He nodded slowly, reaching into his pocket to hand her some cash before shutting his eyes.

A sure sign he was in trouble. He never would have agreed to let her go into the store alone if he'd been thinking clearly.

She left Lenny in the back seat as a guard dog and quickly jogged into the market. She grabbed a hand basket and scanned the aisles for makeshift medical supplies. Aspirin, gauze pads—lots of them—Betadine to clean the wound, and Krazy Glue. She grabbed a couple of items from the pet aisle, a couple of packs of trail mix and Gatorade, and a clean T-shirt for Dade from a souvenir rack by the door.

She quickly paid for it all and jogged back to the car, half expecting to find Dade either unconscious or gone.

But he was just as she'd left him, breathing heavily in the front seat, a lose grasp on the gun in his lap.

"You okay?" she asked, as she slipped into the driver's seat again.

"Peachy," he breathed out.

She quickly put the car in gear, pulling out of the lot and driving south. Two blocks down, she found a Presbyterian church. She pulled around the two-story building, parking in the rear in the spot reserved for clergy. A dim light peeked out from the street lamp on the other side of the church building, creating a shadow over much of the lot. But it was enough light for what she needed.

"Get in the back seat," she told him, switching seats with Lenny herself.

Dade managed to slip out the passenger side door then collapsed into the back.

The car smelled like leather, sweat, and the salty fog filtering in off the Bay, ripe with ebbing seaweed. Dade's eyes were closed, his head lulling backward against the seat. He could have been sleeping, were it not for the rapid in and out of breath from his nostrils as she worked.

She tried to move quickly, not only to close the wound before he lost too much blood but also to minimize the pain. While he was a silent patient, his breath came harder when her fingers hit the wounded flesh, his chest rising and falling rapidly.

She started by crushing up two tabs of aspirin into a powdery mix then applied the paste to the wound. It was a poor substitute for local anesthetic, but it would have to do for now. Thankfully, it looked as though the bullet had grazed his shoulder rather than lodging there. A good thing. If it had been there, she would have taken him to the hospital no matter how much he protested. Despite the heroics shown on TV cop shows, digging into someone's flesh to pull out a bullet usually resulted in ruptured arteries, nerve damage, or other internal bleeding. All of which she was ill-prepared to deal with.

She soaked a gauze pad with Betadine and applied it to his shoulder. He winced but didn't move. Next she pulled out the tube of styptic powder that she'd bought in the pet care section.

Dade looked down at the picture of a dog on the tube.

"What's that?"

"Styptic powder."

"Which is?"

"It helps clotting. You use it on overtrimmed nails."

"There's a picture of a poodle on it."

"It's for dogs' nails."

"You're giving me dog medicine?"

"It's not medicine. And it'll work for you, too."

She grabbed the tube of Krazy Glue and applied it to the sides of the wound, leaving a small opening at the top, where she applied more of the powder. Closing it entirely left no room for drainage to avoid an abscess. This way the wound might weep a little, but it would heal faster.

She worked quietly, holding the side of the wound together for several seconds, willing the glue to take. Dade's skin felt warm underneath her fingers. She hoped it was the strain and not an infection brewing.

"You almost done?" he breathed out. His eyes were closed again, his head leaning back on the seat. The gun was completely abandoned at this point, shoved somewhere in his pants. His hands were limp. His arms lax.

"Almost." She removed the pressure from his shoulder and was glad to see the skin holding together. She finished off by applying more Betadine to the outside then taped a gauze bandage over the top. It wouldn't heal pretty, but it would heal. And it avoided the hospital.

She sat back, using gauze to clean his blood off her hands, and realized she too had been sweating.

Dade opened his eyes. He looked down at the white square on his shoulder.

"Thanks," he said.

She met his eyes, softer now, spent with the energy of forced vulnerability. She nodded and handed him a Gatorade. "You're welcome. Drink this."

He did, taking small sips from the bottle. She could feel him watching her as she gathered the used gauze into a plastic bag, cleaning up their make-shift operating room. Lenny barked in the front seat, sniffing at the steering wheel.

"The dog," Dade said. "You named him Lenny?"

Anna nodded. "After Sugar Ray Leonard. They're both boxers."

Dade grinned. "Cute."

Anna shifted in her seat, not sure how she felt about that assessment.

"How long have you been in the business?" she asked, taking his chatty mood as an opportunity to learn what she could about him.

He shook his head. "Long enough."

"You're American? You were trained here?"

He nodded silently.

"Military?" she asked, even though she knew the dog tags in his bag had proven that.

"Marines."

"How long did you serve?"

He took a long breath, and she wasn't sure he was going to answer.

"Ten years."

"What made you leave?"

He rolled his head to the side, pinning her with a long look. Not information he was willing to share.

"So, now you're in the private sector?" she pressed.

"Yes."

"Why turn private?"

"Politics." He closed his eyes again, leaning on the seat. "Politics dictated my every move. I was tired of seeing the bad guys get away because they had good friends."

"So now you hunt the bad guys yourself?"

"Something like that."

"Bad guys like me," she said, her voice low.

He opened his eyes. "Christ, what do you want me to say? Have you read your file?"

The comment made him angry, color pinking his cheeks. Good. That honestly scared her less than the listless Dade.

She nodded. "I can imagine what's in it." She paused. "How old were you when you went in the military?"

"Twenty-one."

"I was thirteen."

He turned his head her way. "Seriously? Shit."

"My parents died when I was too young to remember them. I grew up in a group home near the city center. One day a man from the government office came and gave us each a written test. I guess I did well, because he said he had somewhere special for me to go. From then on, Petrovich basically raised me."

"Your handler?" he asked.

She nodded. "He taught me everything I needed to survive in the KOS."

"How old were you when you made your first kill?" Dade asked, his voice softer. Something flickered behind his eyes. If she had to guess, it was pity.

She hated pity.

"Old enough to know right from wrong."

"But you did it anyway."

"I had orders to follow. I didn't have much of a choice."

"You always have a choice," he countered.

"So I deserve this? Being hunted down now is my ill-earned fate?"

"Is it?" he asked, his eyes boring into her.

That was a loaded question. Had she killed people? Yes. Definitely. Had they deserved it? Probably. Maybe. Did anyone really deserve to be killed? Justice had been served at her hand. She was sure of it. But so had the personal interests of her sponsors. She'd been too young to be able to distinguish one from the other at the time, but in hindsight she had no idea how many innocent people had been given to her as targets that threatened some unscrupulous person's way of life.

And Dade was after *her* now. Did that make him an instrument of justice?

She realized she had no answer to that question any more than she had one to his.

She shrugged. "We're all bad. We're all good."

"That was a cop-out."

She smiled at him. "Yes, it was."

She could see something warring behind his eyes. If she had to guess, he was trying to decide how much of what she'd told him was truth and how much was designed to sway him. She wasn't sure what he finally settled on, but he nodded and asked, "What made you leave?"

"I wanted a life."

"Have you had one?"

She shook her head slowly side to side. And that was the raw truth. Deep down she had always known this day would come, and she'd have to run, to start again. Living with that knowledge was no more a way to live than being under the KOS's control had been.

"We should go," he said. "As long as we keep moving we make it harder for them to find us."

She nodded. "Do you want me to drive?"

He shook his head. "I'm fine."

He didn't look fine, but the conversation had put some of the color back into his face. So she didn't protest, instead slipping from the back seat, switching seats with Lenny again, and sliding into the passenger side of the SUV.

Dade got behind the wheel. But before he started the engine, he slid something across the console toward her.

She looked down.

It was her Glock. She glanced up, sending him the silent question.

"You're going to need it when we find them," he said.

She nodded. "Thanks."

Anna slipped the gun into her waistband. It felt heavy, comforting. Like an old friend. It was easy to wear. Felt secure against her body. She leaned back against the seat, feeling more of the old Anya come back to her than she ever thought she'd see again.

And hoped she wouldn't have to use the gun on the man beside her.

CHAPTER TWELVE

———

They spent the night driving the City, up and down winding roads—some empty as their inhabitants slept, some filled with the nightlife spilling from bars, clubs, and diners. They stopped at a gas station around 3am where they refueled and Dade made a decision and picked up a burner phone. Around dawn, Dade pulled into the parking lot of a Denny's where he spent the last of his cash on breakfast and walked Lenny around the back of the building to do his business. Anya fed him some water then walked him up and down the block to stretch his legs.

Dade leaned against the car, watching her. With his good arm, he pulled his cell from his back pocket and dialed. His contact answered on the third ring.

"The job done?" was his clipped greeting.

"No," Dade said.

There was a pause. "When?"

"I need to speak to our employer," Dade countered.

"You know that's not possible."

"He better make it possible. There's been a change of plans."

Dade could feel the man on the other end tense. "What kind of change?"

Dade took a deep breath. He'd never done this before, and he wasn't entirely sure it was the right thing to do now.

"I'm not finishing the job."

The silence on the other end did nothing to reassure him.

"Did you hear me?" Dade asked.

The man's voice came slowly and deliberately. "Not finishing isn't an option."

Dade knew. These weren't the kind of people who let bygones be bygones. When they made a contract, it was honored. One way or another.

"I'm not doing it," Dade told the man. "Tell our employer the deal's off. The deposit will be returned to the account it was wired from."

Again the silence on the other end stretched far longer than comfort would have dictated. Finally the man sighed. "Our employer will not be happy. We were told you were supposed to be professional."

"I was *supposed* to be the only one on the job. It was *supposed* to be clean and simple. Our employer should have given me all the facts, not just the ones he wanted me to believe."

"You had what facts you needed to do the job you were hired to do."

"Look, I'm not doing anything until I know who else is after Anya, why, and which side I'm on."

"You're on the side of the man who paid you."

"He doesn't own me!" Dade shot back.

The man sighed again. "He won't be happy."

"Tell him to join the club," Dade said then stabbed the *Off* button. Then he tossed the cell into the trash can beside the restaurant.

He exhaled deeply, running a hand through his hair, knowing he had just painted a target on his own head the same size as Anya's.

He watched as she approached, the dog ambling along on the end of her lead. Her eyes were shielded from the sun by a pair of cheap sunglasses they'd picked up at the gas station, and her hair was hanging loosely around her shoulders, blowing in the early morning breeze.

She'd had the opportunity to run last night. She could have easily left, let him bleed out, fend for himself. She'd stayed. He didn't know what to make of that. Some sort of strategy on her part? Did she need his protection? He didn't know. What he did know was that there were two people out there who wanted her dead. Somehow she was a danger, a threat to them.

What he'd said to Anya last night had been true. He'd entered into this line of work as a sort of extension of what he'd done in the military. Fixing what was unfixable through the bureaucracy of government channels. Of course, it wasn't *just* altruistic heroics. He did take a hefty fee for his services, but he chose his jobs carefully. And it bothered him that he'd chosen incorrectly in her case. Bothered him enough that he wasn't ready to walk away just yet.

At least, not until he knew what he was walking away from.

* * *

When Anna finally dragged Lenny back to the SUV, she found Dade at the rear of the car, the back door raised. A laptop, printer, and a couple other small black boxes filled the trunk. If pressed, she'd guess at least one was a police scanner. All seemed out of date by at least ten years.

"Nice toys," she commented, sarcastically.

Dade shot her a look over his shoulder. "*I* think so." He had the laptop on, typing a sequence of numbers onto a black screen. Anna noticed the cords running between each of the machines.

"Not a fan of Wi-Fi?"

He shook his head. "Not when I'm trying to be invisible." He looked up long enough to give her a wry smile. "This stuff may be old, but it works. And it leaves a hell of a smaller digital footprint."

"What are you doing?"

"I have a sudden shortage of funds. I'm securing more."

"Stealing?" She craned her neck to get a better look at the screen, but the numbers meant nothing to her.

"Borrowing."

"From?"

He pulled a couple of newspaper pages from the trunk and handed them to her. The paper was today's, likely purchased from one of the coin-operated boxes at the entrance to the Denny's. The pages were folded over to a section revealing last night's winning numbers to the California lottery.

Anna raised an eyebrow. "You're going to steal from the lottery?"

"Borrow."

"So, you'll be giving it back?"

He nodded. "Eventually."

She wasn't sure whether she believed him or not but let it go.

"Won't they notice the money missing?"

He shook his head. "It's not going to go missing. It's going to be paid out to a winner." He took the paper back, eyes scanning the list of winning numbers for the SuperLotto.

"How?" Anna asked.

"On any given day there are hundreds of winners of small amounts—twenty dollars here, fifty dollars there. Combinations of three or four winning numbers can often result in smaller payouts. For any payout less than six hundred dollars, you can take your ticket directly to the store it was purchased at for payment, bypassing the state lotto offices."

"And stringent security," she said, nodding. It was a good plan. There was just one flaw. "But you have to have the actual winning ticket to take in, right?"

Dade nodded. "And I will."

Even as he said it, Dade switched screens, pulling up a graphics program with a facsimile of a California SuperLotto ticket already loaded. Juggling between his sequence of numbers and the graphic, he quickly input a series of numbers onto the ticket.

"You've done this before," Anna said, more a statement than a question.

"It's not a way to get rich, but there have been times in the past when I've needed cash without a traceable trail. These will get run through the state lotto machines. As long as the numbers and the bar code on the ticket match the one in the machine, no one's going to look too closely. The clerks are working for minimum wage, and the store owners all get compensated by the lotto anyway, so no one really cares. As long as the machine spits it back as a winner, that's all that matters."

"Clever," Anna admitted, wishing she'd thought of it. She watched as Dade's screen of numbers generated a bar code. He quickly transferred it onto the ticket face.

"They teach you that trick in the military?" Anna asked.

"No," he answered without looking up. "Juvie."

Anna paused. "You've been in jail?"

"Juvie," he corrected. "Whole different ball game. Record expunged when I was eighteen."

"So what did you do to end up in juvie?"

He shrugged. "Truancy, vandalism. Usual rebellious teenager stuff, but I had to take it to extremes, you know?"

No, she didn't. She didn't know the first thing about "usual teenager" things. But she nodded anyway as she watched him hit a button that whirred the old printer to life. He must have had special paper loaded in already, as it quickly spit out a perfect copy of a winning lotto ticket.

He held it up to the light. "A little on the pale side, but it'll do."

He turned to her. "Let's go win the lottery."

* * *

Anna waited in the car, listening to Lenny munch on dog chow in the back seat as she watched through the front window of the convenience store on the corner of 19th and Sanchez. Dade stood in line behind a young guy in droopy jeans, his fake winning ticket in hand. She stuck a fingernail in her mouth and chewed, a nervous habit she hadn't indulged in in years. She wasn't sure about this idea. Granted Dade had told her the ticket he'd made up was only worth a hundred dollars, hardly enough to hit anyone's radar, but it was still stealing. From the government. Putting money back into that system would be trickier than taking it out. That is, if Dade really had any intention of ever paying it back.

She couldn't get a handle on him. Clearly he was dangerous, well trained, not to be messed with. But he didn't seem to have a temper or kill indiscriminately. In fact, she could almost understand why he did what he did. A killer with a social conscience, maybe? Yet, here he was stealing. And not for the first time, it sounded like.

So was he a good guy or a bad guy? Friend or foe?

She wasn't sure. All she knew for certain was that she sorely wished she'd been able to grab ammo for her Glock from her duffel before they'd fled the motel last night. Riding around with a guy like Dade would feel a lot more comfortable if she were armed with more than one bullet.

Anna watched as the guy in the sagging jeans left the store and Dade stepped up to the counter. He exchanged a few words with the clerk, handing over the forged ticket. The man took it and turned his back to Dade, inserting the ticket into a machine behind the counter.

Anna held her breath, waiting. Ears straining for the sound of sirens coming to take him away.

Instead, the clerk stepped away from the machine, opened the cash register, and counted five twenty-dollar bills out into Dade's hand. She watched Dade flash the guy a smile and thank him before exiting the store.

He jogged up to the car and slid into the drivers' side.

"Got it?" Anna asked.

Dade nodded. "Piece of cake."

Anna felt relief flood her system as Dade started the car, pulling back out of the lot and heading north toward Market.

"So where are we going now?" she asked.

Dade stared out the front window as he drove. "Shelli was clearly the leak in your life. The question is, who does she work for?"

Anna nodded. "Unfortunately, she knows we're looking for her. And she's probably deep in hiding by now. There's no way we're going to find her."

"I agree. But the postcards in her place," Dade said. "If the locations were meeting points of some sort, I'd be curious to know who she was meeting."

"Fisherman's Wharf, Chinatown Square, and Coit Tower," Anna repeated from memory.

Dade nodded. "I say we visit Coit Tower first. Least busy, most likely someone noticed her. Possibly noticed who she was meeting."

"Agreed."

*   *   *

Coit Tower sat atop Telegraph Hill looking over the eastern side of San Francisco. Dade found a spot to park on the street two blocks from the landmark and got out of the car, surveying the area slowly. Anna did the same, scanning the street for anything out of the ordinary. No sign of Shelli's now–jet black hair, no sign of the men in black from the night before, no flash of silver muzzles pointed her way. Still, the solid length of her Glock at her side was reassuring.

As they approached the tower, the crowd was nothing like Pier 39 had been, though there were still a fair number of people filtering in and out of the historical sight. A small circular building sat at the bottom of the architectural marvel, housing a gift shop. Dade approached the man behind the counter, asking if he'd seen anyone matching Shelli's description lately. Unfortunately, the man only spoke broken English, shaking his head in the negative at Dade's request. Dade bought tickets from the man for the both of them to ride to the top of the tower. Anna scanned the faces of each person enjoying the wall murals as they waited for the antique elevator ride to the top.

The tower was built in 1933 by Lillie Hitchcock Coit, who had been saved as a child from a terrible fire by city firefighters. She had then dedicated her life to those same firefighters, often riding along in her petticoats on the engines. When she died, she commissioned the tower as a dedication to those who served in San Francisco.

At least, that was the history that the docent riding the elevator with them recited. It wasn't until the doors opened and the crowd dispersed onto the viewing areas that Dade got a chance to question the woman alone about having seen Shelli. No, she hadn't noticed anyone fitting the description—either with long red hair or short black hair. Dade thanked her, moving on to a security guard near the railing.

Anna wandered to one of the tall windows along the tower's perimeter and stared out at the vast array of buildings before her. The City looked like a doll's village, the tiny rooftops and miniature trees jutting up from sloping hillsides. She took a moment to take in the scenery, awed by the sheer volume of people packed so densely into one square of earth. The perfect place to hide.

"No one's seen her," Dade said, coming up behind her. "If this was a meet point, no one remembers Shelli. Let's try another spot."

As reluctant as she was to leave the moment of serenity, Anna knew he was right. She followed his lead as he turned back to the elevators.

Half an hour later they were parked at a garage on Kearny, just kissing the three blocks-wide section of SF known as Chinatown. Grant and Stockton ran through the middle of the neighborhood, which boasted the largest Asian population outside of mainland China. Which left them a lot of ground to cover.

The photograph on the postcard showed the Dragon Gate at Grant and Bush. It was at least a starting point. Mingling scents of savory food and sweet incense hit Anna's nostrils as they approached the first gift shop on the narrow street. Again, Anna let Dade do the talking, questioning the woman behind the counter. No, she hadn't seen Shelli either. Or if she had, Shelli's face had blended in with the hundreds of visitors she saw every day.

He did a repeat at the next half dozen shops along the street, coming up with exactly the same answers.

They were looking for a needle in a haystack. Anna was about to give up hope when they stopped a street vendor selling spiced nuts. He was an older man with a weathered face and unnaturally dark hair from a box.

"Excuse me," Dade said.

The man looked up. "Nuts?"

Dade shook his head. "Actually, we were wondering if you'd seen a friend of ours come through here." He gave the man a quick description of Shelli.

He squinted up at Dade then shook his head. "Sorry, I don't remember seeing her here today," he said in heavily accented English.

"What about on a different day? Has she been through here at all recently?"

The man shrugged. "Sorry, I see a lot of faces. They don't all stick, you know?"

Anna felt her hopes sinking. It had been a long shot anyway, but it still felt deflating.

"Was your friend here the same day you were?" the man asked.

Dade paused. "Which day would that be?"

"Last week. I remember seeing you here then."

Dade cocked his head to the side then slowly said, "I wasn't here last week."

The guy shook his head, soft jowls wobbling on either side of his chin. "No, no. Of course not. But you," he said, pointing at Anna. "*You* were here."

CHAPTER THIRTEEN

———

Dade spun on Anna. "When were you here?" he demanded.

She could see whatever tentative bond of trust they'd forged rapidly disintegrating.

"No," she quickly said, shaking her head vehemently from side to side for emphasis. "I've never been here before and certainly not last week."

The man looked from Dade to Anna. "I don't wanna get in the middle of anything," he said, "but I'm sure it was you."

"When?" Anna asked. "When was I here?"

The man bit his lip. "'Bout three days ago, I'd say."

"What did I do?"

The guy cocked his head at Anna.

"Humor me, okay?" she said. "When I was here before, what did I do?"

"I don't know, shopped, ate. What do people do here?"

"Was she with someone else?" Dade asked.

The man shook his head. "Nope. Not as far as I saw."

"No one met her here?" Dade asked.

Again, the man shook his head. "Not that I saw. She was alone as far as I could tell."

"Exactly what did she—what did *I* do?" Anna asked.

The man shrugged his shoulders. "Walked around a bit. Stopped at the souvenir place over there." He pointed across the way at a store front filled with "I heart San Francisco" T-shirts and postcards.

"Did she buy anything?" Dade asked.

He narrowed his eyes, as if trying to see the scene again. "Actually, yeah, she did. I think she bought a magazine. She sat on a bench over there by the tea shop and read for a few minutes. Then she left."

Anna felt Dade straighten beside her. He caught on the same detail she did. The magazine.

The postcards hadn't been telling Shelli where to meet *someone*, but to find *something*.

It would have been the easiest thing for whoever was controlling her puppet strings to write instructions somewhere in the margins of a magazine, then slip it into the back of the rack, leaving it for Shelli to buy and read later. Clerks were trained to watch for people shoplifting, but no one in the store would have noticed someone leaving a magazine behind.

"Do you still have the postcard?" Anna asked Dade.

He nodded, pulling the stack from his back pocket. He handed the one for Chinatown to her.

Anna read over the script again. "The magazine she bought. Do you remember what it was?" she asked the man.

He shrugged. "One of those gossip magazines."

Anna stabbed her finger at a line on the postcard.

You must come next time to check out the people.

"There! The postcard was telling her what magazine to buy. *People*."

Dade nodded. "Her instructions were in the magazine," he said as they stepped out of the vendor's earshot again.

"No wonder Shelli didn't care about leaving the postcards behind. If she came disguised as me, there'd be no link between her and the drop spots."

"And if she took the magazines with her, there's no information left at any of the points," Dade finished, his eyes cutting to the souvenir shop.

Anna felt disappointment welling inside her at losing their only lead.

"Shelli's contact wouldn't want to chance someone else buying the doctored magazine. They would have planted it as close as possible to her pick up." Dade's gaze was still on the shop.

"What are you thinking?" Anna asked, scanning the storefront herself.

Dade pulled out the burner phone she'd seen him buy earlier. "Security footage."

She looked more closely at the store and saw what he'd seen—a small, red light glowing at the corner nearest the store entrance. A telltale sign of a security camera.

"Can you access it from that?" Anna asked, gesturing at the phone.

Dade nodded. "Maybe. It all depends on how careful the owners were when they set up their system and how much security they have on their network."

Anna knew that while digital security cameras were getting cheaper and more accessible to the masses, their wireless feeds were also much more vulnerable to hacking than their older, analog counterparts. Anyone with a Wi-Fi connection could in theory access your data. One reason she'd decided to forgo the digital surveillance outside her own apartment.

For all the good it had done her.

"Nice." Dade smirked.

"What?" she asked, leaning forward to see his screen.

"They kept the default login credentials."

"Does that mean you're in?"

He nodded, holding the phone farther from his body to allow her to see. The screen showed a live video feed of the storefront, including images of the two of them.

Anna felt a tingle shoot down her back, realizing just how easily anyone could access images of her anywhere. It was unnerving at best.

"Can you access historical footage?" she asked, her eyes darting from side to side, suddenly feeling vulnerable and ready to leave.

A few swipes later, Dade answered her by pulling up a screen with a list of dates and times. He scrolled until he had a list of times from three days ago.

"Shelli was at the shelter until five," Anna told him.

Dade moved down the list, hitting 4:45. Footage from three evenings ago came up, showing the storefront in black and white. They watched people filter in and out, most carrying soda cans or souvenirs as they exited. No one entered carrying a magazine.

The footage played for fifteen minutes before ending and kicking them back to the menu with times listed. Dade hit 4:30, watching a similar set of footage.

He did the same thing for the next few times listed. Anna watched for a bit but felt her eyes wandering back to present, scanning the street. They'd been out in the open too long. If Dade could access cameras that easily, what about the people hunting her? There must be a dozen security devices mounted in the area—inside shops, at ATMs, near public transpiration. Not to mention phones, tablets, laptops. Her image could be on any of them right now, being transported to anyone anywhere. She wiped a sweaty palm on her thigh.

"There." Dade's voice jolted her out of her thoughts.

She looked at the screen as he rewound a bit of footage and played it back again. A man in a knit cap and bulky jacket walked into the store. Two minutes and fifteen seconds later, he walked out again empty handed.

"His jacket looks lighter," Anna said, catching the same detail she assumed Dade had.

He nodded, replaying the clip again. The man held his jacket closed to his body when he walked into the store, but the sides flapped freely in the breeze as he exited. He'd been hiding the magazine in the jacket.

Dade zoomed in on the man's face. "Know him?"

Dark hair peeking from under the cap, facial hair a week or so past needing a shave, eyes downcast so she couldn't tell the color. Nothing about him struck a chord of recognition. She shook her head. "Sorry."

Dade let the footage play, watching the man until he walked just to the edge of the camera's range. He paused a minute at the left corner of the building near the street, his back to the camera, before moving on and out of the shot.

Anna looked up from the device, following the eyeline to the left corner. A parking meter sat at the street, just outside the building.

"The meter." She looked up at Dade, feeling hope flutter in her belly again. "You think there's a chance he parked there?"

He nodded. "It's possible."

She watched him pull up another screen on his phone. "The smart meters scan the license plates of every car that parks near them. If the owner doesn't pay, they're mailed a ticket." He looked up and gave her a wry smile. "No meter maids needed anymore."

"Where do they store the plates?" Anna asked. She had to admit, Dade had a leg up on her when it came to this. Her training had been pre-smart anything. And while she'd tried to keep a small digital footprint over the last few years, she hadn't been focused on finding anyone else's.

"Cloud storage." His eyes were back on his screen.

"Where?"

He paused, swiped a few screens, stabbed a few numbers out. "Here."

She leaned over to look. Somehow he had gotten into the parking authority's system, and she was looking at a list of plate numbers for the day in question.

"What was the footage time stamp?" she asked him.

"2:45." He pointed to a license plate number that had occupied the space in question between 2:47 and 2:54.

Anna couldn't help the smile that curled her lips. "Gotcha."

Ten minutes later, they were back in Dade's car, keying an address near the marina into his GPS. It was a holding for an Ace Industries, the business on the title of the car associated with the plate number, at least according to the DMV records Dade had invaded. They rode in silence, Anna trying not to hold her breath as she prayed they were on the right track. She felt anticipation building in her stomach as Dade parked outside a warehouse situated along the Bay, just below the freeway overpass, that matched their destination address. It was an older building, originally painted white, though rust had long ago taken over as the predominant color. The building was two stories tall, squatting in the middle of an industrial area, with a corrugated roof and an abandoned forklift parked outside.

"You think this is it?" Anna asked. Honestly, it didn't look any different from dozens of other buildings along the water.

But Dade nodded in the seat beside her, his eyes focusing on the far side of the warehouse. "I know it is."

"How can you be so sure?"

Dade lifted a hand and pointed at the building. "Because Shelli just came out of the side door."

CHAPTER FOURTEEN

———

Anna watched a woman with long, chestnut brown hair emerge from a side door then put a cell phone to her ear, speaking rapidly into the device. She'd changed her clothes since the airport the day before, swapping her baggy sweatshirt for a fitted trench, along with the obvious addition of a wig. But as she turned her face toward the sun, Anna could clearly make out Shelli's features—upturned nose, bright green eyes, and a smattering of freckles that gave her face a deceptively friendly appearance.

She talked rapidly into the phone for a minute then stabbed it off before reentering the warehouse the same way she'd come out.

Dade reached across Anna's lap and opened the glove box, quickly pulling out a box of ammo. As he loaded bullets into the magazine, Anna felt the weight of the one shot left in her own Glock. She hoped it would be enough.

"You have a plan?" Anna asked.

Dade shook his head. "Not necessarily. But whoever is bankrolling Shelli also hired those guys to come after us last night."

"And you think he's in there?"

Dade shrugged. "I don't know. But I want to be prepared either way."

Dade locked the magazine into place and stuck the barrel of the gun into his waistband before jumping from the vehicle. Anna followed his lead, a step behind him as he casually walked the few yards between the SUV and the chain link fence surrounding the property. Dade glanced over both shoulders before quickly scaling the fence, dropping easily on the other side. Anna followed, hitting the ground a few seconds later.

Dade didn't speak but pointed her toward the right side of the building, while he disappeared around the left side, his 9mm held tight to his body, a deceptively relaxed grace moving his limbs as he circled around to the back of the warehouse.

Anna tried to match his stride, but relaxed wasn't in her repertoire at the moment. Nervous, anxious, unprepared for whatever lay ahead. She looked down. God, her hands were even shaking. She shifted her weapon to her left hand, shaking the right vigorously to try to gain some control over herself again. She'd had control once. But that was way too long ago now for her body to recall on its own.

Anna moved quickly, rounding the right side of the building. Windows lined the upper story of the warehouse, likely giving way to offices of some sort. Halfway down the length of the building Anna spied a door with another small window at the top. Silently, she jogged toward it, and stood on tiptoe to see inside.

The interior of the warehouse was stacked with cardboard boxes. It was hard to tell the contents from here. But from the varying sizes and shapes and Asian lettering printed on the sides, she guessed this to be some sort of importing business. Though whether it was legal or not, she couldn't say.

No people were visible from her vantage point. Though, as suspected, she spied offices built onto a second-story catwalk running the perimeter of the building's interior.

And in one of the offices the light was on.

She stepped back from the door. It was small, painted white like the rest of the building, with orange rusted hinges. It looked doubtful it would even open, but she put her hand on the knob, turning clockwise. Surprisingly, it moved. The hinges groaned as Anna pushed, the sound echoing through the warehouse. She cringed, hoping whoever was in the office couldn't hear from up there.

As soon as she had the door open enough to slip inside, she did, quickly closing it behind herself again. She took a minute to let her eyes adjust to the darkness, a sharp contrast from the bright sunlight magnified by fog outside. She listened for any signs of life on the main warehouse floor, but the only thing she heard was her own breath, coming hard in the silence.

Once she trusted her eyesight again, she navigated the maze of boxes toward the far side of the warehouse where she'd seen the light on.

Her steps were light, though every one seemed to echo off the concrete floor. Or maybe just through her own head, filled with hot breath and nerves. She felt sweat trickle down her back, despite the cool temperature, as she neared a metal stairway leading up to the catwalk.

Anna took one tentative step, then another, bending low at the knees to distribute her weight evenly enough with each step so as not to cause the stairs to creak as she ascended. As she reached the top, sweat fairly dripped down her back, dust tickling her nose, but she continued silently, slipping past two dark offices before nearing the one with a light emanating from the window.

Thin curtains covered the glass, but as Anna crouched below the sill, she could make out two figures inside the room.

The first was easy to identify, with her long chestnut wig. Shelli. She had her back to the window, talking to another person across the room. The other person was closer to the shadows, angled away from the window. Anna leaned forward, craning her neck to get a look at his face. It was a man, she could tell that much from his shape. He was dressed in slacks and a dress shirt—nothing unique or distinguishable that she could tell.

Shelli was speaking to him, her hands moving animatedly as she did. The windows were too thick and the walls too well soundproofed for Anna to hear what she was saying, but the man answered calmly, causing Shelli to gesture even more wildly. At least that part of Shelli's personality hadn't been affected.

Anna wondered suddenly how much was. She wasn't used to being on this end of a professional. Most of the targets she had contact with had been exactly as they'd appeared to be. *She* had been the chameleon, the one who was not what she pretended to be in order to get close enough to them to strike. She preferred that position to the one she was in now, not knowing who was who or what she could trust to be real about them. If anything.

Shelli moved toward the door, and Anna tensed. Shelli's companion moved backward toward the corner of a desk that Anna could barely see behind the curtains. He put a large brimmed hat on his head, obscuring any chance Anna might have had at ascertaining his identity. The two moved toward the door, and Anna quickly ducked down, diving into the open doorway of the dark office to her right.

She watched as Shelli and the man exited, the man turning left, toward the stairs, and Shelli heading right, in the direction of Anna's position.

Anna crouched lower then froze in the dark, willing Shelli to walk past her. She held her breath, trying to keep her raw emotions from ringing out as the woman walked by the office.

Shelli moved along the catwalk, passing within a foot of Anna's hiding place. Anna watched her, eyes glued to Shelli's back as she silently counted off seconds.

One, two, three…

Shelli didn't turn around, and Anna let out a slow, evenly modulated breath as she watched Shelli follow the catwalk to the far left side of the building, exiting out into the sunshine through a second story door to the outside.

Anna waited only long enough to see the door swing shut before springing up and running after her. Shelli was a pawn in all this, Anna knew. Anna wanted the person who was orchestrating her movements, the one who had put the target on Anna's head for whatever unknown threat she posed to him. But she also knew the quickest route to that person was Shelli.

Anna jogged down the catwalk, quickly hitting the outside door. She pushed it open, eyes squinting against the sudden onslaught of light as she scanned the grounds for Shelli. She spotted her quickly, staying close to the side of the building as she made her way across the dirt property toward a gate in the chain link fence. She walked purposefully, completely unaware of being watched. Anna followed, keeping to the shelter of the building, the abandoned forklift, the shadow of a lone tree hunkering in the corner of the property to avoid being out in the open should Shelli turn around.

But she didn't.

Shelli made her way to the street, following it east to the corner, then turning left. Anna held her gun to her side, trying to make it as inconspicuous as possible to passing motorists as she followed Shelli, turning onto a street filled with single-story machine shops and mechanics' garages.

Shelli was half a block ahead when she paused at a small brick building and slipped into an alleyway between the structures. Anna jogged toward the alley, pausing to peek around the corner before following. She made it as far as the back of the building before Shelli jumped out from behind the brick, a gun pointed straight out in front of her.

Anna froze, watching as Shelli's upturned nose wrinkled in disgust, her eyes hard, cold, and flat.

"Anya," she said.

It was one word, but it told Anna all she needed to know. Shelli knew who she was. There was no doubt she had been hired to spy on Anna. And that she was working for someone from Anna's past.

Anna's fingers tightened around her Glock.

Shelli must have noticed, since she yelled, "Drop it!"

Anna did, hearing it clatter to the pavement beside her. "So, it's true," she said. "It was all a lie."

"You're one to talk," Shelli countered. "*Anya*."

"I left that life a long time ago."

Shelli smiled. "You should know better than anyone that you can never leave that life."

Anna swallowed, a sudden lump in her throat reminding her just how true that statement was.

"Who?" Anna asked. "Who are you working for?"

Shelli opened her mouth.

But Anna never heard the answer.

Instead, pain exploded behind her ear, her vision blurring, and blackness closing in on all sides as the ground tilted up to meet her.

* * *

Anna blinked her eyes. Or tried to. Pain shot through her head with the effort of moving, every breath in her chest pounding against her skull. She lay perfectly still, trying to get her bearings. The floor beneath her was cold, concrete if she had to guess. She could smell the Bay nearby and hoped that meant she hadn't been moved far. Voices came from very far away, speaking in a foreign language, though they sounded garbled, as if her reception needed tweaking. She took deep, slow breaths, trying to fill her brain with enough oxygen to gather her wits without letting the nausea in her stomach take over. She slowly wiggled her fingers and toes. Nothing felt broken or beyond repair, though she quickly ascertained that her wrists had been bound behind her back with something thin and plastic that bit into her skin. Slowly she cracked one eye open, ignoring the pounding behind her eyelids. Through slits of light she could see boxes, dust, a dirty floor. The warehouse. Shelli had brought her back here.

Shelli and her partner, she realized. The man. He must have followed Anna as Anna had followed Shelli. Shelli's partner? Or employer? Anna blinked, opening the other eye, her gaze scanning the warehouse. She was lying on her side on the floor, dumped beside a tower of boxes. The voices were coming from a few feet away, she realized, the forms of Shelli and her companion taking shape. Shelli was again waving her arms, shouting. The companion was quiet, calm, his voice a low hum as he responded. It took Anna a minute to realize what was wrong with their garbled speech, but when she did it hit her with shocking clarity. They were speaking Serbo-Croatian. Or at least a variant of it, throwing in Slovenian and Albanian words to make their own bastardized version of the language. Anna was familiar with all three, a long-dead portion of her brain clicking on to translate the conversation. She was slow. Rusty. It was her native language, but she hadn't used it for years. And coupled with the fog still slowly lifting from her head, she missed half of what they were saying. But Shelli was clearly angry. She hadn't expected Anna to come here. The other man? He had. He'd been ready for her. "Waiting" was the literal translation of the word he used. She wondered if she had somehow telegraphed her movements that clearly or if he was just experienced enough that he always expected the unexpected.

As Anna strained to hear more, she realized they had stopped talking and were facing her. They'd noticed she was awake.

The man mumbled something to Shelli, and she turned around, her green eyes flashing at Anna as if somehow all her troubles were Anna's fault.

Who knows? Maybe they were.

"She's awake," the man said in English. "We should have a little chat with her."

Shelli stepped toward Anna, but the man put a hand on her arm to stop her. "No. Let me."

Shelli looked disappointed, something flashing behind her eyes again. She shot a look of disdain at Anna.

But she stepped aside, allowing her companion direct access to Anna. He stepped close, the tip of his black, leather shoes coming to the tip of Anna's nose before he crouched down and tilted his head to the side to match her angle.

"Hello, Anya," he said, his accent thick, his voice hauntingly familiar, as if years and lifetimes had not hung in the air between them.

Anna swallowed. Her eyes adjusting to the unreal sight of the person before her.

Her former trainer. Goren Petrovich.

The most dangerous man she had ever met.

CHAPTER FIFTEEN

———

Anna blinked, staring at the ghost. That was the best word she could think of to describe him. Goren Petrovich was supposed to be long dead, killed years ago, half a world away.

After Anya's last hit, she'd spent a month in Switzerland, recovering from the burns she'd received after setting the car bomb. She'd had an escape planned well before she'd killed Fedorov that night, but even following her best laid plans, she knew she wouldn't be getting away unscathed. It hadn't mattered. A few burns, a sprained ankle, and a bullet lodged in her shoulder had all been a small price to pay for the hope of a new life. To be honest, she'd been prepared to pay higher.

Once she'd left the private hospital, she'd traveled Europe as a "student," staying a week in a hostel here, a couple weeks camping there, always on the move, always alert to being followed. Always conscious of the KOS's shadow looming just behind her.

She'd known when she left that the men who'd sponsored her actions were vying for political power in a game they couldn't win. If her line of work had taught her anything, it was when to get out. Factions had been warring internally even before the government had started to crumble. And once it had, power had been as unstable as the quaking ground San Francisco was so famous for. Several people she'd known to be agents had been captured as prisoners of war. Some "disappeared" at the hands of their captors, and some were traded as currency between warring factions.

Others were tried for crimes against humanity and executed. Odd to think of it when they had believed *their* actions were executing those whose crimes had been inhumane.

Or maybe that had just been a line told to young recruits like her to help them sleep at night.

After six months of constant travel and constant looking over her shoulder, Anna had read about the body of a business owner from Belgrade being found. He'd been shot dead in his store, a local bakery, seemingly a robbery attempt.

Seemingly.

But Anna knew better. She'd recognized the store as a front, the owner as Petrovich. She cried for a full day, expelling a host of conflicting emotions. He'd trained her to kill, sent her to what could have been her death several times, had been the monster at her back the last six months, spurring her to move forward, never stop running because he could have been a step behind her. He'd also been the only father she'd ever known. Protected her, trained her to survive in a world where few did. His death had left a confusing taste of love and hatred in her mouth and had also served as the final severed tie between Anya Danielovich and Anna Smith. Anna had left for the United States after that.

Only, it appeared, so had he. Because here he was. Standing over her.

Very much alive.

"Untie me," Anna demanded, her voice holding much more bravado than she felt.

Petrovich smiled and shook his head slowly from side to side. "I'm sorry, Anya. That wouldn't be prudent."

She looked from Shelli to Petrovich. "What do you want?"

He crouched down low, making himself comfortable at her level.

"You."

An answer that inspired all sorts of paranoia to gather in her stomach. But she stuck her chin out defiantly. "You have me. Now what?"

"Now, now. All these years and this is the greeting I get?"

Considering he'd been the one to knock her out and bind her, she didn't think he was in the position to lecture on manners.

However, she let the comment slide. Mostly because she was too well bound to do otherwise.

"Let's go into the office where we can talk," he said. Though clearly it was not a suggestion.

He nodded at Shelli, who hauled Anna up by her armpits, her strength surprising for someone so petite. Anna looked into her former friend's face, trying to gauge her. But Shelli didn't look at her. Wouldn't turn her face toward Anna at all. She was stone.

Anna glanced at Petrovich. Had he trained Shelli, too? Was this who she worked for? Who had been stalking her like prey?

Petrovich led the way back up the metal staircase and down the catwalk to the open office again. A metal desk and nondescript fabric-covered chairs filled the room, along with a couple of tall filing cabinets that looked like they'd been collecting dust for some time. On the desk sat Anna's Glock.

One bullet.

If she could just get to it, she would make the most of that one shot.

Petrovich gestured to one of the chairs, and Shelli deposited Anna into it.

She couldn't say that the vertical position was any more comfortable than lying on the floor, but at least it put her eye to eye with Petrovich as he sank into a chair opposite her.

He smiled at her, a fatherly gesture that was completely at odds with their current situation. "How have you been, Anya?" he asked, his voice low and soothing.

She shook off the tingle of familiarity and tried to ignore the inappropriate sense of nostalgia that accompanied his voice. How many nights had she arrived back at her training camp, getting away from a job with barely her life intact, to hear the comforting murmur of that same voice telling her she'd executed a job well?

"I've been better," Anna answered truthfully.

Petrovich smiled. "You always did have a sense of humor."

"You are supposed to be dead," she said. Not that she really wanted to walk down memory lane with the man, but considering her current position, she knew the more she could get him talking, the better.

He nodded. "I am." He paused. "As are you."

She narrowed her eyes at him. "Are you talking about the car wreck in Kosovo or the attack on the hotel last night?"

He grinned again. "What makes you think I was behind that?"

"The fact that you didn't just ask 'what attack.'"

He laughed out loud, his voice rumbling off the walls. "Very well done. All right, I admit, I had a hand in that. But you misunderstand my intention, Anya."

"Anna," she said. "It's Anna now."

He cocked his head at her. Then the corners of his mouth tugged upward in a patronizing grin. He reached one hand out and trailed the back of his knuckles down her cheek. "Oh, *dragi*, you will always be Anya to me."

His hands were rough and cold, the contact making her shiver.

"What do you want?" she asked. "Why am I here?"

"You're here because I didn't want Shelli to shoot you."

Petrovich sent the redhead a look that was clearly laced with reproach. But Shelli didn't answer, a slight sneer of her upper lip her only response.

"You didn't want Shelli to shoot me, yet you hired men to kill me?"

Petrovich shook his head. "No, no. You misunderstand. I never wanted you dead. I wanted to get your attention."

She raised an eyebrow at him. "Well, you have it," she responded. Not that she believed his intentions for a second.

He sighed and leaned back in his chair. "Right. Enough with pleasantries. Down to business it is. I am very glad to see you alive, Anya. I had hoped the men I hired would not kill you. That you had not really lost all that I'd taught you—just buried behind that veil of civility."

She clenched her jaw. "So this was all what? Some kind of test?"

"If you want to call it that."

"Did I pass?"

He grinned. "You're alive, aren't you?"

"And if I had failed?"

He shrugged. "I had faith you would not fail."

A lie. No one would have set up such an attack if he'd really had any sort of faith. He'd wanted her dead. She was his loose end. Whatever he had planned next, he hadn't wanted to take the chance that anyone would be alive to complicate it.

But Petrovich was nothing if not adaptable. She'd escaped his attempts—twice. But he had her here now. At his mercy. And clearly he thought he saw an opportunity in the present situation.

"What do you want with me?" Anna asked again.

He leaned forward, clenching his hands in his lap. "I have a job for you, Anya."

She let out a bark of laughter. "You've got to be kidding me."

"I am not joking."

And by the hard look on his face, she could tell he was not.

"I don't do those kinds of jobs anymore," Anna said, a mixture of dread and curiosity brewing.

Petrovich ignore her protest. "I work in the private sector now," he explained. "I have a small crew, but most are new. American military-trained. Not the same level of discipline we had back home."

Home. She had never thought of the training compounds as home. In fact, as far back as she could remember, nowhere had ever felt like home. Funny that he should use that word.

"At home, we were single-minded," he continued. "We had discipline, drive, the greater good in our hearts. My crew, they are good. Don't get me wrong. But not as good as you."

"Clearly," she said, surprised to find her voice shaking. "Or I wouldn't be here."

He grinned, showing off two rows of small, yellow teeth. "Yes." He was pleased she understood. "I need the best. I want you back, Anya. I want you to come work for me."

Anna looked from him to Shelli. The other woman's face was still stone. Clearly she worked for him. Clearly she was one of the American trained people he thought so little of. Anna wondered how Shelli felt about that.

"You worked for him all along?" Anna asked, addressing Shelli.

The redhead didn't acknowledge her, kept her eyes straight ahead as if Anna hadn't spoken.

"How did you find me?"

Petrovich's eye hardened at this.

"I'm not the only person who knows where you are. You have gotten sloppy, Anya."

Dade. Petrovich knew about Dade.

"That man you were with at the hotel. He's no friend to you, Anya."

"I know. He's been hired to kill me," she stated matter-of-factly. Which clearly surprised Petrovich, his poker face slipping for a split second. Good, it gave her satisfaction that he didn't know everything about her before she did.

"So you know who he is?"

"Yes," she said, even though that was only half true. She knew what his mission was. Who he really was remained a gray area at the moment. As much as whose side he was on.

She'd known men like Dade. He might have been willing to work with her to find Petrovich, but she knew he wasn't in this to do her any favors. He had his own agenda, his own reasons for being here. And his own job to finish.

That is, if she got out of here.

Anna wiggled her wrists, testing the bonds. They were tight enough to cut into her skin. No way was she going to wriggle out of them. Whatever she did, she was going to have to do without the use of two independent hands.

She let her fingers explore as far as they could reach, coming up against the metal rungs of the chair behind her. Nothing she could use as a weapon, nothing sharp enough to cut the plastic ties at her wrists. She had to stall.

She looked at Shelli again.

"So you work for him now?" she asked. "You were his agent this whole time?"

Shelli blinked but kept her eyes straight ahead.

"You lied to me about everything. You tricked me. You were undercover, spying on me this whole time."

Nothing. No reaction.

"Spying on me just so he could recruit me to replace you?"

Shelli's head snapped toward her that time, eyes dark, nostrils flared. Anna had hit a nerve. Good.

"That's enough," Petrovich said. Though he was grinning again. Clearly he was enjoying the battle for teacher's pet going on between his pupils.

Shelli squared her jaw and turned her face away from Anna again. Though Anna noticed the barely contained contempt made her chest rise and fall a little higher with each breath.

"Anya, you never give up, do you?" Petrovich asked.

"You should know. You trained me."

"Yes, I did." He nodded. "And I'll tell you, I didn't believe it when they told me you were still alive. 'That can't be,' I said. 'Anya—my Anya—would never betray me like that.'"

"Betray you?" she couldn't help choking out. "You used me."

"I trained you," he shot back, fire flashing behind his eyes, breaking his cucumber-cool exterior for a moment. "I taught you everything you know. And you left me."

"I didn't have a choice," she said softly. Which she knew was the truth. She'd been an instrument of a government losing its power, slowly slipping toward a bloody dissolution. Had she stayed, she would have outlived her usefulness in a matter of months, maybe weeks. She'd been living on borrowed time, if what you called her life then was living at all.

"You lied to me," Petrovich spit out. "I grieved for you. Thought you were dead. And then, what do I find? You're living the high life in San Francisco."

It was hardly the high life, but she didn't argue the point.

"What do you want me to do, Petrovich?" she asked instead.

He took in a deep breath, reining in the anger he obviously still felt toward her. "I want you back. Working under me again. I trained you, honed your skills. You owe me the benefit of them now."

"I owe you nothing," she stated flatly.

But he ignored her. "As I said, I have a job."

"A job," she said. "You mean murder."

He gave her a hard look. "You know that's not a nice word."

"Killing people isn't very nice work."

"People like you and I provide a *service* to those who are in need. We solve problems."

"No," Anna corrected. "People like *you* provide this service. I wash dogs. I don't kill people."

Anymore.

But she shoved that thought down.

"My *dragi*, you are not in a position to take a moral high ground now, are you?" he asked, gesturing to her bound hands.

"There is no way I will go down that path again," she said vehemently.

"You don't have much choice."

"You can't make me pull the trigger."

Petrovich nodded. "True. But the alternative hurts my heart."

"The alternative?" she asked. Even though she knew. She knew he was alive, knew where he was, knew about Shelli and his "private service" organization. No way was that the kind of information he would let her walk out of here with.

"You know the alternative. I can't have you working against me, now can I, Anya?"

"Against you?" she sputtered. "I'm not working at all. I wash dogs. I put them up for adoption. I am not working anywhere."

Petrovich cocked his head to the side and gave her a sad smile.

"Anya. Stop fooling yourself. We both know who you are. What you do. You can hide, you can—" His hands waved in the air, as he searched for the right translation. "—playact at this nice life you have cultivated. But we both know this isn't you. There is no escaping your past. No pretending you are anything less than you are. It's in you. You are who you are, Anya."

She felt a lump form in her throat. He was voicing every fear she'd harbored since that fiery night in Kosovo. She was who she was. There was no escaping her nature. No escaping the fact that every instinct she had was honed for one purpose.

She could run, she could hide, she could pretend to start over. But the truth was inside her. This was her life. And, as she stared into his dark, deadly eyes, she realized he was right.

She would always be Anya.

"What's the job?" she asked quietly.

He grinned. "That's my girl." She detected a slight shift in Shelli's demeanor across the room, but the woman didn't say anything. And Anna didn't dare take her attention off Petrovich now.

"Senator Jonathan Braxton," he said. "You know who he is?"

Anna nodded. She knew of him, as did anyone with a television lately. A senator from California, he was one of the two frontrunners for the Republican presidential nomination. He'd been either on the news or engaging in televised debates every night of the week. "I know the name," she answered.

"He has several big ideas for reform," Petrovich went on. "Some of which make people nervous. People with deep pockets and big agendas of their own. They would very much like to make sure that Braxton and his reformation plan disappear as quickly as possible."

Ann nodded. "So, you want me to kill the senator."

"I want you to take care of the problem."

"By killing him."

Petrovich nodded.

The words hung heavy in the room. Anna grasped her fingers tighter around the chair rails behind her.

"When?" she asked.

"I have a time and a place in mind, but those are details we can discuss at a later time."

"I'd like to discuss them now."

Petrovich smiled. "When did you become so demanding, Anya?"

She shifted her weight forward toward the edge of the chair.

"There's a lot that's changed about me."

He nodded. "Yes. I can see that."

"But you're right about one thing," she continued. "There is no escaping my past, is there?"

He shook his head slowly. "No. There is not."

"Anya will never really be dead."

Again he shook his head, agreeing with her.

"I can't change that fact."

He watched her, his eyes assessing, seemingly wondering where she was going with this.

She tightened her fingers around the highest chair rung, shifted her weight onto the balls of her feet.

"The past is what it is, and all I can change now is the future," she said.

Petrovich's smile was a thing of the past, his features stony.

"What are you saying, Anya?"

"What I'm saying is that in the future, neither Anna nor Anya will ever work for you again."

His jaw tightened, accentuating the loose flesh the years had put there. "This was not the outcome I had hoped for."

"Me neither," Anna said. Then she grabbed the chair rung with both hands, shifted her weight to her feet, and quickly swiveled to the right, whacking Petrovich in the side of the head with the chair.

He fell to the side, hitting the floor, stunned momentarily.

Unfortunately, Shelli was not. She sprang into action, jumping at Anna, body slamming her full force and knocking the chair from Anna's hands as they both fell to the ground.

Anna pulled her knees up in a tight fetal position then shoved them at Shelli, catching her squarely in the chest. Shelli hit the edge of the desk, grunting as the corner bit into her back. But she recovered quickly, grabbing Anna by the armpits and hauling her up to her feet. Anna spun right, breaking from Shelli's grasp and coming around with a roundhouse kick to her head. The force threw Shelli against the wall, her head making a loud thud as it hit the brick.

Anna lunged forward, toward the desk. And her gun. She was a foot away when she felt Shelli's arms on her again, spinning her around.

Anna whipped around to face her, quickly feeling the force of Shelli's fist connecting with her jaw. Anna's head twisted left, her body crumpling on the floor before she could stop herself. Trying to shake off the swaying room, she struggled to her feet.

Shelli charged at her again, her mouth set in a grim line of determination.

Without the use of her hands, Anna's balance was sorely off. As Shelli lunged forward, Anna knew she didn't stand a chance against the full force of the woman's weight coming squarely at her. Anna planted both feet shoulder width apart, then pushed off to the left at the last minute, letting Shelli's body glance off her shoulder. Anna used the momentum to spin around, catching Shelli square in the back with another kick.

Shelli fell forward onto the ground, hands in front of her to catch her fall. Without missing a beat, she kicked backward, sweeping at Anna's feet, knocking them clear out from under her.

Anna fell backwards, landing with a jarring thud on her butt. Her teeth clacked together, and she bit her tongue, tasting blood in her mouth.

She quickly rolled over onto her stomach, pulling her legs up under her like an inchworm and leaping to her feet.

Only to face the barrel of Petrovich's gun.

"Enough," he yelled.

Shelli stood behind him, panting, blood trickling from a cut at the corner of her mouth. She was glaring daggers at Anna, clearly wishing Petrovich had stayed out of it and given Shelli the satisfaction of ending Anna herself. Gone was any trace of the woman Anna had shared so many easy moments with in the past months. The hatred in her eyes was clear as day, cutting through the room. Anna wondered if Shelli hadn't been secretly hating her this much the entire time. What it must have taken out of her to sit there and pretend at being friends, waiting for the word, waiting until her employer told her she could finally act on that resentment at never being good enough to fill Anna's role in Petrovich's eyes.

Shelli was close to Anna's age—maybe a couple years younger. At what age had Petrovich started grooming her? Did she see him as the father figure Anna once had? As her protector, only to one day be here—his victim, at his mercy, no more protected by his brand of love than the people he had trained her to kill. It was different here, he had said. Compliance not a given, no undying loyalty, and no promise of a swift death if orders were not obeyed to the letter. Shelli could never be Anna, and she knew it.

And she hated Anna for it.

"I'm disappointed in you, Anya."

Anna turned her attention back to Petrovich.

He, on the other hand, showed no emotions. Whatever he had felt for her a moment ago—or a lifetime ago—he felt nothing now.

Numb. Just go numb, dragi.

"I know," she said quietly.

"You know the penalty for traitors."

She nodded. From the time she had come to live with him, he had drilled her fate into her. She'd been too young then to realize that traitors were everywhere. When governments changed hands daily, there was no such thing as loyalty, only survival.

Petrovich cocked his head to the side. "I am sorry, Anya." But again his eyes held no emotion as his finger tightened on the trigger.

Maybe he was incapable of showing emotion. Maybe he really was numb.

Anna steeled herself for the sharp fiery sensation that she knew would accompany his bullet. She resisted the urge to shut her eyes, forcing herself to face her fate head on.

A loud shot splintered the dusty air inside the warehouse. Anna started, expecting to feel pain. But none came.

Instead, the office window shattered, and she watched the gun drop from Petrovich's hand, sliding across the floor under one of the filing cabinets, as blood gushed from a wound at his wrist. Someone had shot him before he'd had a chance to pull the trigger on Anna.

She whipped her head around.

Dade.

CHAPTER SIXTEEN

Anna didn't waste a second. As Shelli ducked down behind the desk, taking cover from the gunfire, Anna spun around, throwing herself backward until her fingers connected with her gun on the desk. She grabbed it, then quickly wiggled her arms low over her butt, slipping her legs down through the opening. Not an easy task when they were bound together, but, oddly enough, not the first time she'd ever done it either. She shifted, holding the Glock in her hands, straight-armed in front of her, pointed at Petrovich.

He was cradling his injured hand in the other, his eyes trained on Anna, as if wondering just how she had pulled that trick off.

"You have a partner?"

Partner was a stretch, but Anna nodded. "Yes."

"You always liked to work alone."

"Things change," she said. She shifted her attention to Shelli, who dared to venture out from her cover again. She moved slowly, her eyes still scanning the warehouse for the source of the surprise interruption. Though, nowhere in their depths did Anna see a white flag just because she was the one being held at gunpoint.

Not that she expected to.

"Back up," Anna demanded, taking a step toward Shelli.

She did, taking two steps backward until she was flush against the wall.

"You, too," she told Petrovich.

He complied as well, taking a place next to Shelli. His eyes were still stone, void of all emotion.

No, not quite void. Somewhere in them she thought she saw a flicker of pride.

She'd surprised him. Not an easy task when he'd taught her everything she knew. He was impressed. It sickened her that some small part of her was pleased to see that. That a part of her felt like she had done well and deserved his silent praise.

"Now don't move!" she yelled, knowing that her anger was more directed at herself than them. Clearly neither of them was stupid. As long as she held the gun, they had no intention of moving.

Anna sidestepped slowly to the left, keeping her weapon on the pair. She would have liked to end them both right then and there, but she only had one bullet and two targets. No matter who she used it on, the other would drop her before she could flee.

"I'm leaving now," Anna said, backing slowly toward the door. "I'm backing out of here. My gun will be pointed at this door until I leave the warehouse. If I see anyone in the doorway, I shoot. Understood?"

Petrovich nodded. "Understood," he said calmly, as if comprehending a lesson from a textbook and not the rules of his own death.

Shelli said nothing. Didn't move. Her eyes still searching for escape.

Anna slowly walked backward, praying Dade was smart enough to have gotten out of the warehouse and started the car. She paused a moment in the doorway, calculating just how far it was to the door down the catwalk. Could she make it before Petrovich and Shelli bolted from the office?

She didn't really expect them to stay put. She knew that Shelli must have a weapon on her somewhere. Likely more than one. But as long as Anna's hands were bound, there was no way for her to search one while keeping a weapon on the other. As soon as Anna was out the door, they would both be coming after her.

The question was, could she outrun their bullets?

She took one last step backward, over the threshold.

She locked eyes with Shelli. Shelli knew as well as Anna did what the odds were.

She stared Shelli down for only a second.

Then she ran.

With the gun tucked up tight against her chest, she took off at as close to a sprint as her awkward position would allow toward the door to the outside of the warehouse. As she'd guessed, she could hear Shelli springing into action behind her, feet clanking on the metal catwalk, Petrovich yelling after her something that Anna didn't take the time to translate.

She was two feet away from the door when a bullet hit the wall in front of her, embedding itself in the wood, sending splinters flying into the air and a spray of dust along with it.

Anna's instinct was to stop, duck, look for cover. But she knew if she did that, she'd be dead. Instead, she kept running, willing her feet to move faster, tucking her hands up close to her body as she ran the last couple of steps to the door.

Three more shots rang out, pinging against the metal railing, the wall, the door ahead of her. Anna sprinted to outrun them. Another one hit the door in front of her just as she threw it open, sudden sunshine assaulting her as she got her bearings.

She tumbled through, rushing blindly away from the building, all the while listening for the sound of Shelli a step behind her. She raced forward, down the flight of steps, panic starting to build as she remembered that the SUV was parked a good ten yards away.

She'd never make it. Shelli would surely be on top of her by then.

But she kept running. It was the only option she had.

She ducked around the forklift, circling the corner of the building, and almost cried in relief when she saw the SUV idling just ahead.

Dade had been ready for her. He'd created the distraction he knew she'd needed then provided a quick getaway.

She sprinted toward him, pulling energy from pure adrenaline. She heard the warehouse door slam behind her and Shelli racing down the stairs after her.

"Drive, now!" Anna yelled, coming up alongside the SUV.

Dade didn't wait to be told twice, putting the car in gear as Anna threw herself into the back seat of the car, her legs still dangling out the open door as it lurched forward.

Tires spun, dirt kicking up as they surged across the property, throwing Anna onto the floor. She spun around, dropping her weapon and grabbing for the fully loaded one stuck in Dade's waistband instead. She aimed it at the warehouse, firing off four shots through the open door. Two went wild as she got her bearings. One hit the side of the building, taking out a chunk of brick and causing Shelli to crouch low on the metal staircase.

Anna continued firing as Dade put distance between them and the scene until she ran out of bullets and caught sight of Shelli running the opposite direction, a wisp of brown hair flying after her. Anna may have escaped, but so would Shelli and Petrovich.

Anna pulled herself back onto the passenger seat as Dade flew down the road, tires spinning, taking the corner with such force the back end of the truck spun out. She managed to grab the door and pull it shut next to her, her balance impaired by being trussed up like an inchworm.

Three blocks later, they hit city traffic again, and Dade was forced to slow down.

Anna glanced in the side mirror. She wasn't sure what she was looking for, but she didn't see any women in wigs driving bleeding old Serbian men, so she took that as a good sign.

"Glove box," Dade said, his hands gripping the wheel. "There's a pocketknife."

She dropped his gun on the console between them and flipped open the box, pulling out a green army knife. She managed to open a blade, and hand it to Dade.

"Do the honors?" she asked.

He did, quickly cutting through the plastic bands, before handing it back. She flexed her hands, shaking circulation back into her fingers.

"Nice shot back there," she said, watching a VW inch toward the red light in front of them.

"I know."

Anna let herself smile.

"I wasn't sure how much you'd gotten from him at that point, so I figured it was better to aim low." He paused. "You did get some answers from him, didn't you?"

She nodded, relaying the conversation she'd had with Petrovich. Even as she recounted the scene to Dade, it hit her that Petrovich really had seemed surprised that she wouldn't join him. Had she changed that much? Or had he never really known her? For that matter, had she ever known him? Not really. She knew what he'd wanted her to know, what he'd pretended to be. And maybe vice versa, now that she thought about it.

"He's going to kill the senator," she said, knowing for certain just how true that was. "He wanted me to do it, but I have no doubt he'll take it upon himself."

Dade was quiet for a moment, eyes straight ahead. "That doesn't have anything to do with us," he said, his voice flat.

Anna nodded. "No," she agreed. "But we're the only ones who know."

Dade didn't answer.

"Petrovich said something in there," she went on. "He said I can't outrun what I am. Who I am."

Again, Dade was silent, eyes straight ahead. Not that she expected an answer. She was talking to herself almost as much as to him, letting the realities of that future she'd talked about in Petrovich's office fall into place as she spoke them out loud. Of what it could be if she planned her moves very carefully now.

"He was right, you know," she continued, watching Dade closely. "If the past two days have taught me anything, it's that he was right. I killed twenty-four men. Did you know that?"

"Yes." The answer came quickly, clipped. He had definite feelings on the subject, she could tell.

"I *am* a killer."

Dade turned to her. "So you want to kill Senator Braxton now?"

She shook her head. "No. And if I do nothing now, aren't I doing just that?"

Dade gave her a hard look. Then he turned his attention back to the road.

"I'm not trying to make up for the lives I ended," she continued. Which was true. She knew there was no making up for those. As a young agent she'd told herself the targets she was given were bad people who deserved to die. It's possible that was really true. She'd never know now. "But I have a chance to save one."

"Bullshit," Dade said, eyes still straight ahead. "You're trying to save yourself. Let me tell you something—it won't work. You can save a hundred lives, and those kills will still haunt you."

Anna bit her lip, watching the taut line of his jaw, the twitch of nerves just below the growing stubble on his chin.

"That may be true," she agreed. "But if I do something now, at least Senator Braxton's death won't haunt us, too."

The use of the pronoun was deliberate. Us. Dade was a killer, too. Whether he woke with nightmares of conscience like she did or not, she didn't know. But she'd thought she'd glimpsed a moment of humanity in him. Maybe just enough that he would listen to her appeal.

Because she needed his agreement if this was going to work.

It took several beats of silence before he finally opened his mouth to answer.

"So what do you want to do?"

"Warn him."

"And tell him what? That we know he's about to be killed because you were hired to do the job?"

She nodded. "Good point."

"We don't even know where or when Petrovich plans to strike."

"What if we could figure it out?"

He paused. "How?"

"Where would you do it?"

He breathed in deeply and exhaled through his nose. "Okay. I'd do it somewhere public. A large crowd to get lost in."

"I'm sure the senator makes plenty of public appearances."

"Outside," he added. "Harder to keep security tight."

Some of the tension was disappearing from his face. This he knew how to do. Plan the perfect hit. This was his comfort zone.

Anna nodded. "Okay, a large, outdoor, public gathering." She paused. "Can I see your phone?"

"Why?" he asked, even as he slid it from his pocket and handed it to her.

"Chances are his campaign website has his schedule posted."

Anna quickly found the senator's official website and clicked on a page marked *Appearances* that did, in fact, list the senator's upcoming schedule. She scrolled through the list, quickly dismissing the private fundraising dinners, the expensive golf tournament, and a visit to a children's hospital. Instead, she homed in on a rally scheduled in Golden Gate Park for the following day.

"You think this could be it?" Anna asked, reading the entry off to Dade.

"Short notice. Not a lot of time to plan."

"I have a feeling he's been planning this for a while," she answered. "I was an afterthought in the equation, but I'd bet he's got every other detail worked out to a tee."

He always does.

Dade shrugged. "I'd say it's perfect as far as access and easy getaway go. If it were me? That's where I'd hit him."

Anna nodded. Her, too.

"So we have a pretty educated guess as to when and where. I think it's enough to warn his security staff."

Dade took a deep breath and looked in his rearview for the tenth time in as many minutes. He was antsy, she could tell. Clearly not used to be being on this end of the hunting ground. Being the hunter was a much more comfortable position than being the prey.

"Fine. Do you have a number?"

Anna clicked through to another page, pulling up the phone number and address of the Braxton campaign headquarters in Sacramento. She quickly typed the digits into Dade's phone, waiting as it rang on the other end.

Three rings in, she was greeted by an automated voice giving her a menu of options. Unfortunately, "warning of death threat" wasn't one of them. She hit 0 to talk to an operator and was immediately greeted with a Musak rendition of AC/DC's "Back in Black."

She waited five minutes, listening to the song repeat twice, then hung up.

"Well?" Dade asked.

"No one answered."

He shrugged. "So?"

She took a deep breath. An anonymous tip was one thing, but what she was about to propose was taking it a whole leap further.

"Look, if we're going to do this, we might as well do it right."

"Meaning?"

"Meaning I think we should talk to the senator in person."

Dade narrowed his eyes at her, trying to read her thoughts behind the words.

She put on her best poker face, willing emotion out of her expression. She needed his compliance to pull this off.

"Why?" he asked again.

"I think he'll take us more seriously. He needs to know we're not fooling around, that this is a real threat."

Dade didn't respond.

"And I think we have a better chance of speaking with him directly. Or at least his head of security. Someone in charge. On the phone, it's easy to pass us off to some junior staffer who couldn't give a shit, you know?"

Dade let out a deep breath. Then finally nodded.

"Fine. We'll go to Sacramento."

CHAPTER SEVENTEEN

———

The hour-and-a-half drive between San Francisco and Sacramento was dotted with strip malls, suburbs, and rural farmland. Anna watched them all pass as she leaned her head against the cool window, wondering what it would be like to live in one of those sleepy farm communities. She'd never done the small-town thing before, afraid of being where there were too few people and too many questions. Blending into an anonymous city was much easier.

But maybe a change of pace would be nice when this was all over. Maybe a slower way of life would suit her. For so long she had lived day to day, ready to pack up and leave at a moment's notice. But somehow, knowing that her worst case scenario had already found her, she felt more…secure. Odd that was the word that came to mind when she was riding with a man who'd been contracted to kill her, on the run from an assassin for hire, rushing to stop an assassination that she'd been asked to perpetrate. It was not a situation that she had any control over or any sort of assurances about the outcome.

Yet she felt more secure than she had in her apartment every night, locking the doors, arming the alarm systems, sleeping with one eye open next to her watchdog, just waiting for the day when the unknown would shatter her life.

She was now facing the unknown head-on. Taking something into her own hands.

She planned to end this. To make sure that Petrovich not only never contacted her again but never trained another young recruit to kill for his gains again. It was a wrong she wanted to right for more reasons than one, not the least of which was saving her own skin. She would not let the threat of Petrovich control her life anymore. She was not the daughter he never had, his pupil, his puppet. She controlled her life now. She had a plan.

And it all hinged on Braxton.

* * *

Dade knew nothing about Jonathan Braxton. He was one of hundreds of faceless politicians who thought they were the epitome of importance but really never got much done in the bureaucracy that was designed, in Dade's opinion, to stop any sort of progress at all. Dade had long ago given up following politics. Swap one party for the other, one name for the next—honestly nothing much ever changed in government. The only thing that ever changed was the degree of nastiness in their campaigns. He admitted getting a kick out of the mudslinging sometimes. What he was not getting a kick out of currently, though, was sitting in Braxton's campaign headquarters in a hard plastic chair waiting for someone named "Prescott" to see them.

The woman at the wooden reception desk had politely gone through a list of twenty questions when they'd come in, trying to drag out of them if they were big contributors or no-name protestors. Dade had given her precious little to work with other than he was in possession of information related to Braxton's security that was of the utmost importance. She told him that this Prescott would be with them shortly to discuss his issues. Only Prescott clearly didn't have the same definition of "utmost" that Dade did. They'd been waiting for half an hour. And his patience was wearing thin.

He shifted in his seat, idly flipping the pages of a *Time* magazine from the table in front of him, surveying Braxton's war room. Cheap wooden tables were filled with laptops and college students whose youth made them believe they were making a difference in the world by helping this guy win a nomination. Posters graced the walls, everywhere photoshopped images of Senator Braxton smiling back at them, showing him as the perfect not-too-old, not-too-young, not-too-good-looking, but not-too-plain-looking candidate. Folding chairs mingled with hand-me-down office furniture, giving the place a grassroots feel that said they couldn't afford real furniture despite the fact that

Dade was certain the senator was spending millions on television commercials.

Not for the first time, Dade questioned what he was doing here.

He had enough problems of his own. He certainly didn't need to take the senator's on. Besides, even if they were able to warn the senator away from appearing tomorrow in the park, what's to say Petrovich wouldn't try again? Another time, a new location. There were too many unknowns and not enough concrete details.

And, to be honest, he only had Anya's word that Petrovich was planning to target the senator at all. For all he knew she might well be working for him, might have accepted the contract after all, and this was just a way to get close to her new target.

He looked over at her now, trying to gauge the thoughts behind her expression. She watched the activity in the room, her eyes resting maybe a little longer on each intern than Dade's. She was interested in what they were doing, watching their lips as they spoke, trying, he guessed, to make out conversations. If it was because she was calculating her next move or because she was truly interested in the senator, he couldn't say.

It was a nice idea that she cared about the senator's well-being. Bad girl gone straight. Killer turned savior. But he wasn't sure he bought it completely. Warning the senator about the hit was a singularly selfless act. People on the run for their lives weren't usually known for being selfless. He wondered at her real motives for being here.

Her eyes flicked to his. She'd felt him watching her. Not much escaped her notice.

"How much longer you think they'll keep us waiting?" he asked, trying to cover the fact that he'd been staring at her.

She shrugged. "He's a busy man."

Dade nodded. "So am I."

She shot him a look but didn't answer, instead picking up a magazine at random from the table in front of them, flipping to a page near the front, staring at the type but no more reading it than Dade had been reading his.

They sat in silence another ten minutes before a man finally emerged from one of the back offices and strode purposefully toward them. He was dressed in a charcoal grey suit with a classic white shirt and paisley tie beneath. His blond hair was slicked back from his forehead in a stylish manner straight out of some men's magazine. Way too polished to be the just-one-of-the-people Braxton.

"I'm so sorry to keep you waiting," the man said as he approached, extending his hand first to Anya, then Dade. "David Prescott."

Dade shook the man's hand. His grip was firm and quick…polite, confident, impersonal.

"Anna Smith," Anya offered. "And this is Nick Dade."

"We were hoping to speak with the senator," Dade said.

"I'm sorry, but Senator Braxton isn't available at the moment. Out campaigning hard. You know how that goes," he finished, flashing a smile at Anya.

"And you are?" Dade asked the man.

"I'm the senator's chief executive consultant."

"Which means what?"

The man smiled. "It means I make sure Mr. Braxton wins the nomination."

"We should speak to someone in security," Anya said. "We have some information."

Prescott nodded. "That's what our receptionist told me. Please, come into my office. We can talk there." He turned, leading them back down the small hallway.

"Senator Braxton must have a lot of supporters," Anya observed, gesturing to the row of closed office doors lining the hallway.

Prescott nodded. "He does."

"Are all these offices filled with consultants such as yourself?"

"There are several people working on the senator's campaign staff off and on," he answered noncommittally, opening the last door on the left and gesturing Anya and Dade into his office.

It was small, with a large window facing south. As modestly furnished as the workroom, it held a small desk and a pair of chairs facing the window. Bookshelves lined the walls, and a computer sat open on the desk's surface.

Prescott gestured to the chairs. "Please, sit."

They did, and Prescott took a seat behind the desk before asking, "So, what can I do for you?"

"We have information that makes us nervous for Senator Braxton's welfare at tomorrow's rally," Anya said.

Prescott raised an eyebrow. "What kind of information?"

"We believe there may be an attempt on his life."

If Prescott believed them, he showed no signs of distress, wearing just the same slightly interested look that Dade had a feeling the guy wore whether he was listening to opera or watching porn. It was classic politician-face. Smug, pleasant, never telling.

"May I ask what leads you to believe this?"

"No," Dade broke in. "You may not."

Dade was happy to see Prescott's smile falter for a second before pasting itself back on his face.

"I see. Where did you get this information?"

Instead of answering, Anya said, "What kind of security do you have planned for tomorrow?"

Prescott clasped his hands in front of him. It was a move Dade knew well. It was designed to mask any sort of unconscious tells—gestures, fidgeting, nervous habits. Prescott had obviously been schooled in Lying 101.

"I can assure you that we have taken all possible security scenarios into account and provided adequate means to keep the senator safe."

"Adequate for what?" Anya pressed.

Prescott's smile was showing strain. "Adequate for any circumstance that should arise. I'm sorry, where did you say you obtained information of this threat?"

"We didn't," Dade answered.

"Well, unless you can tell me anything more specific…" Prescott trailed off, clearly inviting explanation.

Dade crossed his arms over his chest, looking to Anya. This was her idea, her gig. He still wasn't even sure what they were doing there. This was exactly how he'd envisioned this interview going—in circles. Surely Anya hadn't been naïve enough to think this guy would jump to cancel the rally on their vague say-so.

Anya took a deep breath. "I'm sorry. I wish we could tell you more, but we don't have details. Just…knowledge of a threat."

Prescott nodded. "And you can't tell me where you heard this threat."

Anya pursed her lips together then slowly shook her head.

Prescott nodded. "All right. Well, I'll tell you what. I'll definitely let the senator's security team know to have their eyes open tomorrow, how does that sound?"

It sounded like bullshit to Dade. Anya nodded, though Dade seriously doubted the guy would do more than make sure reception had their names on the do-not-allow-entry list.

Prescott stood, and offered a hand to Anya, effectively ending the interview. "Pleasure to meet you" he said automatically.

She nodded and smiled. "You too."

He moved around the desk to see them out, holding the door open for them.

But Anya paused on the threshold. "Um, Mr. Prescott, do you think I could use the restroom before we leave? We have a long drive back to the City."

Prescott glanced down at his watch—an unconscious move, a quick slip in his politician demeanor. Never let them see how little they mean to you. Never let them see how they're wasting your time.

"Of course," he answered. "It's just down this hallway to the left. Now, if you'll excuse me, I have a press release I need to prepare. I trust you can see yourselves out?"

Anya shot him a big smile. "Of course. And thank you again for taking the time to see us, Mr. Prescott."

"Sorry I couldn't be of more help," he said, standing in the doorway to his office, watching Anya walk down the hallway the direction he'd indicated. Dade noticed that Prescott waited until she pushed through the restroom door before nodding Dade's way and disappearing back into his office.

As soon as Prescott's door clicked shut, the restroom door popped open again and Anya emerged.

"Have the car ready. I'll be out in ten minutes," she whispered to Dade. Then she quickly moved to one of the other closed office doors. She paused just a moment outside, listening, before she turned the knob and slipped inside.

Dade watched, mental wheels turning.

What the hell was she up to?

* * *

Anna blinked in the dark office space. Unlike Prescott's room, this one held no window—just a desk with a pair of chairs in front and one leather office chair behind. File cabinets lined the walls, bookcases on either side. Nothing fancy, but all the essentials were there.

Including the laptop open on the desk.

She went straight to it, quickly jiggling the screen to life with the keypad. As she'd hoped, it was already logged in to the campaign's internal network, giving her access to the same files the interns on the floor had. Which, she quickly realized, was not a whole lot. However, it gave her an opening to worm through to get to the information she really wanted—Senator Braxton's security schematics.

As much as she'd been honest about wanting to stop the attempt on Braxton's life, she had another motive in coming here—stopping the attempts on her own life. She'd had no delusions that their vague references to a threat would cause the senator's campaign to cancel the rally. It was far too close to election time and far too important a city to ignore. Her real motive in coming here had been just this—to gain access to information about where security would be stationed at the rally, and more specifically, how she could get around it.

Shelli was in the wind. Petrovich didn't even officially exist. The warehouse they'd held her at was clearly a temporary place. Anna was out of ways to track them down. She had one guess where she could find them—at Senator Braxton's rally tomorrow.

And that was where she planned to take them out.

Anna's fingers flew across the keyboard, quickly gaining access to the security files, detailing how much security was expected to be at the senator's side, where local police would be stationed to control the crowds, and what sort of profile would qualify for their seemingly random searches.

Anna committed it all to memory, quickly shutting down the window and digitally erasing any sign of her intrusion. She lowered the laptop screen back to sleep, then got up from the desk and slipped out of the room.

"Anna?"

She started and spun around, finding Prescott standing directly behind her in the hallway, a frown of concern etched on his brow.

Had he seen her come out of the room?

"Uh, hi. I...I think I'm lost," she said, pulling up her best bimbo voice. "Um, where did you say the restrooms were again?"

Prescott's forehead smoothed, a smile replacing the momentary show of real emotion. "Back that way. Take a left."

She nodded. "Right. Thanks," she said, and slipped down the hall to the bathroom. She locked herself in a stall, waited a three count, then walked out into the hallway again. She noticed Prescott's door was open, his eyes on the restroom door as she exited. She gave him a little wave then quickly made her way back down the hall to reception and out the front door to Dade's SUV, which was idling at the curb.

She said a silent thank you for Dade's compliance and slipped into the passenger seat.

"Go," she said. "Before he starts asking questions."

Dade did, pulling away from the curb, pointing the SUV back toward the freeway.

"You want to share what that was really about?" he asked.

His voice was calm, but Anna could feel an edge to it, lurking just below the words. Dade didn't like being out of the loop.

"Security details."

Dade's eyes stayed straight ahead on the road. Though she could tell he was mentally putting pieces together. "For the rally."

She nodded.

"Because you plan to be there."

Again, she gestured in the affirmative.

Dade took a deep breath, letting it out slowly through his nose.

"Look, I'm obviously involved in this up to my eyeballs. I'm seeing it through to the end. But I don't like being kept in the dark."

Anna nodded. "Okay. I understand." And she did. She glanced across the console at Dade. But how much could she trust him?

He'd dispensed with the handcuffs, returned her weapon to her. But had it been out of trust or because he knew she had nowhere to run and only one shot left in her gun? How much of that had been a show to gain her trust and how much was sincere? She didn't know. But at the moment, she didn't have much of a choice. It was trust Dade or work against him. And it was going to be a hell of a lot easier if he was on her side.

If even just for the moment.

She took a deep breath, letting it out slowly. "Okay. Look, Petrovich isn't going to give up. I can either spend my life running from him, or I can face him. He'll be at that rally to kill the senator. I need to be there too. I need to get to Petrovich before he gets to Braxton. I need to end this."

Dade didn't say anything. He kept his eyes straight ahead on the road. Finally he asked, "So what's your plan?"

"Think like Petrovich. Plan the assassination the way he would."

"Only it's not Braxton you plan to assassinate."

She bit her lip. In all honesty, she wasn't sure she could pull the trigger on Petrovich, even if the opportunity presented itself. She wasn't sure she had it in her to kill anymore.

But she nodded anyway.

Dade kept his attention on the road in front of him. His eyes were fixed straight ahead, the line in his jaw tense. She wished she knew what he was thinking, but the thoughts behind his eyes were carefully veiled.

Finally he spoke. "Fine. We'll go to the rally. I'll help you."

CHAPTER EIGHTEEN

———

They settled into silence, each lost in their own thoughts about the following day as farmlands stretched one into another on the drive back to the city.

Anna watched the sun begin to sink into the horizon, creating a mosaic of soft pinks, violent oranges, and deep purple hues shot through with delicate wisps of clouds. She wondered if Braxton was on that same road somewhere. Heading toward San Francisco to get a good night's sleep in some hotel before the rally tomorrow. She wondered if Prescott would tell him about their visit, or if Braxton would take the stage tomorrow blissfully unaware of intentions lurking somewhere in the crowd. Silently, she wondered which was better.

"We need gas," Dade said, breaking into her thoughts as he pulled off the freeway. Farmland flanked the road on either side here, a small service station and an all-night diner planted at the end of the off-ramp the only buildings in sight. Dade pulled down the ramp to the one main road crossing the freeway and into the service station, coming to a stop at the first pump.

As he went inside to pay, Anna got out and stretched her legs. She clipped Lenny's leash on and walked him as far as the patch of grass at the road holding a sign touting the lowest gas prices in the county. He walked in a circle, sniffed at the grass, backtracked again to the sign, then finally squatted down and did the deed. Anna turned a plastic garbage bag she'd found in Dade's car inside out, and used it to scoop his mess, depositing it in a trash can next to the pump.

"Excuse me?"

Anna spun around to find a man in a baseball cap and sunglasses standing behind her.

Too close behind her.

She instinctively took a step away. "Yes?"

"Do you know where Dayton Farms is?"

A lost farmworker. Nothing nefarious.

Anna forced out the breath she'd instinctively held in at the sight of him.

"Sorry. No, I don't."

The man smiled, showing off a mouthful of crooked teeth. "Bummer. I'm supposed to be helping with inventory tonight. Been driving in circles for the last hour."

"Sorry," she said again, shrugging her shoulders. "Wish I could help."

He nodded. "Well, thanks, anyway. Have a nice evening."

"You, too," she said automatically as the man turned around and walked toward a rusted green pickup truck parked next to the second gas pump.

He slid into the driver's seat of the truck and leaned over to the glove box. Probably pulling out a map, she decided. He paused a few minutes. Then Anna saw the lights on his truck turn on, the engine roar to life, and he pulled out of the station, heading toward the freeway.

"Ready?" Dade asked. He was screwing the gas cap back on.

She nodded, bundling Lenny back into the car.

While the road had been dotted with cars on their way to Sacramento, at this time of night most of the traffic was running the opposite direction, commuters who worked in the city driving toward the outlying suburbs where their dollar stretched into bigger homes and better school districts. There were precious few cars traveling beside their SUV, only the occasional pair of headlights piercing the growing dusk to pass them. Dade stuck to the right lane, letting the faster cars go around, keeping to a maximum of five miles over the speed limit.

Anna watched a pair of headlights approach in the rearview mirror. The driver signaled left, pulled around them, and passed.

A few minutes later another pair approached. She watched them grow bigger, the light filling the SUV's cab. It took a moment before she realized they were filling it too brightly. Growing too big.

"Dade?" Anna warned, her eyes glued to the mirror.

Only he didn't get a chance to respond before the headlights surged forward, kissing the SUV's back bumper.

At seventy miles-per-hour, the impact caused the car to lurch forward. Anna watched Dade clutch the wheel to keep the car from swerving out of their lane. He swore under his breath, eyes darting to the mirror.

"What the hell was that?"

The headlights hung back, putting a couple of car lengths between them. Then Anna watched them surge forward again.

This time Dade was watching, too, ready for them. He sped up in response, flooring the accelerator.

Anna held onto the side of the door, bracing herself for impact against the dash with her other hand.

The car behind them sped up to match Dade's velocity, the sound of its engine working overtime, an ominous accompaniment to the headlights bearing down on them. The other driver gunned his engine, jumping forward, and rammed into their bumper again, this time hard enough to whip Anna's head forward. Instant pain shot through her neck, the muscles there involuntarily cramping on her. She felt Lenny slide into the back of her seat, falling to the floor. He barked loudly, a sharp protest to his condition but a reassuring sign that he was okay.

Dade clenched his jaw, eyes intent on the road ahead, both hands holding the wheel in a death grip.

"Hold on," he instructed. He raced forward, pushing the car to its limit. Anna watched the speedometer climb past seventy, hitting eighty, ninety. The car began to shake. Lenny whined in the back seat as he cowered close to the floorboards.

The headlights hung back for a moment, creating a falsely comforting vision before pulling closer again, the driver behind them matching Dade's speed mile for mile.

He was coming in for another go.

Dade's gaze ping-ponged between the road ahead of him and the headlights of the car behind, quickly crawling up their back. Anna felt him ease off the accelerator, letting their pursuer move in closer.

Anna glanced across the cab, hoping Dade knew what he was doing as she watched the headlights catch up to them, moving in closer and closer until she was bracing herself against the dash for impact again.

Dade waited until the other car was almost touching them, headlights filling the cab, lighting it up like daylight.

Then Dade swerved to the left and slammed on the brakes, skidding to a stop on the median in the center of the freeway. Anna watched as the car behind sailed past in the lane to their right.

She sucked in a breath as she got a good look at the driver. It was the guy with the pickup from the gas station. So much for innocent farmworker.

You should know by now. No one is innocent, Anya.

She watched the pickup slow, pulling onto the right shoulder, its brake lights an angry, glowing red ahead of them.

Anna held her breath as the pickup stopped. But no one got out. Nothing moved. It just sat there.

Waiting.

He knew they had to pass him. He was waiting them out. Ready, no doubt, with weapon in hand for his target to drive past his window, giving him a perfect shot.

Dade's breath came hard and fast in the silent cab, his eyes glued to the pickup's taillights. Anna could feel her heart pounding, matching the same pace.

"Now what?" she breathed.

Dade squared his jaw, the muscles in his neck so tense she could see veins pulse with adrenaline there.

"We play his game."

Dade put the SUV in gear, checked the rearview for other cars.

Seeing none, he pulled his M9 from his waistband, holding it in one hand as he clutched the wheel with the other.

"Stay down," he commanded, pulling the car into the left lane. Anna complied, ducking low in her seat.

The pickup was parked about a hundred yards ahead of him.

Dade wasted no time, laying on the accelerator, quickly gaining speed. Aiming his headlights at the back of the pickup.

The driver was ready for them, engine revving, taillights dulling, as he eased off the brakes in anticipation of another race.

Dade, on the other hand, didn't ease up, pulling almost parallel to the other car before yelling, "Down now!" He pointed his gun directly at Anna's head.

She dove for the floor just as he pulled the trigger. Two shots aimed straight out the passenger-side window at the pickup.

Almost simultaneously, the pickup driver fired as well, one shot pinging off the metal door, another shattering the side mirror as the SUV surged past him.

The pickup driver's tires skidded as he pulled onto the road behind them, quickly gaining speed.

More shots ripped through the air, shattering the back window as shards of glass flew through the car. Anna turned away, instinctively covering her face with one arm.

"Take the wheel," Dade yelled at her, twisting around in his seat to return fire.

Two shots splintered the pickup's windshield, causing the vehicle to swerve. But it quickly recovered, signaling the driver was unharmed.

Ahead was an exit, leading right, through more farmland. "Get off," Dade instructed.

Anna did, swerving sharply right, jostling Dade forward and sending the next of his shots wild. She ran the red light at the intersection, quickly pulling onto the one-lane road heading west. It was dark now, streetlights nonexistent this far out from the City. Up ahead she could see a building of some sort, though it was dark, too, likely abandoned at this hour.

The pickup followed her off the freeway, continuing to shadow them, shots bouncing off the back bumper of their SUV. If she had to guess, she'd say the driver was aiming for their tires.

Dade ducked into the cab to avoid a shot that glanced off the side of the SUV, taking a chunk of black paint with it. Anna swerved left, running up on the dried grass at the side of the road before gaining control again.

They passed the lone building, and Anna saw it was an abandoned gas station. The windows were boarded up, though the prices reflected on the sign still standing at the road indicated it hadn't been long ago that the economy had forced its owners out of business.

"Turn around," Dade said, watching the building go by. "Go back."

Anna scarcely had time to turn the wheel before she felt Dade's foot on the brakes, tires spinning as they flipped around one hundred and eighty degrees.

The pickup sailed past, shots hitting the driver's side of the car with shattering dents. Anna craned her head around, watching out the now nonexistent back window as the driver applied the brakes, spinning his car opposite with the same force Dade had.

It idled for only a moment before the driver accelerated again, heading straight toward them.

Anna reached over the console with her right foot, moving to stomp on their accelerator.

"Wait," Dade said, stopping her.

His eyes were on the rearview, watching the pickup approach.

"Just wait."

Anna bit her lip and turned around in her seat again. Her heartbeat sped up in time with the acceleration of the pickup, bearing down on them. Lenny whined in the back, too scared or nervous to bark, picking up on her feelings as she watched the headlights grow closer, glowing right at them.

"Dade…"

"Wait! Just wait for it."

The car was just feet away from them now. Seconds from impact.

"Dade!" Anna repeated, hating the panic in her voice.

"Wait," he commanded. "And…now!"

She stomped on the accelerator with all she had as Dade pulled the wheel sharply left and shot his torso out the driver's side window.

He fired off three quick rounds right through the hole where the pickup's windshield had been. The SUV swerved left, jumping out of the pickup's path.

The pickup didn't change course, didn't swerve, didn't turn. Just kept accelerating forward.

As it shot past, Anna caught a glimpse of the driver, slumped over the wheel.

Dade's aim hadn't failed.

The pickup continued to accelerate right past Anna and Dade.

In a straight line, directly toward the gas station.

Anna watched as the pickup bounced off a garbage can, ramming straight into one of the gas pumps as it came to a final stop.

For a moment the only sound was the hard panting of their breath in the cab.

For a moment.

Then an explosion rocketed through the silence, the pickup jumping in the air, a plume of fiery red and blue bursting out from beneath it, engulfing the car, the pump, the entire gas station.

Anna ducked down, covering her face as instant heat burned her cheeks. A moment later she heard metal debris rain down on the roof of Dade's SUV.

They sat in stunned silence for a full minute, staring at the place where the truck had just been, before Dade sprang into action.

He slid back into the driver's seat, quickly putting the car into gear. He shot forward, navigating around the fire, back toward the freeway. Caution about going over the speed limit was a thing of the past as he put distance between them and the wreckage as quickly as he could.

He was just screeching onto the freeway on-ramp again when Anna heard sirens wailing in the distance. Not surprising since Anna was pretty sure that the fire could be seen from three towns over. She waited until the sound faded behind them before breaking the silence.

"He's dead," Anna said quietly.

While she knew it was kill or be killed, the idea of someone she had just been talking to suddenly not being there was still unnerving.

Dade nodded. "Yeah." He looked in the rearview where a tall plume of smoke could still be seen. "Very dead."

"You shot him?"

"Probably."

His jaw was tight, the angles there hard. His emotions—if he felt any at all—were totally unreadable.

"He won't ever give up, will he?" Anna asked.

Dade glanced her way.

"Petrovich," she clarified. "He sent that man after me. He knew where we'd be. He knows every move I make."

"Calm down," Dade said quietly.

She realized her voice had been rising as she spoke, her breath coming faster. She closed her mouth, willing herself to take a deep breath in and out.

"He knows what my car looks like," Dade said. "He's got his people watching for it. It was probably dumb luck that guy spotted us."

Anna nodded. Right. That made sense.

"Besides," Dade continued, shooting a look her way, "we can't be sure it was Petrovich."

"Who else would it be?"

He paused a moment before answering. "In case you haven't noticed, I've defaulted on my job."

She glanced his way. "I had noticed that."

"And my employer was none too happy about it."

Anna watched his features closely in the shadows. "Why?" she asked.

"Why was he pissed? Take a wild guess."

"No. I mean why did you quit?"

He blinked in the darkness, eyes straight ahead on the road. "I changed my mind."

She nodded, knowing that was about all she was going to get out of him for now. "Thanks," she said quietly, trying hard to cover any emotion in her own voice.

He turned to look at her.

"For changing your mind," she added.

He held her gaze a moment then nodded in acknowledgment before turning back to the road.

CHAPTER NINTEEN

———

It was late by the time they got back to the City, the lights of the buildings in the distance twinkling like tiny fireflies as they crossed the Bay Bridge. The air was cool, fog rolling in from the ocean, the crisp, salt-scented wind chilling Anna's cheeks through the SUV's perpetually open windows.

They'd agreed that a motel wasn't safe, that the fewer people who saw them the better. They had no idea how wide Petrovich's network extended—or who Dade's employer might have on the take—and they'd both had enough gunfire for one evening. Instead, Dade pulled into an abandoned drive-in movie theater and parked near the boarded-up concession stand.

Overgrown bushes flanked the asphalt, four large, dormant white screens rising up from the wildlife like giant ghosts in the night. It was quiet, like a forgotten patch of earth hidden away in the middle of the city.

Anna got out and stretched then fed Lenny their last handful of dog chow before walking him around the grounds. When she got back to the car she saw that Dade had pushed the back seats of the SUV down, flattening them into a makeshift bed in the back. A sleeping bag lay over the seats, unzipped into a flat blanket big enough for two. Dade sat on the left side, his eyes concentrated on the screen on the phone in his hand.

"What are you doing?" Anna asked, unlatching Lenny's lead.

He hopped into the car and immediately curled into a ball on the front seat, looking as drained as Anna felt.

"Trying to track down my employer."

Anna climbed into the back, gingerly slipping beneath the sleeping bag, careful not to touch Dade as she did. It felt oddly intimate lying down next to him, and she didn't want to get any closer than she had to.

"How?" she asked.

"I was hired through a third party. If I can get to him, I can get to whoever hired us both."

"So who is the third party?"

His eyes met hers for a second then quickly looked away. "I don't have a name. Just a telephone number."

She narrowed her eyes at him. "So, you took the job without knowing anything about the people hiring you?"

"Look, I don't usually care who hires me. The reason they want a target neutralized doesn't matter. I take a job based on the target. The reasons behind the hire mean nothing to me."

Anna couldn't help but notice his language. Target. Neutralize. He was impersonalizing the people he killed. She wondered if it was deliberate or an unconscious act of self-preservation.

"Don't you ever get tired?" she asked.

"I'm getting tired now," he answered the edge still present in his voice.

"No, I mean of this. Running."

There was a pause. "I'm not running, Anna."

"That's a lie. Anyone who lives this life is always running. There's always someone at your back, looking over your shoulder, just around the corner. Tell me you don't sleep with your gun at your side and one eye open?"

Again with the pause. Then, "You're right."

Anna closed her eyes and leaned her head back on the seats. She inhaled deeply the scents of leather and damp salty air. "I just thought…I thought I could start over. That maybe one day I could sleep. I mean really sleep. Deeply. Calmly. Without fear of what will happen when I wake up."

She heard him set his phone down, plunging them both into sudden darkness in the back of the car.

"You can't go back," he answered.

"I know." She nodded. "I know that now. But…but where do I go forward from here?"

She wasn't sure why, but her voice cracked. She hadn't meant it to. She hadn't meant to get deep or emotional at all.

Especially not with Dade. She bit her lip hard, willing the sob in her throat to subside, not to escape.

"Are you okay?" he asked.

Dammit, he'd heard her. She took a second, feeling tears heat behind her eyes.

"Yes."

"Liar."

The sob popped out.

She shut her eyes tightly to stave off tears.

In the darkness, she heard Dade shift, the polyester of the sleeping bag crackling as his body moved closer to hers. In a moment, his arm was around her. She didn't want comfort. She didn't want to get close. But she couldn't help pressing her face to his chest all the same, the warmth like a beacon to her.

Tears trickled down her cheeks, wetting his shirt—she was sure—but he didn't say anything, didn't pull away. He just held her. His arms that had seemed like fighting against steel only yesterday were now a welcomed strength—holding the good in, holding the bad at bay.

And so she clung to him. Her arms going around his solid torso, holding on for dear life.

His hand went to her hair, stroking it back from her forehead.

"Hey. It's okay," he whispered to her.

She nodded. But the tears flowed down her cheeks just the same.

"You're going to be okay. I promise."

She gulped, tried to take a deep breath to still her throat. She nodded again. "I know." She sniffed, even though the promise was as hollow as her tears felt. "I'm sorry."

"Don't be," he quickly told her.

"I hate crying."

"Me too."

She choked back a laugh. "Sorry," she whispered again. She pulled away. Even as warm and wonderful as his body felt, she forced herself to pull back.

His hand went to her hair again. "Hey, really, it's okay. I cry."

She scoffed. "Really?"

Only he didn't laugh. Just nodded.

"When?"

"When I got back from Afghanistan. Hell, I cried every night for a while."

She had a hard time picturing that. And the disbelief must have shown on her face as he added, "Everyone I knew was dead, Anna. The whole squad."

"What happened?" she asked softly.

She half expected him to clam up again, but instead he lay his head down on the seats, facing her.

"Ambush. We were bringing supplies to troops at an outpost along the Pakistani trade route. We were attacked. By the time backup came, five of us were pulled from the mess. Five who hadn't been killed immediately. By the next morning, only four were left. As I lay in the hospital bed I watched them die around me. Slowly. From infections, internal bleeding, wounds too severe to be repaired. Each morning I would wake up and refuse to open my eyes. Draw it out as long as possible before I had to face who had gone in the night. And when I was the only one left, each night I went to sleep sure that I would be gone by morning. For two weeks I did this, expecting each morning to wake up dead. Then I was discharged and sent home."

"I'm sorry," Anna said quietly. She didn't know what to say. Comfort was something she didn't really know how to give. She'd been too long away from people, she realized. Too long making sure she kept her distance that even now, in the intimate confines of their makeshift bed, his face inches away from her, hearing words she was pretty sure he'd never spoken to anyone else, she wasn't sure how to receive the closeness. "I'm so sorry," she said again.

Dade shook his head in the dark. "It's not a sob story. Everyone has their own trauma in life. I'm not unique in that. But it was hard. I was pissed, felt guilty, angry, and just sad. Sad that so many good people had died for no reason. So, I cried. It's okay to be sad. It's okay to be scared sometimes."

She nodded. She knew that. But it didn't change the fact that she hated those feelings. Feeling scared meant she wasn't in control. And when all else in her life was in chaos, the very least she wanted to do was control her own emotions.

In her former life, she had often prayed to feel human, to feel the compassion for her fellow man that she knew she should.

Of course, at first that was all she could feel. She'd been sick the first time she'd put a bullet in someone's chest, seen the blood ooze out, watched the life drain behind his eyes as the realization dawned on him that he was dying. She'd stood frozen, watching him fade, wasting so much time she'd almost caught a bullet herself. But she hadn't been able to leave the man until she knew he was gone, the thought of him dying all alone too much to bear. She hadn't slept for a week after that first time. The images coming back to her as soon as she closed her eyes, the man haunting her dreams as soon as she drifted off. He'd been an arms dealer, someone who had been responsible for countless deaths himself. But it hadn't negated the way he had looked at her as his soul had slowly slipped away into whatever oblivion awaited him.

After that first time, Anna had forced that part of herself to shut down. To turn off all emotion, become numb, as Petrovich had told her time and time again.

And she had. Soon enough she'd been so numb she didn't know how to turn *that* off. How to feel human again. Nerves she sometimes felt, anxiety, fear of being killed herself. But in that instant where her fingers locked on the trigger, squeezed, shot the life out of someone as they sat unsuspecting before her, she'd been trained to feel nothing.

And she had hated it. Hated that they had taken the one thing she had left that was hers—her humanity. She prayed to feel, and when she'd stopped believing in anyone to pray to, she'd hoped, begged, pleaded with herself to feel something. She'd forced herself to look in their eyes as they died, to watch the life slide away from them. But she'd felt nothing.

And now…in the cold, in the dark, beside a man she shouldn't trust, she couldn't stop feeling. Couldn't stop the tears from falling for every person that she'd been numbed beyond humanity toward.

For herself.

For Dade.

Without thinking, Anna reached a hand out toward him. In the dull moonlight filtering through the windows, his face was in shadow, the hard angles of his profile softened in the dark. She trailed her fingers across his cheek, tracing the outline of his jaw, feeling his rough stubble on the pads of her fingers.

She heard him draw in a breath, sharp and sudden. But he didn't move. His body was still, tense beside her.

He didn't know how to do close, either.

But suddenly she wanted close. Was desperate for it. For the chance to be, for just one night, a part of something other than herself.

She leaned forward in the dark, touching her lips to his.

At first he was stone, unmoving. He didn't even breathe as far as she could tell.

She flicked the tip of her tongue out to lick his lower lip, softly opening her mouth to taste him.

And he responded.

His lips moved slowly at first, softly, tentatively, as if not sure how deep he wanted to get himself into this. She inched her body closer to his, feeling his warmth beneath the sleeping bag.

She felt the moment when he gave in, the moment when he decided that he would allow himself this vulnerability. His arms went around her middle, crushing her to him. His hand went to her hair, not stroking gently now, but tugging, stinging her scalp. His kiss deepened, his breath coming hard against her cheek.

Anna closed her eyes, lay back on the leather seats, and gave in to the feeling of…feeling. Feeling every touch of his body, every muscle pressing against her, every sensation of his rough cheeks brushing against her neck, his wet tongue running over her lips, his hands warm and strong, running up her thigh, down her back, beneath the hem of her T-shirt.

She closed her eyes. And let it take over.

* * *

Anna lay in the dark. Crickets chirping in the tall grasses nearby created a symphony that she swore was just for her. Lenny snored in the front seat, a rhythmic, comforting sound. And Dade breathed softly beside her, his bare chest rising and falling in the moonlight. She couldn't help grinning, laying a hand on his skin. He was warm. Solid.

She closed her eyes. It was the first time in years that she had felt sated and relaxed. Her mind was as calm as the night, her body at ease. She lay still, enjoying the long forgotten sensation.

Though, had she ever really felt this?

Maybe. She couldn't really remember now. But there might have been moments as a child when she'd felt warm, secure. Happy without any qualifiers attached.

She closed her eyes, allowing sleep to come naturally to her.

But it never got there.

Because as soon as her lids dropped down over her eyes, the sound of gunfire tore through the side of the SUV.

CHAPTER TWENTY

———

Dade woke instantly, rolling over on top of Anya in a protective instinct. He fumbled in the dark for the gun tucked into his pants. It took him a second to realize he wasn't wearing any pants. He was groggy, out of it, a state he wasn't used to being in.

Anya wriggled out from beneath him and emerged with his M9 in hand. She shot two rounds out the shattered back window.

Dade scrambled over her, grabbing a handful of clothing in the process, diving toward the front seat. He was about to turn the key in the ignition, when shots sprayed the hood of the car, crawling up to explode the windshield in front of him.

He ducked down and quickly scrambled to the back of the car, keeping low as the gunfire continued to hail on them from the driver's side.

Anya had shoved herself into a pair of jeans, had her shirt half over her head. She was still pointing the gun out the back, sending rounds toward their unseen attackers.

Dade pushed the back passenger side door open then shoved Anya out ahead of him. He felt Lenny following a step behind, instinctively sticking close to the couple.

Dade crouched low, sticking behind the SUV's tires. He grabbed his gun from Anya, ducking out around the back end of the car and shooting off another couple of rounds. He was almost out of ammo, he knew.

"Into the bushes," he commanded, shoving Anya ahead of him again.

She went, grabbing Lenny by the collar as she did, diving into the overgrowth to their right. Dade provided cover, shooting out at unseen attackers until his gun reported a hollow click. He was out of bullets. It was a footrace now.

He dove into the bushes after Anya, a hail of gunfire following him.

He couldn't see where she was, but he could hear her crashing through the underbrush of the overgrown landscape. He followed the sounds, painfully aware that his pants were still in his hands as he raced away from the scene.

He felt himself gain on Anya, the sound of her feet slowing as he approached.

Unfortunately, in the distance, he also heard another set of feet entering the brush. Or two sets. More? He couldn't tell, the noises all running together.

"Dade!" he heard Anya call ahead of him.

"Right behind you. Don't slow down."

She didn't answer, but he heard the sound of her feet picking up pace, Lenny's bark echoed in the darkness as the pair hit the edge of the clearing.

Dade caught up to Anya just as an explosion rocketed through the sky. Heat hit his back, knocking him to the ground. He turned around just in time to see orange and red flames reaching up into the air where his SUV had once been.

He scrambled to his feet, quickly shoved his legs into the pair of pants, threw a shirt over his head, and tucked his M9 into his waistband.

"Was that…?" Anya asked.

"Yeah. Let's get out of here."

The drive-in gave way to a service road that ran along the edge of a row of brick office buildings. The windows were all dark at this time of night as Anya and Dade ran past them. A shot whizzed past Dade's ear, hitting the building and tossing chunks of brick into the air. He ducked his head down to avoid shards in his eyes, instinctively putting himself between their pursuers and Anya as they ran. He pushed her sideways at the corner, veering left, then quickly right again into an alleyway leading north.

More bullets followed them, pinging off the side of the building. Dade dove behind a dumpster, pulling Anya with him. A break in a chain link fence behind them led into a yard beyond. Dade quickly pulled at the break, creating a hole large enough for Anya to crawl through. He shoved Lenny through ahead of him before following them both, feeling the rough links scratch at his back as he crawled over the earth on his belly. Dade sprang to his feet on the other side, grabbing Anya by the hand again and pulling her with him as he ran through the yard, back out onto the main street.

Keeping behind the line of parked cars, Dade heard gunfire shattering windows as they raced past, one after another, car alarms blaring from the vehicles. Lights turned on in windows, the commotion drawing people out of bed.

Dade turned right at the corner then made a sharp left and another right.

They raced another three blocks zigzagging through neighborhoods and yards, Lenny loping along at their side, until the sound of car alarms began to fade in the distance and the hail of bullets stopped whizzing by their ears.

"Wait," Anya said, collapsing behind a car.

She was breathing heavily, sweat running down her cheeks, her chest rising and falling rapidly.

"I'm not used to this anymore," she panted, doubling over at the waist.

He stood beside her, one arm draped around her shoulders as she caught her breath.

"We need to keep moving," he said. They'd outrun their attackers for now. But that wouldn't be true much longer. They had a car, which Dade and Anya now did not.

Anya nodded. "I know," she panted. She held up one finger and leaned her head back, taking two big deep drags of oxygen, in and out. "Okay," she said, "let's go." Though he could tell she still hadn't caught her breath.

Dade grabbed her hand, speed walking with no real destination in mind.

He heard a car behind them as they turned onto the next street, and he pulled Anya to him, flattening her against the side of the building behind a trash can. Headlights approached, and he held his breath. He could feel Anya tense beside him.

The car passed. An old VW bus.

Relief drained out of Dade. He took Anya's hand again, making tracks forward.

They walked in silence, keeping to the shadows whenever a car approached, until they hit a more populous area where nightlife was still out and alive. Homeless people roamed the streets, the lights of all-night convenience stores blinking in neon, the bar crowd still stumbling home as early risers went in search of their first lattes.

Dade led the way to a BART station at the end of the block. Anya needed a chance to sit and catch her breath. If they boarded the train, at least they could keep moving while she did. He wasn't sure where to go, but putting distance between them and the neighborhood was a good start.

He purchased tickets from an automated machine, immensely relieved to find his wallet and phone still in the back pocket of his pants, and the three of them descended the escalator into the lower level to wait for the subway.

The next train was heading east toward Oakland. Dade stood on the platform, waiting an excruciating five minutes for the train to arrive. He felt open. Exposed. If anyone had seen them enter the station, they were sitting ducks.

Anya shifted from one foot to the other beside him. Her skin was pale, and she was chewing on her lower lip.

He put an arm around her shoulders, drawing her into him. "Your shirt's on backwards," he mumbled into her ear.

She looked down. Then back up at him, grinning. "You're not wearing any shoes.

She was right. In his haste to flee, he'd been lucky to manage pants.

He leaned over and kissed the top of her head. "You okay?" he whispered.

She swallowed hard. Then nodded.

The train carriage arrived, a whoosh of sound filling the tunnel, and Dade quickly ushered Anya in ahead of him, followed by Lenny.

They settled into a pair of seats near the back of the car, facing the doors. Dade let out a breath he didn't realize he'd been holding when the doors finally slid shut. No guys with guns had entered. No one was shooting at them. They were safe.

At least for as long as it took to get to the next station.

The car was scarcely populated at this time of night, occupied only by a couple guys in baggy jeans who'd obviously been drinking heavily enough to leave their cars behind, and a guy in an overcoat reading a paperback. The guy in the overcoat looked up when they entered, staring at the pair.

Dade realized they must have presented an odd sight, both sweating, out of breath. Anya's arms wore scratches where branches had hit her during their flight. Dade could see the same on himself. Not to mention he was barefoot.

Dade didn't realize it, but he must have stiffened, as Anya leaned in and whispered beside him.

"He's looking at Lenny. Dogs aren't allowed on BART unless they're in a carrier."

She reached down and scooped the animal into her arms, holding him securely.

The guy shot her a look but seemed reassured enough that he wasn't going to get bitten that he quietly went back to his novel.

They rode in silence, exhaustion hitting Dade as he realized that he now had no vehicle, no computer equipment, and a gun without any bullets. In the long run, most everything in his SUV could be replaced. But at the moment, they were items he sorely needed if they were going to make it through the next few hours alive.

It was closing on 4:30 am. Braxton's rally was scheduled for one that afternoon.

While he'd agreed that Anya's plan to meet Petrovich head-on was a hell of a lot better than running from him forever, there were a couple things it didn't take into account. Dade, for one. And his former employer, who was still waiting to see Anya become a problem of the past. Dade knew as long as she was alive, they would both continue to have targets painted on their backs, with or without Petrovich in the picture.

Dade glanced over at Anya. Her head was tilted backward, leaning on the seat's headrest.

It had been a long time since he'd cared about someone else's safety. Since he'd cared at all about a woman. He hadn't lived a celibate life, but it had been a long time since he'd really been there with someone. Sex had been a release, an escape. Kind of like a bottle of wine. Smooth, enjoyable, but once it was empty, it was empty, and he moved on to the next one.

He looked over at Anya.

Her skin was beginning to regain an even color now, the bright pink on the apples of her cheeks fading, the white around her eyes darkening. Her chest was rising slower, the jittering in her feet still now. She closed her eyes, and her lips parted just the slightest as she breathed. He felt a sudden urge to lean over and kiss her.

But he didn't.

He couldn't.

Not knowing what he had to do this afternoon.

Instead, he leaned his head back against the seat, listening to the steady rhythm of the train on the tracks, trying to reconcile what he'd just done with Anya at the drive-in with what had to be done at the senator's rally.

* * *

Lenny wriggled in Anna's arms. She absently stroked his fur, her hands running down the length of his back as she watched the multicolored tile walls stream past her windows. It felt safer down here, like she was in some sort of cocoon in the tunnels, protecting her from the rest of the world. The warm, relaxed feeling she'd felt just hours ago—hours? God, it felt like a lifetime—was a thing of the distant past, a moment that she should probably never have indulged in and knew she wouldn't let herself again. But the immediate adrenaline was starting to fade from her system, allowing her to gain control of her limbs again.

Lenny whined, probably hungry. She rubbed the back of his neck to calm him. He could feel the tension in her, she knew. Animals were intuitive in that way, much more so than humans. They could feel their surrounding. Anna wished she could do the same. Maybe then she would have felt the attackers coming at her, had had some warning. Maybe she would have been able to get them out of there before they'd lost Dade's car.

Lenny wriggled again beneath Anna's touch.

"Shh," she commanded. She ran her hand in smooth, soft strokes along his spine, over the top of his head, around the side of his neck.

And that's where her fingers felt something.

She opened her eyes, running her hand along the side of his neck again. The folds of skin around his neck were thick, but as she smoothed them out against his body with her hand, she felt a lump. Small, almost indistinguishable from the rest of his skin, certainly hidden from view.

But it was there.

"Sonofabitch," she breathed.

Dade instantly tensed beside her, his hand going to the band of his pants. "What?"

"Look," she said, smoothing the skin out again so that Dade could see the lump.

He looked then shrugged. "What?" he asked again.

"Give me your hand."

He did, and she ran it over the spot on Lenny's neck. "Feel that lump?"

He nodded.

"It's a locater chip."

He blinked at her. "You're serious?"

She nodded. "Owners have a version of this injected into their dogs so that if they run away, a shelter can scan the chip and know who they belong to."

"And this one?"

She felt around. "Same location, but it's bigger. If I had to guess, I'd say GPS."

Dade breathed out a string of curses. "That's how Petrovich keeps finding us."

She nodded. "And why Lenny was left alive in the apartment to begin with. Petrovich knew I'd come for him."

"We need to get it out."

Anna nodded. She held Lenny close, again angry at herself for not seeing this sooner. It hadn't been dumb luck that the dog had escaped notice in her apartment. It was ridiculous, she now realized, to believe that it had been. They'd torn apart every corner of her apartment. Had she really thought they'd missed a seventy pound, barking mess of slobber? But she'd been so relieved to see him that she hadn't questioned it.

No more mistakes. You're better than that. Stay sharp, Anya.

They exited the train at the next stop, Montgomery, and climbed the escalator to ground level. They were in the financial district, fast food places and coffee shops mingling with high-rise buildings. A block down on Market, they found a convenience store on the corner.

Dade waited outside with Lenny while Anna went in and purchased a pair of nail clippers, NyQuil, duct tape, paper towel, three pieces of beef jerky, and a pair of canvas shoes for Dade.

Once outside, she gave two pieces of the jerky to Lenny, finishing them off with a NyQuil chaser. Dade picked him up and carried him back to the BART station, finding an unoccupied restroom on the ground floor. They pushed inside, and Anna locked the door behind them.

After fifteen minutes the NyQuil began to take affect, Lenny's eyelids drooping. Using the nail clippers, Anna carefully cut into the top layer of Lenny's skin. Dade held the dog still, but even with the medication, she felt Lenny wince, and cringed. "Sorry, pal," she mumbled. She forced herself to continue clipping at the thick skin until her fingers felt the plastic edge of the locator chip. She grabbed onto it with the edge of the nail clippers, pulling it free. She then quickly folded the paper towel into a square and applied it to Lenny's cut. It wasn't deep or long enough to require stitches, but she knew he wouldn't be happy when he woke up. She took a generous hand with the duct tape, wrapping it around his neck to secure the paper towel. A patch job, but it would have to do for now.

She put the third piece of jerky in her pocket, promising Lenny a treat as soon as he woke up.

"What do you want to do with this?" Anna asked, handing the chip to Dade as they exited the station.

Dade turned it over in his hand. It was a small cylindrical capsule, less than an inch long.

Dade looked down the street. The sun was just starting to show above the horizon, the sky turning a dusky pink. Cars were already lining the street, early commuters trying to get a jump on the inevitable traffic. Down the block was a bus stop, picking up where the subway left off. On a bench at the stop sat two Asian women, one with a shopping bag and the other a large, red purse clutched on her lap. A couple guys in suits stood nearby, thumbs glued to their phones. A large orange and white bus was just pulling up.

"Hand me the duct tape," he said.

Anna did, passing over the bag of supplies. Dade took it and jogged across the street to where the bus was opening its doors to let morning passengers on. He rounded to the back, crouching down low to stay out of the driver's line of vision. He quickly ripped a length of tape off the roll with his teeth and attached the chip to the underside of the bus's wheel base.

It only took a moment, but Anna held her breath the whole time, sure that someone would spot him. That the people on the receiving end of the transmitter would screech up to the station any second. That they had stayed in one place too long and this was it.

Dade stepped away just as the doors of the bus hissed shut. A cough of smoke churned up from the tailpipe where he had just been, signaling movement again.

He grinned as he jogged back to Anna. "That should keep them busy for a while."

She nodded, watching as the bus pulled away, taking the tracking device with it. "Now let's get the hell out of here."

CHAPTER TWENTY-ONE

————

"I need to speak to our employer." Dade shifted his phone to the other hand then punctuated his request with a sharp, "Now."

The man on the other end sighed. "I told you that is not possible."

Dade looked across the expanse of damp grass at Anya. She was walking Lenny in slow circles, the "slow" part a clear sign the dog was still shaking off the medication. He stumbled a little, listlessly sniffed the grass, clearly groggy. In the distance, across the lawn, Dade could see workers erecting the stage Senator Braxton would be standing on in a few short hours.

"Bullshit. I want to speak to him," Dade said.

"Whatever you have to say to him, you can say through me," the man countered.

Dade looked down at the readout on his cell. The tracking app was homing in on his location. The man was in the City. That much Dade could tell. If he could keep him talking another two minutes, he'd have an address. "Fine. Then tell our employer that I've had a change of heart."

The man paused. "*Another* one?"

"Very funny."

"I'm not laughing, Mr. Dade."

"Yeah, well, neither am I. Nothing about this job has been particularly funny, the least of which this conversation. Give me his name."

"As far as our employer is concerned, your relationship with him terminated when you reneged on your contract to eliminate his problem."

Dade looked across the lawn at the "problem." She was leaning down on one knee, feeding the dog a slice of jerky. She rubbed the fur on his head, made some sort of baby-talk face, and grinned at him.

Dade forced himself to look away.

"I'm ready to take care of his problem now."

"I'm sorry, but it's too late. He's already hired a replacement."

"No shit! Speaking of which, you can tell our employer that I don't appreciate being shot at."

"I'm not sure our employer cares what you appreciate anymore, Mr. Dade," the man on the other end said.

Dade looked down at the readout. The guy was downtown.

"Does our employer still care about Anya? Because I can deliver her."

"I told you. Other arrangements have already been made. Your services are no longer required."

Dade could feel the man hanging up.

"Wait!"

There was a sigh on the other end. "Yes?"

Dade looked down. The man's location was narrowed to a two-block radius. He just needed a few seconds more…

"The payment. I wired it back to our employer. Did he get it?"

The man on the other end paused a moment. This was clearly not the question he'd been expecting. "Yes," he said slowly. "The refunded deposit was received as promised."

"Good. At least you know my word is good."

"Honestly, Mr. Dade, I don't care about your word, and neither does our employer. Our business with you is finished. Good-bye," the man said, then hung up.

Dade looked at the readout. A red dot flashed at four-fifteen Sutter, just across from Union Square Park.

Dade grinned. "Gotcha."

"Got what?"

Dade looked up to find Anya jogging toward him, dragging Lenny along on his lead.

"What did you get?" she asked again.

Dade shrugged. "Information on another job."

For a moment, her eyes clouded. As if the mention of his work suddenly jolted her back from some spot just this side of reality.

"Oh."

"And there's an errand related to that job that I need to run now."

She bit the inside of her cheek. "Errand."

"Yeah. I'll be back before the rally. You'll wait for me here?"

She paused just long enough to make him nervous before slowly nodding.

"I'll be here," she said.

In anyone else, he might have doubted the sincerity of the statement. But he knew how badly she wanted to corner Petrovich, and knowing he would be at the rally, Dade trusted that Anya would be, too.

"One o'clock. I'll meet you back here."

She nodded. "One o'clock."

Dade hoped he could trust her.

*   *   *

Dade jumped on the light-rail, heading toward Sutter. He stopped off only once, at a gun shop off Geary to purchase more ammo. Then he rode the line until it dropped him off just a block from the tall glass building matching the address on his phone. He entered the lobby and paused at the directory of offices housed inside. There were several investment firms, a couple of tax consultants, a few start-ups, and one attorney's office. Dade took a stab in the dark and entered the elevator, hitting the button for the fifth floor that housed the attorney's office. The man on the phone had immediate knowledge of the funds transfer, which led Dade to believe he was the one setting up the overseas accounts for his employer in the first place. If it were Dade, he'd have hired a lawyer to do that.

Dade was alone in the elevator, listening to the Muzak being piped in through hidden speakers. Instead of being soothing, the soft rock was just irritating, adding to his antsy mood. Normally he would finesse someone for the type of information he needed now. But he was out of time for that sort of option.

The elevator doors slid open to reveal the lobby of Johnson, Davidson & Burke. A large, modern desk in an oval design took up most of the area, a woman in a headset behind it, fingers clacking away at her keyboard. She looked up briefly, but Dade plowed past, not bothering to make eye contact, his cell already out and in hand as he dialed the number for his contact.

"Dade," the man said, clearly not excited to hear from him again. "I told you we're done."

"I'm giving you one more chance," Dade told the man as he walked onto the main floor of the offices. Cubes filled the center of the room, admin and junior members of the firm humming with activity. "One chance to tell me where I can find our employer."

"Now you're just wasting both of our time."

Dade quickly walked the maze of cubes, watching faces, scanning for anyone talking on their phones. "What you're wasting is an opportunity to see this mess taken care of for our employer."

Along the perimeter of the room sat glass-walled offices, home to those promoted out of the sea of cubes. Dade could see at least three senior members inside their offices on phones. He approached the first, where a man with grey hair in a navy-colored suit was talking into a Bluetooth, arms waving animatedly in the window.

"Our employer is well able to take care of matters himself. You've proven yourself unstable. We're through."

"What if *I'm* not through?" Dade said.

The man paused, and Dade could hear his breath coming hard through the phone.

But the guy in the suit kept talking into his Bluetooth. Not Dade's man.

"Is that supposed to be a threat?" the man finally asked.

"Take it however you like," Dade said, moving on to the next window. A woman with a handheld receiver sat at her desk. He quickly moved on. In the next office, Dade could see a man with dark hair standing at the windows, his back to the main floor. He had a cell in hand.

"I'm going to say this once more and only once more. Your contract is terminated. Our employer wants nothing more to do with you. You are to lose this number and forget you ever knew it."

"Give me a name," Dade barked out, watching the man with the dark hair closely.

The figure in the office shook his head in the negative.

"You know I can't do that."

"Last chance." Dade took a step toward the office door.

"Good-bye, Mr. Dade."

The man in the office pulled the phone from his ear and hit the *Off* button.

The line in Dade's ear went dead.

"Don't say I didn't warn you," Dade mumbled under his breath, quickly shoving through the door.

The man with the dark hair spun around, phone still dangling from his hand. "What the…"

He didn't finish the statement, his eyes immediately going big and round as he recognized Dade.

"How the hell did you get in here?" he asked, taking a step toward his desk.

But Dade was faster, drawing his gun from his waistband and pointing it at the man. "Don't."

The man froze, his eyes going from the gun in Dade's hand to the windows behind him overlooking the sea of cubes.

"Don't move," Dade instructed. "Don't speak. Don't even think of alerting anyone out there."

The man's eyes flickered to the glass once more, but he nodded.

"Now, go close the blinds. Slowly," Dade added.

The man nodded again, crossing the room to the glass windows and letting down the horizontal privacy blinds.

"Lock the door," Dade said.

The man did, hands shaking as he turned the latch. "What are you going to do?"

"I'm going to ask you nicely to tell me who our employer is."

"You know I can't—" the man started.

But Dade was already across the room, pinning the man to the wall, the muzzle of his gun pressed against the man's temple.

"Yes, you can," he ground out.

The man let out an involuntary whimper.

"And if you're smart, you will."

"Please," the man said.

"This is not an idle threat," Dade told him, pressing the cold steel into the man's skin until it turned white from the pressure. "I kill people for a living, and you're just one more number to me. I'm out of time, out of options, and out of patience. You can either give me the information I want, or I can shoot you and tear your office apart until I find it myself. Your choice."

The man's breath came fast and hard. "I can't," he whispered. "He'll kill me."

"So will I."

"Someone will hear you," the man said, his voice going higher. "They'll hear the gun shot and come running."

"You really think that concerns me now?" Dade asked.

The man looked up into his face. "You're crazy if you think you'll get away with this."

"Last. Chance." Dade ground the words out through clenched teeth.

"You can't do this…"

"One," Dade counted off.

"No, please. You don't understand…"

"Two."

"I have a family…"

"Three."

Dade changed the angle of the gun, aiming at the wall behind the man, and fired. The loud report went off right in the man's ear, the bullet shattering a diploma of some sort hung in a frame on the wall, glass crashing to the polished hardwood floor. The man let out a strangled sort of sob, and Dade saw a wet trickle of liquid soil the inside leg of his pants.

"Oh, Christ. Oh, God, please don't shoot me. Jesus," the man whimpered.

Dade moved the gun back to the man's temple. "A name."

The man closed his eyes, his Adam's apple bobbing up and down.

"Demarkov."

"Demarkov what?"

The man swallowed again. "Vladimir Demarkov is his name."

Dade narrowed his eyes at the man. "Call him," he demanded.

"I don't have a number."

Dade pressed the muzzle harder into his flesh.

"I swear I don't have one! He conducts all business in person. If I had a number, don't you think I'd tell you?"

"I don't know," Dade said, pressing until the man's head bowed under the pressure. "Would you?"

"Yes! Jesus, yes. Look, he..." He faltered, swallowing hard again. "He's always at his club. Moonlight. It's a strip club in the Tenderloin. He had me set up accounts, gave me the job details, and told me to find someone to make it happen. Which I did." He paused. "Or at least, I thought I did. You came highly recommended."

"I know about me," Dade said. "Tell me about Demarkov."

He swallowed. "Okay, um...he's older. Graying hair. Thick accent."

"What kind of accent?"

He shrugged. "I don't know. European maybe?"

"Go on," Dade prompted.

"Look, I don't know much more than that. When I need to talk to him, I go to the club. He's always there."

Dade opened his mouth to ask more, but a knock at the door stopped him.

"John?" came a woman's voice. "We heard a loud noise. Everything okay in there?"

Dade gave the man a hard look.

"Uh, yeah," the man called back. He cleared his throat, trying unsuccessfully at an even tone. "Yeah, I'm fine. I just...broke a picture frame. That's all."

"You need me to call janitorial?"

"Uh, no. No, I'm fine. Thanks."

Dade waited until he heard high heels retreating before he spoke again. "Where is the Moonlight Club?"

"Between Polk and Hyde. Just east of Van Ness."

Dade nodded. He could find the place easily enough.

"One last thing," he said, easing up on the pressure of his gun.

"You're going to lend me your car."

The man spun around. "I'm going to what?"

Dade took a step forward.

"Right. Great. Okay," the man said, quickly pulling a set of keys from his pocket. "Lexus in the garage around the corner. Second level. Knock yourself out."

Dade took the keys and grinned. "See? Now was that so hard?"

* * *

While it was still morning outside, the interior of the Moonlight was bathed in a dim light that made it completely impossible to distinguish day from night, one hour from the next. The ceilings were low, the lighting sparse, creating a false air of intimacy to sell a fantasy to the smattering of businessmen in suits at the few occupied tables.

Their eyes flickered to the stage, registering only mild amusement, as they talked, drank, and negotiated. One guy in a windbreaker was seated next to the raised stage, eyes riveted upward on the woman dancing in front of him, one sweaty palm clutching a fistful of dollar bills while the other was busy in his pocket.

Dade looked away.

On the stage two women worked a pair of metal poles. One had short, platinum hair—a home dye job. She was topless, wearing only a turquoise G-string that clung to her ample hips as a means of collecting bills. The second woman was completely nude, and Dade could see silvery stretchy marks running along her lower belly. She stumbled, her eyelids at half mast, clearly on something. These were the 11:00 am. girls, the bottom of the stripper food chain.

Dade let his eyes adjust to the dark as he made his way through the mostly empty tables to a purple, vinyl booth at the back of the club.

Just as the lawyer had said, an older guy with graying hair was in residence. A pair of younger men in dark suits sat beside him, with a bottle of bourbon between them on the table, glasses out, cigars being smoked as they talked animatedly, completely ignoring the dancers onstage.

Dade walked straight toward the group, one hand hovering over his weapon.

As he approached, their low conversation ceased, all eyes turning his way.

The man nearest the end of the booth slowly put a hand to his waistband. Clearly Dade wasn't the only armed man here.

The older guy in the middle raised one thick eyebrow at Dade.

"Can I help you?" he asked. His voice was, as the lawyer had said, heavily accented.

"Actually, I believe I can help you, Demarkov."

The man froze, registering clear surprise. Though he didn't act rashly, as one might expect. Quite the opposite. Instead he sat back in his seat, eyes slowly assessing Dade, taking their time to decide just what kind of threat he might present.

"And you are?" he finally asked.

"Nick Dade."

Recognition dawned behind his eyes, and he nodded, almost as if he had expected the visit.

"Ah. I see."

"You hired me to do a job for you."

He nodded. "I know. One that is not done, is it?"

"No, it's not."

"One that you failed at."

"I resigned. That's different than failing."

"Resignation was not an option."

"I know."

Dade stared at the other man, knowing they were each sizing up the other, each trying to silently intimidate the other and each trying to decide just how well it was working.

Finally Demarkov spoke, "What are you doing here?"

"We need to talk about Anya."

Demarkov frowned and shook his head. "You gave up the contract. I have nothing to say to you."

"I've got Anya Danielovich."

The man shot a look to his associates then back at Dade. He leaned forward.

"I'm listening."

"She's yours if you want her."

"You have her now?"

"Yes."

"Where?"

"Somewhere safe."

He paused, his eyes narrowing, assessing Dade slowly and quietly again as the moments stretched on. He was waiting Dade out, hoping he would give away something in the silence.

Dade stood still, calmly letting his eyes meet Demarkov's gaze. Playing his game of silent chicken.

Finally Demarkov cracked first.

"She is still alive, then?" he asked.

Dade nodded.

"But you wish to finish the job after all?"

"I wish to be finished with this mess."

"Why the change of heart?" the man probed.

"I'm tired of running," Dade answered truthfully. "Tired of being a target. I'll give you Anya, but once I hand her over, I'm done. I walk away from the situation, understood?"

Demarkov paused only a moment before nodding. "Understood." Dade could hear the lie in the man's voice clear as a bell. Dade had already proven himself to be unreliable in their eyes. There was no way they would let him walk away now, no matter what kind of deal he could make with them.

But he had to chance it.

"Where is she?" Demarkov asked again.

"I want to know what she is to you first," Dade said.

"She is a loose en—"

"Besides a loose end," Dade broke in. "Who is she to you that she needs to be eliminated?"

Demarkov chewed the end of his cigar. Clearly he was not a man used to explaining his actions to anyone. But, considering he likely planned to have Dade killed anyway, he finally answered, his voice deep and thick with feeling. "Anya Danielovich killed my half-brother."

"Your brother?"

"Anton Fedorov. A general. A highly respected military man," Demarkov explained, obvious pride ringing through in his words. "He was trained in the KOS, the same as I was, and rose through the ranks even more rapidly. Only his rise made enemies within the organization. It wasn't long before he was discharged, then became one of their targets."

Dade recognized the name from Anya's file. Demarkov's description of him was kind. From what Dade had read, Fedorov had deserved the fate he'd gotten and then some. But he kept those thoughts to himself.

"Anya was sent by the KOS to kill your brother?"

Demarkov nodded. "I didn't find out about the hit until it was too late to do anything about it. But Anya was supposed to have died that night, too."

"Only she didn't. When did you find out?"

Demarkov shifted in his seat. "Recently certain other members of the former organization have resurfaced, leading me to believe the past wasn't as buried as I'd hoped."

Petrovich.

As he'd suspected, it was no coincidence that two people from Anya's past had found her at the same time. Demarkov had somehow gotten wind that Petrovich was looking for her, and followed his lead, one party's eminent strike spurring the other's.

"So this is about revenge?"

Demarkov leaned forward. "Where is Anya now?"

"One o'clock," Dade said, instead of answering. "I'll be at Senator Braxton's rally in Golden Gate Park. I'll hand her to you there. You personally," he added, shooting a look at the two lackeys.

"That's a very public place," Demarkov hedged.

"I don't trust you," Dade answered truthfully. "The more public, the better."

Demarkov nodded.

"We have a deal?" Dade asked.

Demarkov looked to his associates again. Dade couldn't tell what silent exchange was going on, but a moment later Demarkov nodded. "A deal. But this time, I expect you to finish what you start."

Dade nodded. "Me too."

CHAPTER TWENTY-TWO

———

Anna sat on a bench across the park from where the rally was set to start in a matter of minutes. People were filling the viewing areas near the stage—families with young children, college students relishing their first taste of being a part of the political process, older couples standing hand in hand at the fringes of the crowd. Sprinkled throughout the group were men in dark suits wearing earpieces—the senator's security. Anna was glad to count at least three canvassing the east side of the park. That was one more than the schematics she'd seen. Prescott must have taken the threat seriously after all. That would make her job easier.

She rubbed her hands together, feeling empty without Lenny's leash to hold. She'd tied him up in the shade, next to a playground on the other side of the park. He had enough water for a few hours, and a soft place to rest his head. She hoped anyone passing by would assume he belonged to one of the families pushing their kids on the swings or traversing the jungle gym. Because no matter what went down here today, she didn't want him caught in the crossfire.

Her plan was to alert security to Petrovich's presence as soon as she saw him. A man with a gun in the crowd would be threat enough for the police to detain him, and once they started asking questions, started delving into Petrovich's background and taking his fingerprints, it was all over. Best case scenario, he'd be deported back to Serbia, left to be dealt with by the government he'd abandoned. Worst case, he'd be tried here as a war criminal. Either way, he would not be chasing Anna down anymore.

She realized her entire plan depended on knowing the nature of the man after her, that Petrovich would, in fact, go after Braxton himself and that they had picked the right event where he'd strike. It was a very educated guess, but she knew it was still a guess. She just hoped to God she knew Petrovich as well as she thought she did.

And that she could trust Dade.

She wanted to trust him. But when he'd left her earlier that day, she realized just how little she really knew about him. She'd met him less than three days ago, and half of that time he'd been bent on killing her and she'd been trying to escape. That wasn't exactly the makings of a solid partnership.

She'd wanted to believe him when he'd said he had business to take care of on another job. She'd wanted to believe that the hard look in his eyes as he'd said it had nothing to do with her and their fate at this rally. She wanted to believe he would be back here any minute to help her execute her plan and that he hadn't taken off to save his own skin, rented a car, and driven halfway to Mexico by now.

But as the minutes stretched on without a sign of him, the belief slowly began to fade and doubt grew to take its place.

She felt sick that he might have played her. And then sick all over again that she suspected it, that the idea had even popped into her head. She wondered if there would ever be a day when she wouldn't automatically assume the worst of people. If she might someday actually trust someone. She *had* trusted him. For that all-too-short instant when they were at the drive-in, wrapped up in each other and the moment. She wanted to believe that moment had been real, that she might see it again when this was all over.

Even though she knew better than that.

When this was all over, she was putting as much distance between herself and San Francisco as possible. She was a ghost again, disappearing, becoming someone else, starting over again just as she always had. Alone.

"Hey."

Anna's head jerked up to see Dade jogging toward her.

Relief flooded her system, though the surprise that he was actually coming back for her must have shown on her face as he said, "Don't tell me you didn't think I'd come back."

Anna swallowed hard, ignoring the lump that had suddenly formed in her throat. "Of course not."

"Good." He shot her a quick grin before looking to the growing crowd. "Ready to do this?"

It's now or never, Anya.

She nodded. "Let's get it over with." She stood.

But Dade put a hand on her arm, pausing her movement. "Hey."

She turned to face him.

His eyes were suddenly soft, open, filled with more emotion than she would have guessed him capable of. They were a whole different color brown like this. Darker, warmer. He reached a hand out and trailed the back of his knuckles down her right cheek. "Good luck," he said softly.

She swallowed. "You, too."

He nodded. Then abruptly turned away, letting a long breath out through his nose. "Let's go, then."

Dade put a hand at the small of her back, slowly leading her through the crowd of supporters. Anna scanned the faces of each person for any sign of Petrovich. Security was tight on the east end of the park, though, according to the information she'd gleaned at campaign headquarters, there were noticeable gaps in security on the west side, where vendors were set up selling hot dogs, popcorn, and cold sodas. That's where she would have broached the crowd if she were Petrovich. Which is what she did now, eyes peeled for both security and her target.

Most of the people pushing in toward the stage were young, idealism written clearly on their acne-stricken faces. Some hard-core politicos were mixed in, carrying signs both for and against Braxton. Most were enjoying the sunshine and the rare warm day in August. Anna hardly saw any of them, her eyes scanning the group for her former handler.

"This way," Dade said, nodding his head to the left. "I see a spot where we can get a good view of the crowd."

Anna nodded, following as he led the way around the left side, past the vendors, to a slightly elevated area by a grove of oak trees.

A few spectators had found the higher ground with the view of the stage. A couple of families, one twenty-something couple, and two men in dark sunglasses.

Anna immediately homed in on the two men. One was older, had graying hair, a paunchy middle. He wore slacks and a blazer, even in the warm sun, his wingtips sinking into the muddy grass. His companion was dressed similarly, standing just a hair behind the older man, shifting from foot to foot on the lawn.

They didn't look right. They didn't belong here. Red flags began waving all over her psyche.

Especially when the older guy saw them approaching and called out to Dade.

"You're late," he said, his voice heavy with a Serbian accent that transported Anna seventeen years back in time.

Anna felt her limbs stiffen, her eyes whipping from the man to Dade's face. Gone was the warm, dark brown in his eyes, instead left in its place was a black, hollow look that held zero emotion.

And zero explanation for the dozens of ugly questions racing through her mind as Dade's hand clamped down on her arm, forcibly propelling her toward the two men.

"Dade?" she asked quietly.

But he didn't answer her, wouldn't even look at her, instead keeping his eyes straight ahead on the two men.

"I don't like to be kept waiting," the older man told Dade.

"I had business to take care of," Dade answered. His voice was flat, words clipped.

Panic began to rise in Anna's throat.

"This is Anya?" the man asked, gesturing to her.

Dade nodded. "As promised."

"Then you will get your payment as promised, too."

Anna felt a breath escape her before she could rein it in. It was true. Every horrible doubt she'd had was true. Dade had never meant to help her, to save her, to see her out of this alive. All he'd ever meant, from the very beginning, was to finish the job he'd started.

He'd lied to her.

And she'd bought every stupid word of it.

You are a fool, Anya. You know better than that. No one will ever save you.

"Now I walk away," Dade told the man. "Our contract is fulfilled, and I don't ever want to see you or your associates again. Understood, Demarkov?"

The man nodded, a small smile playing at the corners of his thin lips. "Understood."

Dade shoved Anna forward, pushing her into the waiting arms of the younger man. The guy grabbed onto her arm with one hand, the other shoving the muzzle of a gun concealed beneath his jacket sharply enough into her ribs to make his point clear. There was no running now.

Anna felt the weight of her Glock, shoved into the top of her right boot, but knew it was useless to her now. Even if she could get to it before either of the men fired on her, she had one bullet and two captors. It didn't take a genius to do the math there.

"Good-bye, Mr. Dade," Demarkov said.

Anna watched as Dade turned and quickly walked away, feeling that panic rise into her throat, begin to choke her. She had no doubt these men meant to kill her.

Demarkov waited until Dade's back had retreated into the crowd of supporters before he turned to his companion and barked out something in Serbian. It had been a long time since Anna had spoken the language, but it came back to her with startling clarity, as she translated the phrase: "Follow him. Kill him."

The younger guy nodded, handing Anna off to Demarkov and disappearing the same way Dade had.

For a moment Anna had the irrational urge to cry out to Dade, to warn him. Immediately she hated herself for caring. He had betrayed her as sharply as anyone in her life ever had. The KOS, Shelli, Petrovich.

Petrovich, who was somewhere in this crowd now. He was here, armed, intent on shooting down the senator, and now he was going to get away with it.

As if in response to her thoughts, a voice came over the loudspeaker, one that Anna instantly recognized.

"How is everyone today?" asked Prescott.

Anna turned her gaze to the stage and watched as a cheer rippled through the waiting crowd in response to the man's question. "Are we ready to meet the man of the hour?" he asked.

Again cheering erupted, people edging closer to the stage. The family behind Anna surged forward, jostling her elbow.

Demarkov's grip tightened on her, drawing her into him. He smelled like expensive alcohol and cheap aftershave. She fought down the urge to run, knowing his bullet was much faster. Instead, she frantically scanned the growing crowd around her; faces, the backs of heads, stature, posture, anything she could see to distinguish Petrovich from the crowd.

A presidential song started playing from the speakers, and Braxton emerged from behind a red, white, and blue curtain, waving to his assembled supporters. They cheered back at him, some waving American flags, others clapping. A couple boos from the protesters in the back were barely heard above the noise and quickly drowned out by shouts of encouragement.

Anna felt her heart pound in her chest, her body hyperaware as she watched Braxton. How many minutes did he have left? If it were her, she wouldn't wait. As soon as she had a clear shot, she'd take it. Too many unknown factors to risk otherwise. Any second Petrovich's bullet would tear through the man waving to his hordes of devotees.

Anna's eyes scanned the tree line on the other side of the clearing. There? Was he hiding in the natural cover?

She looked north. Or was he there, inside one of the buildings at the edge of the park, a scope in hand, aiming his crosshairs at the "man of the hour"?

Maybe he was in the crowd, hiding out in plain sight, ready to lift a pistol to the stage, fire, and disappear into the chaos before anyone noticed.

"Good afternoon, everyone. Thank you so much for coming out on this lovely day," Braxton said to the crowd. His voice was deep, evenly modulated, friendly yet commanding at the same time. He was average height, his inoffensive features giving him a generic look that was more classically handsome than character driven. Brown hair, navy slacks, button-down shirt, but no coat or tie. Professionally dressed, but not so dressed up as to appear above the jeans and T-shirts most of the crowd wore. *I'm like you, only slightly better*, his outfit said.

Anna could see already that he'd make a good politician. If he lived.

CHAPTER TWENTY-THREE

———

Dade watched through his scope as Anya stood next to Demarkov.

They'd been pushed forward by the surging crowd to the very edge of the tree line, clear of any branches obscuring his view. Demarkov's hand was firmly wrapped around Anya's upper arm, keeping her close.

Anya's hands clenched and unclenched at her sides. She bit at the corner of her lip, her nerves translating clearly onto her face. Her limbs were fairly vibrating with the effort to keep them still, stay in one place. She wasn't used to surrender, and it wasn't coming easily to her.

"Steady, girl," he whispered.

He watched her eyes scan the crowd, no doubt looking for Petrovich. Not that there was anything she could do if she spotted him.

At least, not now.

Demarkov's hired gun returned to the pair again, his hands gesturing as he spoke to his boss. Demarkov replied calmly, nodding. Then he gestured to Anya.

He couldn't hear the man, but he could well imagine what he was saying. They needed to get Anya out of there. Transported to somewhere much quieter and more private to dispose of their problem.

Dade found himself silently praying to someone he'd long ago stopped believing in as he let his gaze leave Anya.

He'd done what he could for her. Her fate was her own now.

Instead, he moved his scope a half inch to the right and trained it on Braxton.

Time to finish this.

CHAPTER TWENTY-FOUR

———

"I tell you, he disappeared. Dade's not here." The younger Serbian man gestured to the crowd. "I looked all over. He's gone."

It pained her how relieved she was to hear that statement as Demarkov nodded at his associate.

"Fine. Then we go," Demarkov told the man. "We'll deal with Dade later."

Anna's eyes whipped from one face to the other. If they left, she was dead. The public crowd was her only hope for survival.

"Wait," she said.

Demarkov raised an eyebrow at her. "Wait?"

"I…" She had to stall. Had to come up with some reason to keep them there a little bit longer "…I have to go to the bathroom."

Demarkov scoffed and gave her a look that said he was almost disappointed that was the best she could do.

"You can wait."

"No. I really have to go. Nerves make me have to pee."

"Hold it."

"I can't. I'm telling you, you make me get in a car with you, and I'll pee all over your leather seats before you get the chance to shoot me."

Demarkov paused. He cocked his head to the side, studying her. She stuck her chin out defiantly. And crossed her legs.

"Fine," he finally said, nodding. Though if he believed her or was just amused by her desperate attempt to stave off the inevitable, she wasn't sure. "You can 'pee,'" he said, mocking her with the word.

He pushed her ahead of him, steering her toward a row of portable bathrooms set behind the vendor carts.

Anna stumbled along with his quick step, all the while keeping one eye on Braxton.

Get off the stage.

He was outlining his strategy for providing new jobs in the city. If the crowd's reaction was any indication, it was a good one. Cheers, hollers, and "Yes!"s punctuated each new point he made.

He'd been up there for five minutes now at least. In the spotlight. A clear shot.

His seconds were numbered.

They reached the line of green outhouses, and Demarkov shoved her toward the nearest one.

"I'll be waiting here," he said. "Take your time. But remember, plastic is no match for bullets, yes?" He grinned at her, showing off a row of yellow teeth as he patted the bulge beneath his jacket.

She fought down nausea and nodded, her head spinning, tossing out one impossible escape plan after another.

She stepped into the stall then turned, facing toward the crowd as she moved to shut the green plastic door behind her.

And that's when she saw it.

It was just a flash of light. Sunlight reflecting off polished steel.

But Anna knew that sight well, had been trained to spot it from any distance. It was a gun muzzle.

The flash faded as the gun moved position, and Anna homed in on the person holding it. He was older, short, wearing a windbreaker, and hiding behind a baseball cap and pair of dark glasses.

Petrovich.

He was standing on the edge of the crowd, at the head of the vendor line. Long sleeves of a blue windbreaker covered his arms, but Anna could see a bulge in his right sleeve.

A gun.

"What is the problem now?" Demarkov barked at her.

But Anna stood transfixed in the doorway, watching in horror as Petrovich pulled the gun from his sleeve. No one around him noticed, every other eye in the park focused on Braxton. Petrovich, lifted his arm, moving to take aim.

Only he was a second too late.

Before he could line up his shot, a loud crack exploded in the air.

Anna's gaze whipped to the senator just in time to see the man fall backwards, his feet sliding out from under him as his head hit the metal stage with a sickening thud.

He'd been hit.

CHAPTER TWENTY-FIVE

———

Chaos hit immediately, people in the crowd screaming, running, shoving into one another. Anna watched Petrovich stare at the stage, a frown etched on his face before Anna's view was obscured by people running every which way. If he hadn't taken the shot at Braxton, who had? Anna didn't know. And, at the moment, she didn't care. All she cared about was Petrovich. He was here. And she had to get to him before he disappeared again.

Demarkov grabbed Anna by the arm, pulling her from the restroom door, and dragging her to his side. "What was that?" he hissed, as if the shot at the senator were her fault.

Anna shook her head, wincing as the man's grip tightened.

A security agent appeared to their right, hand to his ear, listening to instructions.

Demarkov shot a look his way, quickly turning to move in the opposite direction.

Anna looked from Demarkov to the agent.

Now's your chance.

"Gun!" she screamed as loudly as she could. Demarkov turned on her, his eyes blazing.

"Gun!" she screamed in his face. She kicked at his shins, wriggled from his grasp as people bumped into her from all angles. "He's got a gun!"

Several people nearby heard her, parroting the phrase until it spread like wildfire.

Demarkov's partner reached for his weapon.

But he didn't get to shoot it as security were bearing down on the man in seconds. Men in suits tackled Demarkov's partner, dropping the man to the ground. Demarkov froze, hands going in the air, as guns pointed his way.

"He shot the senator," Anna shouted, pointing her finger at Demarkov. "I saw him fire as I was getting out of the port-a-potty."

"She lies!" Demarkov growled, making a move for her.

"Freeze!" the security instructed him.

Demarkov froze, his eyes shooting daggers at Anna.

She backed up, melting easily into the crowd as they swarmed him. She waited just long enough to see handcuffs clasp around his wrists before turning and running for the spot where she'd last seen Petrovich.

She had to find him. If he got away, she'd never be safe.

The crowd was thick, running in all directions at once, yelling, shouting, the police unable to control the mass fear that was quickly taking over. Anna fought through them, getting knocked to the ground, picking herself up, pushing through again. Finally she fought her way to the spot near the popcorn cart where she'd seen Petrovich take his aim.

Only he was gone.

She whipped her head wildly left then right, scanning the nearby area. People filled the space everywhere, running, shoving, taking advantage of the chaos. It was impossible to see them all, to look at each face passing her. She moved north, along with the flow of people toward the edge of the park, letting the crowd carry her as she scanned for Petrovich. She couldn't leave without him. This was her chance, her only chance. If he left the park, she knew she'd never catch up to him. He'd be a ghost again.

The crowd carried her near the stage. She'd been unable to see anything after Braxton went down, an army of guys in dark suits swarming him, then quickly pulling him back behind the curtain again. The stage was eerily empty now, the one spot not crammed with bodies.

"Anya."

Anna froze, the cold barrel of a gun suddenly poking into her side.

"Gotcha," Petrovich whispered, his hot breath on Anna's neck. She turned to face him, coming nose to nose with the man. His sunglasses had been knocked off somewhere in the chaos.

The ball cap was pulled down low over his forehead, shadowing his features.

But even through the shadow, she could see the fire in his eyes.

"You shot Braxton," he hissed out.

Anna let out a sharp bark of laughter. "Me? I told you I wasn't doing this job. You were the one who wanted him dead, not me."

Petrovich searched her eyes, trying to read her.

This was one time she didn't need to hide her thoughts from him. What she'd said was the truth. She had no idea who had taken Braxton out. She could guess...but at the moment, all she cared about was taking care of the man in front of her.

The man who, thanks to his confusion over the hit, was off guard. Vulnerable.

"You've lost your touch," Anna said, leaning in so close to the man she could smell the lamb and garlic he'd eaten for lunch.

She saw something flicker behind his eyes.

"You're old, Goren," she continued. "And you're getting sloppy."

He gritted his teeth, all but snarling at her, and opened his mouth to respond.

But she didn't wait, instead sliding her right foot down the inside of his leg and stomping on his instep as hard as she could.

As she hoped, he cried out, lurching forward in pain. She grabbed at the wrist holding the gun, quickly twisting until she heard metal clang onto the sidewalk.

Unfortunately Petrovich's moment of vulnerability was just that—a moment. He quickly recovered, his free hand coming up to grab Anna's neck, pinching the bundled nerves there. It was a move he'd taught Anna her first week with him; it didn't take brute strength to bring a man to his knees, just a working knowledge of human anatomy.

Anna buckled under the pressure, falling to her knees on the ground. Around her, the crowd still surged, bodies packed tightly against one another. Anna felt her vision go fuzzy as Petrovich continued to apply pressure, felt the blood supply being cut off to her brain, the ground rushing up to meet her. She blinked, struggling to maintain consciousness. Just when the black at the edges of her vision started closing in on her, the pressure let up completely.

Anna fell forward onto her hands with the relief, taking in big lungfuls of air as she tried to regain her bearings.

She looked up. Petrovich was gone, his back disappearing through the crowd.

She quickly jumped to her feet, pulling her Glock from her boot, and shoved her way forward, keeping one eye on the baseball cap bobbing through the masses.

As he reached the edge of the park, the crowd began to thin, and he moved faster, breaking into a run as he hit Lincoln.

Anna sped up, sprinting after him. Sirens sounded as emergency vehicles tried to converge on the area. Anna could only imagine how many were injured from the virtual stampede out of the park. But she was only interested in one person now.

She watched Petrovich turn a corner, moving onto a side street beside a coffee house. Anna raced forward, needing to catch up before he turned another corner. If he took off down an alleyway, she'd never find him.

She rounded the coffee house just in time to see Petrovich slide into the passenger seat of a silver sedan. The driver scarcely waited for his door to shut before pealing away from the curb. Through the back window, Anna could see the short, black hair of Petrovich's companion.

Shelli.

He'd had an escape planned. He'd had someone waiting for him.

And he's getting away.

Anna felt desperation bubble up in her throat. As she watched the car pull away from the curb and speed down the street. They made a right turn at the corner, tires screeching.

But Anna didn't break her pace, continuing to chase after the car on foot. She made a right into the alleyway. At the end she swerved left, out onto the main street just in time to see the tail of Petrovich's car swerve left again, heading toward 19th.

She sprinted after the sedan, passing lines of cars parked at the side of the road. A guy in chinos and Birkenstocks was just getting out of a Subaru parked at a meter beside a sandwich shop.

Without even breaking stride, Anna plowed into the man, grabbing at the keys in his hand.

"What the hell, dude?" the guy shouted.

But Anna didn't stick around to answer, sliding into the driver's seat and pulling away from the curb before the guy could even get his cell out to call the theft in.

She scanned the street in front of her, eyes locking on the sedan a block and a half ahead. She swerved into the left lane, surging forward. Then cut off a pickup by swerving right again.

Shelli must have seen her, since she changed course, merging right and running a red light. Anna followed, narrowly avoiding being sideswiped by the opposite traffic. Horns blared, drivers yelled, and somewhere in the background she heard a police siren begin to wail. But she didn't care. All she cared about was the car in front of her. She gunned the engine, taking the corner on two tires, screeching down the side street after Petrovich.

He was not getting away this time.

Anna sped up and rammed the bumper of the sedan. Her head whipped forward, teeth jarring together.

But the sedan didn't stop. Instead it surged ahead, turning left sharply, the wrong way down a one-way street.

This time Anna didn't follow, instead passing to the next street, turning with the flow of traffic. She swerved right, jumping onto the sidewalk, her speedometer hitting sixty as she flew past the other cars. She hit a pair of trash cans, sending newspapers and empty soda cups flying into the street, but she didn't slow down, laying on the accelerator the full way down the block. When she hit the intersection, she pulled the wheel hard to the left, praying her timing was right.

It was.

Petrovich's sedan emerged just at that instant, and Anna plowed right into the side of it.

The sedan skidded sideways, pinned against the side of a brick building by the Subaru.

Anna jumped from the driver's seat as soon as her stolen car skidded to a stop, the sound of sirens still following her in the distance.

She watched as Shelli climbed out the driver's side window, tripping onto the asphalt, clearly dazed. Shelli paused a moment, looking from Anna to Petrovich, but she must have heard the approaching sirens, too, as she took off in the opposite direction, half running, half stumbling toward the end of the block.

But Anna didn't care about her. Her sights were set on Petrovich, shoving at the twisted metal of the passenger side door. It whined, metal scraping on metal, but complied, opening in time for Petrovich to jump out and run back down the alleyway without missing a beat.

Anna followed, her legs pumping, her heart racing. Petrovich's legs were longer, but Anna was younger. In three quick strides, she was on top of him. She flung herself at his back, catching his shoulder and shoving him to the ground.

He yelled out as he fell forward, left hand going in front of himself to catch his fall, the right reaching down his leg.

But she was faster.

"Don't move!" she shouted, her gun shoved into the back of his skull.

She knew he was reaching for the pistol strapped to his ankle. She knew his every move before he made it. Because it was the same move she'd make. He'd molded her in his own image. His downfall. He could never surprise her.

She stood up, towering over him as she allowed him to roll over and face her. She planted one boot in the center of his chest, both hands clutching the Glock held straight-armed in front of her, listening to the sirens bear down on them both.

"Don't move," she repeated.

Petrovich stared up at her. She could see his chest rising and falling as rapidly as she could feel her own move.

"Anya," Petrovich breathed, his eyes on the gun barrel. "I see I taught you well."

"You did," she agreed.

He smiled at her. "This is the real Anya. This is who you are."

"No. You're wrong," she argued, shaking her head. "This was never me. This was who you wanted me to be."

His smiled slowly faded. "You won't shoot me, Anya."

She raised an eyebrow at him. "No?"

He shook his head slowly from side to side. "No. You're right. Things have changed. You've changed. You're soft now, Anya. You're emotional."

Anna shifted her weight, willing his words to roll off her. Willing herself not to analyze each one for how much truth she knew it held, and how disconcerting it was that he did know her after all.

"You've lost your training, Anya," he continued. "You've lost your urge to kill."

"I never had the urge," she shot back. "I never wanted to kill. I had no choice."

"I know," he said softly, as if he was almost sorry. "But you were young then. You are your own woman now. And I know you can't shoot me."

Anna squared her jaw, forced her grip tight on the gun, tried to block out his words even as they saturated her brain.

"Be quiet."

"Anya…" Petrovich said.

"Numb," Anna whispered.

Petrovich raised himself up on his elbows. He smiled at her. "My *dragi*. My Anya."

"Just—" She breathed out slowly. "—go numb."

Anna pulled the trigger, a sharp pop echoing off the buildings as one neat little red hole appeared in Petrovich's chest.

One bullet. That's all you need.

He froze in place, sucking in a sharp breath, eyes slowly tilting downward to see deep red liquid seeping from his chest. He looked up at her, surprise clear on his face. It wasn't often he was wrong. But she'd had one kill left in her after all.

Anna didn't move, didn't speak. Just watched as Petrovich's eyes started to cloud over, then slowly went flat, before he fell back again, his head smacking against the pavement in a final blow.

CHAPTER TWENTY-SIX

———

Anna sat forward in her plastic chair, watching a television mounted to the ceiling in the corner of the waiting area at Gate 72. A news program was on, giving live updates on Senator Braxton's condition. The reporter was slim, blonde, in her forties, and completely interchangeable with any other correspondent at any of the other four major networks airing the same story.

Senator Braxton had sustained a gunshot wound to the shoulder in the park the previous week. He'd been shot with a long range rifle found on the roof of the next building over, believed to be fired by an as yet unnamed associate of Vladimir Demarkov, a war criminal who had long eluded the authorities. Demarkov had been apprehended by authorities at Senator Braxton's rally and had since not been cooperating with police. He was currently being held at an undisclosed detention facility while both Serbian and U.S. officials fought over who got the pleasure of trying him first.

Braxton's gunshot wound was being described as minor, luckily having missed all major arteries and nerve pathways. But the minor injury had major implications in the upcoming race. Braxton's popularity had jumped a full ten points in the polls the first time he'd been seen on TV in his new sling. The sympathy vote seemed to have sealed his party's presidential nomination, and Braxton was now using his own injury and subsequent hospital stay to illustrate just how important health insurance reform was to every American citizen.

There was no mention, Anna noticed, of the unidentified body of a man found in an alleyway just blocks from the park that same day, though Anna had read about it in the *Chronicle* the morning following the incident. The body had been found near a stolen sedan with no ID. Authorities were "looking into it," though they had warned the *Chronicle* reporter that several John Does died in the City every year, and without further funding, the police force was just not able to put names to every one. Likely, the body would remain unidentified and the crime of his death unsolved.

The screen switched to a commercial for a mortgage broker, and Anna let her gaze wander out the window to the tarmac where airplanes were lining up at various gates, slowly taxiing down runways bound for destinations all over the world.

Including one that would soon be carrying her.

"This seat taken?"

Anna looked up and blinked, as the man didn't wait for an answer, instead sliding into the seat beside her.

"Dade," she said quietly. She should have been floored to see him there, but oddly, she wasn't completely surprised.

He smiled at her, a tentative thing. She never would have imagined he did anything tentatively, but there it was.

"How are you?" he asked.

She nodded. "Alive."

The corner of his mouth tilted upward ever so slightly. "That's a good way to be."

"It's not something I take for granted, that I'll say." Her eyes searched his, looking for the answers to questions that had been plaguing her for the last week.

As soon as Petrovich had asked her who shot Braxton, she'd had a suspicion it was Dade. Why, how, and to what end, she hadn't known until she'd collected Lenny from the park, dared to access her bank accounts to check into a motel that night, and turned on the news. As details about the shooting had trickled in, veiled as they were behind the media's spin, small pieces had started to fall into place. As Dade well knew, there was one surefire way to keep a person from taking a hit—shoot at his target before he had a chance.

"You outsmarted Demarkov, I see," he said, gesturing to the television where the story had just been playing.

She nodded, slowly.

"I knew you would."

"You did?" Did she believe him? She wasn't sure. It was an easy thing to say now that they'd both gotten away. "I appreciate the vote of confidence," she finally said.

He grinned a moment before his eyes turned serious. Dark and intent. "I never would have let him hurt you."

Anna swallowed. "You handed me over to a man who wanted me dead."

"I had a scope on you the whole time. If he'd have tried to take you out of the park, I'd have taken him out."

Again, she wanted to believe him. But so much had happened in the last two weeks that she didn't know what she believed anymore.

After the park, Anna had cried in her motel room for two days straight, only pausing to sleep when exhaustion consumed her. She'd given herself that time to grieve for everything that she'd lost—her faith in Shelli, the fleeting closeness she'd felt with Dade, the betrayal that seemed to be all around her. And even for Petrovich. For two days, she'd cried every tear she had in her, but that was all. Just two days. Then she'd forced herself to find new identification and make arrangements to leave the City.

She realized Dade was still watching her, his expression somewhere between a plea for forgiveness and a look of a stranger assessing her for the first time.

"Demarkov was the man who hired you to kill me?"

Dade nodded slowly. "Apparently you killed someone close to him. His half-brother, Anton Fedorov."

Anna nodded. "I remember him." Though, honestly, she felt little remorse about what she had done in his compound that night long ago. Sadness that it had been necessary at all but certainty that, at least that time, she had acted for the best.

She listened as Dade recounted Demarkov's account of his brother's rise and fall, and the man's grudge against Anna for her hand in it.

When he was finished, she let it all sink in before deliberately changing the subject.

"You shot Braxton," she said. It was a statement, not a question. Which is possibly why he didn't answer, just continued to stare at her.

"That was where you were that morning. You had it all planned."

He paused a moment then slowly nodded. "Some of it. There are things you can never plan for. But I think it turned out well."

Anna wasn't sure if adding another kill to her list of sins really qualified as "well," but this was the first time she'd been in an airport in years where she wasn't looking over her shoulder every five minutes. So, things could have ended worse.

"What are you doing here?" she asked, wondering if he'd planned this encounter, too.

"I'd imagine much the same thing you are. Moving on."

She nodded. Moving on. That was a good way of putting it. It sounded so much better than running away, something she'd vowed she was never going to do again.

"Well, good luck," she said, realizing how silly that sounded even to her own ears. She wasn't sure what she was supposed to say, what she was supposed to feel toward him. Feelings were still a bit of mystery to her, and it was going to take some time to sort out what to do with them all again.

But Dade grinned, his eyes going warm as his lips curled at the corners. "You too, Anna." The use of her new name didn't escape her.

They both stood, and before she could decide if this was a handshake situation or a hug situation, Dade leaned in and brushed a soft kiss against her cheek.

"Good-bye, Anna," he said softly as he pulled away. Then added, "For now."

Before she could respond, he turned his back to her and walked purposefully out of the gate, back into the flow of travelers making their way toward dozens of other gates.

And then he was gone.

EPILOGUE

———

The late afternoon sun reflected off the bubbling fountain in the center of the square, almost blinding if one stared at the water too long. The streets were filled with tourists, the adobe shop fronts leaving their doors open today to let in the cool, fall breeze so coveted in Sedona. Wind chimes tinkled from a turquoise jewelry shop down the street, the scents of coffee and the recent rain mingling in the air as the red rocks loomed in the distance, creating a watercolor backdrop.

Anna sipped her cup of tea. Chamomile. It was warm, soothing, and calming, the perfect combination for the perfect setting. She let her oversized sunglasses slide down over her eyes, leaned her head back against her wrought iron chair, felt the cool metal as a soothing contrast to the warm sun shining down on her face. Lenny snored at her feet, only awakening intermittently to bark at a bird or beg for a piece of her turkey sandwich.

"Can I get you anything else, Miss Jones?" her server asked. The woman was young, a college student she guessed, with a thick Hispanic accent and huge brown eyes.

"No, thank you. I'm fine." Anna shook her head, noticing, not for the first time, the absence of hair whipping her cheeks. Her new short, blonde cut was definitely different. She felt as if she were greeting a stranger in the mirror every morning. But different was the whole point. Besides, it was nice to see her natural color again.

Anna yawned, stretched lazily, and leaned down and ruffled the fur on Lenny's head. She'd spent the last few months on something of an extended vacation in the desert—not yet ready to put down roots anywhere but enjoying the calm air of the small, artist community. The vibrant sunsets, sculpted mountains, and clean air had served to heal over some of the wounds of her past. Or at least bandaged them enough that she could begin to lick them and envision a fresh start.

She wouldn't stay here. It was quiet and calm, but it was where people came to escape. Anna wanted to live. Her past was gone. She was free for the first time in her life, free to start over for real, without the fear of demons catching up to her. They'd already done that, and she'd survived. She could survive anything now.

That was something to be thankful for every day. And to know that she could do it again if she needed to.

If.

"Miss Jones?" The server appeared at her elbow again.

Anna lifted her sunglasses and smiled at the woman. "Yes?"

"I have a message for you."

Anna frowned. "For me? Are you sure?" Her eyes instinctively scanned the square. A few tourists. A couple locals enjoying beverages outside. Nothing out of the ordinary.

The girl bobbed her head up and down. "Yes. Anna Jones?" The girl shoved an envelope at her.

Anna stared at it for a moment before taking it in her own hand. "Where did this come from?"

The girl shrugged. "Some guy dropped it off. He paid your bill too," she said, ducking back inside the cafe.

The hair on the back of her neck stood as she once again scanned the benign courtyard. She quickly tore the envelope open. Inside was a single sheet of paper with a phone number on it. She licked her lips, feeling her hands shake as she pulled her phone from her pocket and dialed.

A man picked up on the first ring. "Anna Jones?"

She paused. "Who is this?"

"David Prescott. I work for Senator Braxton."

Anna stiffened, the entire serene scene in front of her freezing in time as old paranoia resurfaced. "What do you want?"

"First, Senator Braxton wants to convey his thanks for your part in thwarting his attempted assassination in Golden Gate Park."

She paused again, answering slowly. "What part?"

"Miss Jones, Senator Braxton is on track to become the next president of the United States. He has the many and varied means of several government agencies at his disposal."

"What are you saying?" she asked.

"I'm saying that playing dumb only makes you look dumb. When a presidential candidate issues an official thank you, just say, 'You're welcome.'"

Despite the jarring presence of Prescott's voice in her ear, Anna felt her voice come calmly. "You're welcome."

"That's better," Prescott said.

"Now what do you really want?" she asked.

"You're very direct. I like that. Okay, I'll tell you. Senator Braxton finds himself in a situation where someone with your particular skill set would be beneficial to him."

"What kind of situation?"

"One that he feels your team would be well suited for."

"Team?" Anna asked, trying to read through Prescott's vague and purposely veiled proposal. "What team?"

"Yourself and Nick Dade."

She bit her lip, not sure how to answer that one.

"Listen, I'd prefer not to discuss this over the phone," Prescott went on. "Is there somewhere we can meet?"

"No," Anna said, automatically. "I don't have any skills that would benefit the senator."

There was a silence on the other end, then, "Listen, Anna. You have an opportunity here to do what few people will ever be able to. You can make a real difference. One that has very immediate, important, and lasting outcomes."

Anna drew a deep breath in through her nose, inhaling the rich scents of the square around her. "This situation. What sort of skills, exactly, are so perfect for its resolution?"

"For one, you don't exist. Neither would any ties between you and the senator."

"So the senator doesn't want voters to know he's hiring a killer?" she said bluntly.

"The senator doesn't want to hire a killer. He wants the kind of security and resources at his disposal that you and Dade can provide. Unofficial, under the radar, problem solvers who can think and act from both sides of the law if necessary."

Anna took another deep breath. Both sides of the law. To be honest, the only law she'd ever followed was the law of survival.

"I've spent too much time working for governments," she hedged.

But Prescott must have sensed the hesitation growing in her voice, and quickly jumped in with, "You wouldn't be working for the government. Officially, you wouldn't be working for anyone at all, though a nicely padded off-shore bank account does come with the job."

Anna raised an eyebrow and glanced down at Lenny. That wasn't altogether an unpleasant thought, she had to admit.

"Will you at least meet with us?" Prescott pressed.

Anna took a deep breath. "Fine. We can meet. But no promises."

"Fair enough," Prescott answered, relief clear in his voice. "That's exactly what Dade said."

Again at the mention of his name, that unnerving feeling resurfaced. "He did, did he?"

"We'll meet you tomorrow at the helipad at the Sedona airport," he said. "Three o'clock your time."

Anna nodded. "But, like I said, this is just a meeting. I haven't agreed to anything, and I likely won't."

"Of course. We'll see you then, Anna."

Then the line went dead.

Anna stared a moment at the phone in her hand before slowly setting it on the table.

A meeting. That was all.

But as Anna well knew, one meeting was sometimes all it took.

"Well, Lenny," she said, leaning down to rub the dog's head, "how do you feel about Washington?"

ABOUT THE AUTHOR

Gemma Halliday is the *New York Times, USA Today* & #1
Kindle bestselling author of the High Heels Mysteries, the
Hollywood Headlines Mysteries, the Jamie Bond Mysteries, the
Tahoe Tessie Mysteries, the Marty Hudson Mysteries, and
several other works. Gemma's books have received numerous
awards, including a Golden Heart, two National Reader's Choice
awards, and three RITA nominations. She currently lives in the
San Francisco Bay Area with her boyfriend, Jackson Stein, who
writes vampire thrillers, and their four children, who are
adorably distracting on a daily basis.

To learn more about Gemma, visit her online at
www.GemmaHalliday.com

Other series in print now from Gemma Halliday...

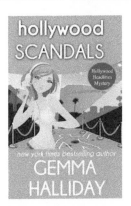

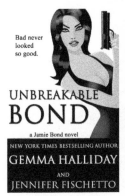

www.GemmaHalliday.com